THE FAE CHRONICLES

Escaping Destiny

AMELIA HUTCHINS

Shaping Destiny. Copyright © February 17, 2014 by Amelia Hutchins

ISBN-13: 978-0991190935

ISBN-10: 0991190939

Amelia Hutchins

P.O. Box 11212

Spokane Valley, WA 99211

Amelia-Hutchins.com

Ordering Information: https:www.createspace.com

Quantity sales. Special discounts are available on quantity purchases by corporations, associations, and others. For details, contact the publisher at the address above.

Orders by U.S. trade bookstores and wholesalers. Please contact Amelia utchins ameliahutchins@ amelia-hutchins.com

Printed in the United States of America.

WARNING

This book contains sexually explicit scenes and adult language, and may be considered offensive to some readers. It is intended for sale to adults ONLY, as defined by the laws of the country in which you made your purchase. Please store your files wisely, where they cannot be accessed by under-aged readers.

~~*~*~*~*~*~*~*~*

This book is not intended for anyone under the age of 18, or anyone who doesn't like lip biting, throw your ass on the bed, tear your clothes off and leave you panting dominant alpha male characters. It's dark, dangerous, intense, gritty and raw book. Scenes are dark, disturbing and scorching HOT. This read is soul crushing, tear jerking, leave you hanging on the edge of your seat, fast paced read. Side Effects may include, but are not limited to: Drooling, lip biting, wet panties, crying and screaming at the author. If any of these things happen, do not seek medical attention—get the next book in the series and enjoy the ride!

~~*~*~*~*~*~*~*~*

The
Fae
Chronicles

Chapter
ONE

Destiny has a way of finding you, even if you've been hiding from it. My destiny was chosen for me and written before I was born. Right after I was born, my parents signed me away. They signed a contract with a monster who in return, stopped harassing our people and freed my brother.

Terrified for my future, they broke the contract and I was hidden among Humans in the least likely place I would be looked for. They created an elaborate illusion so I wouldn't be found, and in doing this, they resigned themselves that they would never see me again. They figured that what they had planned for me was a better future than what had befallen many of the Horde King's other toys. Too bad destiny had other ideas. My parents were only able to hold the illusion together for six short years before the evil, in the form of my brother Faolán and the creature before me, ripped it away. They seemed to be the galvanizing forces that prompted the journey that shaped me and eventually brought me to this cavernous hall, kneeling at the feet of the most feared creature in both this one and the Human one.

Liam, my brother, had been captured, tortured, and broken by the same man who stood before me now.

The Horde King had done everything in his power to ensure I was his. Why? What was so important about me that the Horde wanted me so much?

Children? He had many children, mostly boys, if the whispers about him were correct. Power? It was the most likely reason, but that only added more questions to why this beautiful, deadly creature wanted me as his concubine since I held no power for him to take. Was it to keep my parents under his thumb? Could be, but why did he need to bring them to heel when he could so easily kill them as he had my grandfather?

Nothing made sense, and even now as I knelt at his feet awaiting my fate, I wanted answers that likely wouldn't come. Here was this creature who could easily wipe out anyone he chose to, and for some reason, he wanted *me*. He'd ensured from my birth that I would end up here at his feet. As his slave.

Me. He wanted me.

The room was filled with the noise of the celebrating Horde, while I remained on my knees at his feet. I was still dressed in a beautiful gown, with an almost laughable weapon hidden in the bodice of the dress—one that was supposedly created to kill the Horde King. I had no plans of using it on him. It wasn't because I didn't think I could, I just wasn't stupid or suicidal.

There was no way in hell I could kill him and get away with it. I was going to figure out why the Horde King wanted me, and I was going to escape him. If I used the dagger, I'd be dead before I could figure out the bigger picture, and killing him would seal the fate of too many people who depended on this contract.

I'd lived so much of my life trying to help others, and do what I thought was right. The Guild, with the exception of Alden and Marie, had used my hate and anger for their own purposes and betrayed Adam and me in the end. I hadn't been living then, I'd been surviving. Ryder had been right, and up until I'd met him, I'd merely been existing. It was time to end that part of my life. I'd been going through the motions of living, oblivious to what I wanted for myself. Deep down, I'd known I wanted love; real soul-ripping love.

Blinding love that made you do stupid things, and I had it. I'd fallen in love with a Fairy—I mean, how much stupider could *that* be? In his arms, I felt whole, protected. Sure, he'd given me to Adam to wed, but he really didn't have any choice in the matter and I'd seen the pain in his eyes from doing so. Point? He wanted me for more than just sex.

Yes, Ryder had this need to dominate everyone, including me. But we could work past that, and I was sure I could make him love me. It just really sucked that it had taken me this long to figure it out. I wasn't the key to saving Faery, and that in itself was a huge relief. Unfortunately, that also opened up more questions as to who I really was and what I was meant to do.

In my dream, Ryder let me know that I no longer had to marry Adam. So now, I just had to figure out how to escape what destiny was throwing at me now. The Horde King. I smiled knowing he wouldn't see it. Why I was still staring at his bare feet, which were my sole focal point at the moment.

"Stand up," he ordered, bringing me out of my reverie. His voice was layered, and demanded to be heard. It slithered over my shoulders and wrapped around my spine.

I placed my hands firmly on the ground as I brought myself up to a standing position. I kept my eyes on his feet, because I knew he wanted submission. Everything in his posture and being screamed that he wanted me demure and willing to bend to his will.

Even the blood oath he had me take screamed submission. Ryder had taught me how to submit. He'd made me boneless with the need to submit to him. I could do this, at least long enough to find a way out. Ryder said he would save me, and I believed him. I wasn't sure he could save me from this thought. That meant I had to do it on my own.

"Look at me," he ordered.

I raised my eyes to meet his obsidian depths. The Horde King was beautiful, but often those things which are the most beautiful are the deadliest. He was evil incarnate, and the stories I'd been told by my parents and my brother came rushing back as I met his eyes.

"You are mine," he said softly, his eyes scanning my face as he said it. He was looking for hesitation, or uncertainty, which he would find because I was terrified. I was also uncertain of my fate, and while I didn't want to hesitate, I probably would.

"I am yours," I repeated dutifully.

"Prove it," he replied.

I blinked as what he wanted me to do sank slowly into my brain. I stepped closer, until I was inches from his towering form. His wide wings closed around us the moment I was close enough to touch the pulsating brands on his massive chest. They hid our bodies from those around us. Instantly I was suffocating and choking on his power as it surged through me, blocking off any chance of drawing breath. He was absolute power, and I felt it with every cell of my body.

"Ask me," he growled softly, the vibration sending my skin to a shivering mess.

He was showing me his control, and that it was absolute. He wanted me to know how easily he could kill me, as if I needed a reminder. I lifted my eyes to his and moved even closer until I was pressed against his hard body.

I opened my mouth to ask for permission to breathe, but no words would come. He was preventing them, and his eyes sparkled with amusement at my discomfort.

"Kiss me," he demanded.

I did, knowing that it would bring air, which I needed to draw a breath. Power was corrupting, and this was an example of why he was considered the strongest of the Fae. I stood on my tiptoes and placed my hands carefully against his chest as my lungs burned with the need for oxygen.

His mouth wasn't filled with stench as one would expect from a member of the Horde. Instead, it was clean and minty, and the moment my lips touched his, I was once again able to draw breath—but only barely. I sent my tongue out, knowing instinctively that the deeper I went, the more air I would receive. His arms wrapped around me, crushing me to his body. I reacted to him, easily. Heat rushed through my midsection and the result of my reaction to him made me feel unsure of myself.

He growled against my mouth as his wings caressed my naked shoulders, softer than silk against my flesh. Air came easily as he encouraged the kiss. My hands felt his power as it sparked against the flesh of my palms. His brands even pulsed with it, and my own reacted to it by pulsing and throbbing in response. I moved to step away from him, but his hands lowered to my back and held me there, locked against him.

"I expect you to give me control, Sorcha. You will pleasure me only. You are a Transitioned Fae now. You look of it, and I can smell it on you. I won't damage you, not when I can easily starve you of air, which will no longer kill you, but I promise it will not be pleasurable. Do you understand what I am saying?" he asked as his fingers crept up to touch the torque around my throat.

"If I don't please you, I don't breath."

"Yes," he replied as his hand wrapped around the back of my neck, sending a feeling of hopelessness down my spine. "You will feed me, and pleasure me as is my right. For the blood oath your parents violated, I will seek to punish you. Unlike what many think, you will like my punishments. I know a lot about punishments. There's a fine line between pain and pleasure, and I promise to make you dance on the line between them if you fight me," he whispered with a growl that sent shivers of fear racing down my spine.

I swallowed heavily as fear crept into my veins. "I had no control over what they did. I was only a child."

His lips curved into a wicked smile that was at odds with the hard look in his eyes. He lowered his mouth and pressed his lips against my ear before whispering softly, "Hence why you are still alive, little one. Had you participated in their plans to thwart me, I would have already killed you, Sorcha."

"Syn," I whispered back, not daring to move from the gentle embrace I was wrapped into against his hard body.

"We will sin, of that I assure you. When I am done with you, you will want no other man. That much I promise you."

"What is it you want from me exactly, besides someone to warm your bed?" I asked, unable to stop the words from coming out.

"This," he said, and once again I couldn't breathe, couldn't think past the need for air. He'd taken it all from me, and my lungs burned with fire. I turned my wide eyes to his and watched as he licked his lips. I moved without hesitation. I kissed him, picturing Ryder as I did so. Would he hate me when I submitted to the Horde King? Would he even want me after I'd lain with the King? There was no way I would be able to get away from him; not before he took me, anyway.

I wasn't an idiot. I knew this beautiful creature planned to take me to his bed tonight. I could feel the anticipation in his touch, in his kiss. He liked playing God, and right now, he was. He was giving me air with his kiss, and I wasn't going to be an idiot and suffocate. If I planned to live, I would need to play by this man's rules—for now.

When he finally broke the kiss and pulled away from me, a look passed between us. I got it; he was in control, and if I wanted to make it through this unscathed, I was going to have to give him what he wanted.

"Are you mine, Sorcha, and only mine?" he asked quietly as his hand cupped my chin.

"I am yours in body, but my soul will never be yours," I answered honestly.

His liquid black eyes searched my face for

something, and must have decided against demanding more at this moment, because his wings parted and the brightness of the room blinded me briefly. He continued to watch me before he shouted an order.

"Bring the chains for the Princess," he said to his guards, who were covered from head to toe in a type of form-fitting black armor that was light weight, but looked strong enough to be effective. They all wore black cloaks over the armor and their eyes were the only visible sign that there was a sentient being behind the mask of the helmet. The first male stepped up and took my hands to slip thin silver cuffs onto each wrist, while the other slipped a delicate silver chain through the catch of one cuff and then the other. When he was done, I tested them and was shocked at how strong they seemed.

Well shit, it wasn't looking like I would be getting away from the King unscathed, or without chains. I inhaled slowly and then let it out even slower. My heart was thundering with what was happening. It really was looking like I was on my own now.

The Horde shouted with cheers when their King was handed the length of chain that connected to the cuffs on my wrists. I turned a panicked look at Adam, and blinked as he disappeared from sight, only to appear in front of me as he pushed me back and away from the Horde King.

He moved so quickly that I was having a hard time keeping my eyes on him. It took me a few minutes to figure out that he was trying to sift me away from the Horde King. He was shouting, and I couldn't quite make out what he was saying as he repeatedly disappeared, only to reappear and try again.

"Adam!" I shouted as the Horde King moved to attack him. He would be killed!

"I can't let this happen to you, Syn!" Adam shouted as he gave up trying to sift me out and shielded my body with his own. I watched in horror as the deadly wing of the Horde King took aim, and moved with dire intent toward Adam's heart. Adam was immortal, but as I had seen with Liam, the Horde King could do things that other Fae couldn't.

"No!" I cried, allowing the King to hear the terrified plea that filled my voice.

The entire room was silent, as if someone had flipped a switch, and turned all the sound off. The only sound was the beating of my heart as it shattered for Adam and what he'd just tried to do. I stood behind him with my eyes closed as I listened to the steady drumbeat of my heart that was pounding in my ears.

"Boy," the Horde King snarled, which forced me to open my eyes. He held Adam by his dark colored shirt, his spiked wing inches from my best friend's heart. "Kier, I suggest you take your son home, and teach him the ways of our people. Explain to him the exact details of our alliance. It might allow him to make better choices in the future."

"As you wish," Kier said grimly, grasping on to Adam as the Horde King shoved him away. I watched in silence as Adam turned a look of panic in my direction.

"Go; I'll be okay," I told him, and blinked back tears as Kier tightened his grip on Adam and sifted them both out of the room.

Chapter
TWO

I shivered as the Horde King's guards took up positions around me in case anyone else tried to save me. My hands were bound by magical chains. The tingle of the spell they had been enchanted with was palpable against my flesh.

"Remove the necklace and replace it with mine," The Horde King demanded in a tense tone.

My mother stepped up hesitantly and removed the thin necklace with the ruby on it that had kept me from just sifting away. She then replaced it with one he manifested and handed to her. It was thin platinum, bearing a small silver disc with what must be an insignia for the Horde etched into the face. I barely glimpsed it, before it rested against my throat. When she finished placing it on me, she stepped back but lifted her hand to cup my cheek reassuringly.

"We have much to discuss, Alazander. Your guards can watch my daughter while we go over the agreements. Entertainment and a feast will be provided for those guests who wish to indulge," my father said with a note of deference in his voice as he sidled up to stand beside my mother. I could see he was keeping his eyes down so the Horde King wouldn't see how much this entire situation was angering him.

"You think I should keep up my end of the agreement after you so boldly broke the one we had?" Alazander growled angrily. My father's eyes snapped up to meet the Horde Kings. "That I wish to remain for feasting and entertainment after I was forced to wait more than twenty years for what you should have willingly brought me then?"

"I'm willing to give up a few more things to secure peace, if that is your wish. The war, however, needs to cease. The good of Faery must be considered, and each Caste must be willing to make sacrifices for the greater good."

"Show me what you propose," Alazander demanded, indicating with his hand for my father to lead.

"Let me start the entertainment, and we can discuss it over the feast that has been prepared for tonight. There will also be Humans for those of your breed that can feed without killing."

Feast? I blinked. Surely they wouldn't...My father snapped his fingers, and side doors opened. A large group of Humans, who looked very well-kept, walked out and stood in a line. The men and women kept their eyes downcast and their posture stiff. A buzz of nervous excitement seemed to surround them.

"What the hell?" I asked before I could think better of it.

"They are guests in our kingdom that my brother brought back here. They requested to come to Faery. They are happy and never mistreated here, Synthia. I'd like to keep it that way," he said as he narrowed his eyes on the Horde King.

As far as I knew, the Blood Fae didn't go into the Human world very often. Or, that was what I'd been told. But then, the Horde King had been missing, and he'd just popped up in time to claim me. More fae games.

"Your daughter will be seated beside me, and my guards will stay both beside and behind us while we indulge in your celebration," the Horde King said, pulling on the silver chain that was secured to my wrists. I went willingly to him until I was inches from his chest.

This seemed to satisfy him, and I followed him a few short steps to where a long table with a rich crimson coverlet materialized before us. Ornate, high-backed oak chairs surrounded the table, and he indicated that I should be seated in a chair that was pulled out with magic and placed next to the largest, most ornate chair that seemed to dominate and preside over the rest of the seating arrangement. I took my seat as he expected, and it wasn't until the Horde King noticed my father waiting, that he narrowed his eyes on me and spoke to his guards.

"To me," he said barely above a whisper, and a contingent of his guards decked in black armor sifted to him, "five of you protect what is mine. The others come with me."

I watched as he and the rest of his men walked with my father to another table that was not there as I'd been presented to the Horde. My father unrolled a giant scroll across it, and he and the Horde King began discussing the terms. I wondered with a queasy feeling if it had been one of those parchments made from the skin of traitors, or if it was made through less painful means. I scooted up against the main table, which seemed to please my new guards. The table continued to "set" itself as large gold chargers and gold cutlery appeared before us. Well, that was a good sign that there would be more than just Humans for dinner.

I hid my hands under the table and quickly gave a nudge at the bodice, popping the toothpick dagger out of place, and lifted the skirt of the dress to discreetly slide the dagger out. I held it in my hands briefly before dropping it to the floor, and kicking it away from myself and down the length of the table. There was no way in hell I was getting busted with that thing by Alazander. He'd just suck the air from my lungs and I'd be unable to use it on him, and be utterly fucked in the process.

"Synthia," Madisyn breathed with a look of horror in her eyes. She'd been the only one to notice what I'd just done.

"Not like that," I shook my head, knowing the guards were listening to the exchange.

She lowered her eyes and exhaled slowly. "Is he to your liking?" she asked.

"He is what Liam said he was."

She started to reply to my words, but a scream tore through the room, shattering the calm that had settled over it as the Horde began selecting Humans. I was instantly on my feet, but rough hands shoved me back down into the chair I'd just left.

"Stay seated," a rough voice said as startling gray and aqua blue eyes held mine.

"He's hurting her," I snapped.

"She's feeding him," he retorted. "She will scream

in pleasure soon enough, Princess."

"What kind of sick shit—"

"Is there a problem?" Alazander said, taking the seat beside me. He settled in easily, even though his giant wings should have caused him some issues with taking his seat.

"He's hurting her," I answered, unsure of how he would react. This was the creature that sent his own victims back to their families broken and in pieces.

The victim in question chose that moment to start screaming in pleasure. I couldn't stop the blush that heated my cheeks, or the bulging of my eyes as I watched the couple fornicate against the wall, oblivious to everyone watching them. I watched, unable to tear my eyes from where the Fae was drinking her blood as he thrust his need between her thighs. From my vantage point, it was hard to tell if he was actually Horde or one of the Blood Fae.

"She seems to be finding pleasure now," the Horde King said with a twinge of amusement in his dark eyes.

I tore my eyes away from the couple and looked at my hands clasped tightly together in my lap to stop the involuntary quaking. The men behind me snorted and laughed as more cries of pleasure erupted around the room. This was so not cool; definitely not a dinner party I'd ever sign up for.

"Gather the Elite Guard, we're almost done here," the Horde King said in a soft voice to the guard that stood closest to him.

I sat silently, watching those around us; I wasn't winning the fight against my nerves as the room continued on as if this wasn't what it was. A sacrifice. My only hope of escape had been dashed, and it was almost a relief to know he would be safe from this monster before me. I needed to come up with a plan for escape and see it through before I was officially screwed.

I wasn't prepared when he picked me from my chair and sat me on his lap. My entire body trembled from his touch and the electrical pulse that slithered and kissed my every nerve ending. I wasn't fast enough to stifle the moan those electrical currents created. His men snorted and exchanged knowing looks. Crap, with everything that had gone on over the past two days, I must have used up every ounce of energy I had stored up when I fed from Ryder last. Hunger blossomed from my stomach to my panties, or was it the other way around?

His hand moved down to play across the flesh of my leg that the dress revealed. He was testing me, seeing how willing and receptive I was to his touch. I looked up and met Liam's tortured look that was visible in his eyes. I had the strangest urge to reassure him that I was fine, even though I really wasn't.

Liam kept stealing looks at the Horde King that looked like a combination of hatred and confusion until the Horde King narrowed his eyes at Liam, causing him to quickly avert his gaze to the charger in front of him. This just seemed to be getting worse.

I exhaled slowly for courage as the Horde King continued to stroke my flesh, luckily where no one else could see it. His other hand slid up my back until it was resting on my neck—once again showing me how easily he could control my fate. So be it. I'd be damned if he did it here, though. I could see Liam struggling against the urge to jump across the table.

"I'm hungry," I whispered through the growing lump in my throat.

"Dinner will be served shortly. The cooks have prepared a feast of pheasant, quail, roast, and boar for us, as well as delicacies from the Dark Forest, courtesy of the Dark Knight," Madisyn said with her eyes firmly on me. Lovely. I guess it was fitting that in Faery you would have hokey names like the Dark Knight who comes from the Dark Forest. There was probably an Enchanted Forest and a Mount Doom around here somewhere, too. The servers were setting up trays and bringing drinks around to those who had a place at the table.

"Not for food." Not good! It came out quickly. Crap. Involuntary statements like that, combined with everything else my body was doing to me, meant I was going to need to feed very soon.

"We're done here, anyway. It's time to take you to the Horde Kingdom, and I'm sure you are in a hurry to settle into your new home as well," the Horde King replied, releasing his hold on my neck but not removing his fingers from my thigh.

"Good," I said softly, moving my eyes away from him to scan the crowd. Where the hell was my knight in shining armor and why was he late? I hadn't planned on him saving me, but I'd at least expected to catch a glimpse of him before I went to the Horde's stronghold.

"I'm glad to see you willing to serve me," he replied with his mouth against my ear.

I gulped down air as if I couldn't get enough. I turned to look one last time at my mother as the guards easily helped me to stand on my feet. The crowd was oblivious to what was going on until the King growled loudly. The entire assembly of the Horde creatures that had come turned to him, dismissing those they had been feeding from without a second thought.

"Say your goodbyes; you have one minute," he said quietly in my ear. He then moved toward his guards to allow me to step away from him.

He didn't have to tell me twice. I moved toward my family and hugged my mother tight. "I'm going to be okay," I whispered quietly reassuring them.

I smiled at my father, and quickly stepped back to give the Horde King no reason to be upset with me. If I was going to escape him, I was going to need to earn his trust to do so. I didn't want a huge goodbye either, seeing that I'd just been reunited with them and for the most part we didn't know each other. Even though I understood why I was being given to the Horde, it still upset me that within one day of meeting them, we were here with the freaking Horde, and I was being given to their King.

Alazander held his hand out for me, which I accepted hesitantly. As soon as he sifted me, I wouldn't be able to get away from him for a while. Grudgingly, I moved in close enough that he had to pull me the rest of the way into his arms. He pressed me against his chest before he unfurled and swept those huge wings down and launched us off the floor and toward the vaulted ceiling high above us. I was flying! I held onto him tighter without meaning to, and he smiled with approval as I did so. It had nothing to do with him, and everything to do with the fear of falling, or being dropped.

"Hold onto me," he whispered heatedly.

As if I was going to let go?

I felt the weightlessness of sifting take hold and closed my eyes.

Ryder wasn't coming to save me. Not today at least.

Chapter
THREE

The Horde had followed, sifting in behind us as we materialized into an enormous room where even more creatures awaited us. The room was dark and the walls were a light gray stone. Huge glass chandeliers hung from the high ceilings on metal poles that held them firmly in place above the tables. They threw soft, flickering light against the stone and assembly of the Horde creatures that were present. All I could guess was that it was some sort of great hall or a gargantuan meeting hall of some kind. I was still wrapped in the electrical hold of the King as he shouted off orders in a language I couldn't understand. This was odd, as so far I had understood all of the different dialects that the High Fae spoke in Faery. I seemed to be included in those orders as I was quickly pulled away from him by two of his guards, who took me down a long, winding stairway that led to a richly decorated room.

The room leapt to life as the door was opened and I was pushed through the doorway by one of the guards. The stone walls of the vast room sparkled like crystal was embedded in it and reflected the many candles that were scattered throughout the room. I stumbled but easily caught my balance and turned toward the guards.

"Give me your hands," the first one said through the black material that covered the lower half of his face. His gray and aqua eyes searched mine briefly before he stepped forward and grabbed for the thin delicate chain.

He guided me in the direction of the oversized bed, which had to be the biggest Fae bed I had seen so far. Made of oak, and I mean oak trees, each of the four posts was a slender tree that soared up and intertwined its branches with the next tree. Silvery sheets adorned the mattress, with an array of assorted pillows pushed against the headboard in varying shades that matched the wall and sheets.

"Get on the bed; on your knees and face the door," he ordered. I moved onto the bed as he had ordered and sat back on my knees. He looked up and whispered something under his breath, which caused a chain much like the ones attached to my wrist to appear. He attached it to a chain that hung high from the ceiling. He pulled the chain and suspended my arms above my head. It looked like the Horde King liked his playthings tied up and helpless. Shit. It would be just my luck, which at this point was no luck at all.

"Sit up higher," the guard ordered, and I shifted until I was sitting upright on my knees.

I watched him materialize and place thin cuffs much like the ones on my wrists, around my legs, just above my knees. The chain he attached to those cuffs was then secured to the two posts at the foot of the bed. I swallowed as I realized what they were for. The other guard came in, also dressed in the same black armor, his face hidden for the most part behind a black cloth.

"Ready?" he asked the first guard.

"She's ready," he replied, flashing me a look with those gray and aqua eyes. I'd never seen eyes like his, but they looked as if they belonged in this silvery room. "This is only temporary; running is a bad idea where he is concerned," the guard told me softly.

One guard pulled, and then the other. They pulled until my arms were high above my head, but there wasn't pain from it. Then, they started to pull on the chains attached to my legs, and didn't stop until my legs were spread wide apart, and I was completely helpless to do anything but watch them.

"He will be in momentarily to feed," the second guard said as they left me, dressed in all of my finery on the bed, and sifted from the room.

I felt hot tears rush to my eyes, but I refused to allow them to fall. Instead, I raised my eyes to a huge chandelier that had crystals hanging from it that reflected the candlelight into every imaginable color of gorgeous, dancing prismatic patterns. It was beautiful, and could easily be a focal point while I endured the Horde King's attention.

I would have to endure him long enough for him to think I was subdued. Hopefully he would forget all about me once he had his way, and I could leave this place and never look back. First, I had to gain his trust to ditch the chains, since, like the necklace, they probably kept me from sifting.

There was nothing else inside the room; not at first glance, anyway. I could just make out shelves, but couldn't bring the items on them into focus. I was squinting when Alazander sifted in.

He stopped briefly to examine me, and then held his hand up, and a glass goblet rimmed in gold and filled with a light blue liquid appeared in it. He smiled and took a long sip before he brought it down and held it against my lips.

"You will drink," he said after I just stared at him blankly.

"Okay, but shouldn't we get to know one another before you tie me to your bed?" I asked, hoping to find a clue as to his intention beyond his need to abuse my body.

"What would you like to know?" he asked.

"Why did you want me?"

"Why you, what?" he asked me back.

"Why did it have to be the first born daughter of the Blood King that you took?"

There was more to this than I was seeing. The Horde King wasn't stupid, and this wasn't about petty grudges. If it had been, he could have easily demanded my sister, but he hadn't. He had waited until I'd been found, which spoke volumes about what he needed me specifically for.

"What if I took you because I could, and because you were his first daughter? There were other reasons, but nothing you need to worry yourself with," he replied as he sat on the bed and glamoured away his black silk pants effortlessly. I blanched as he sat naked before me. The man was freaking huge. I was fighting to keep my eyes from revealing my inner panic. I had to remind myself to breathe as he moved closer to me.

"So, you took me because you could?"

"Essentially. As I said, there were other reasons," he replied, and held the goblet of blue liquid up to my mouth. I took a sip willingly, and inhaled as he continued to hold the glass up with the intention of me smelling it. The flavor exploded in my mouth, fruity and faintly bubbly. "It is what Humans would call Ambrosia. The nectar of the gods, supposedly. Do you like it?"

"It's very nice," I replied honestly. Maybe if I got drunk I could make it through tonight.

"How long has it been since you have fed?"

"Two days," I replied easily.

"So you are hungry then, yes?" he asked with knowing eyes.

I was. I had been fighting off the hunger in hopes that Ryder could save me. I'd been injured in the explosion, and even though my father had healed it, I really needed to feed. Soon.

"I am going to feed from you soon, so if you have any more questions, ask them now."

"Don't you want to know about me?" I asked, licking my lips nervously.

"Do you like to fuck?" His question made me blush, and a little angry.

"Yes," I replied, unable to lie.

"Good, because I plan to use you—at every opportunity. Tell me, are you looking forward to being my concubine, or do you dream of escaping me soon?"

Fuck a rubber duck! "I don't look forward to becoming anyone's sex slave."

"So you plan on escaping?" he asked as he reached up and pinched my nipple through the dress. I hissed and felt a flash of fear, and anger that I wasn't angry enough. Instead, heat was flooding my body and my cheeks.

"Yes," I blurted out, much to his delight.

"You won't escape me, ever. I'm not easily manipulated by pretty faces either. Tell me something, how many men have you fucked?"

"Two," I said, exhaling slowly as he moved further onto the bed with me. I felt his wings closing in around us again, stealing the air from my lungs.

I inhaled deeply as the oxygen grew thin when they closed fully around us. They were soft, silky warm. The spikes I had seen earlier must have retracted when he felt safe within his own castle. His mouth was inches from mine. The goblet was gone and forgotten as his hands now stroked me through the dress, sending heat swirling through my body. I moaned, unable to stop myself.

"Only two, that's good. How many did you fuck during Transition?"

"One," I whimpered as he lifted the dress, and his hand trailed over the thin panties I wore.

"One?" he asked in surprise.

"One," I confirmed and felt anger at my response to him rise within me.

I shouldn't be feeling anything but hatred for this monster, but here I was, panting like some whore while his finger stroked my pussy.

"You don't like that your body is responding to my touch, do you?"

"No," I replied firmly.

"You're wet for me. Does that upset you; that your body knows you are in need?"

"Yes," I whimpered as he dipped his fingers and pressed them against the silk panties I wore. He watched me as he stroked my core, finding the perfect rhythm as his fingers pushed against my need. My body tensed with want—for him.

"You smell good. Are you going to allow me to fuck you?"

I felt the tears fall. I'd been trying so hard to hold them at bay, but it was a losing battle. I shook my head. "I don't want you," I replied as golden eyes flashed inside my head. "You're not giving me much of a choice, anyway, seeing as how you had to tie me up and all."

"Who is it you want?" he asked, stroking his fingers over the silken nub of my pleasure.

Ryder!

I didn't answer him, not that he expected an answer as he moved closer and the air disappeared. I was left with the option to kiss him, or die. I kissed him, and the moment his tongue pushed through my lips, I sobbed. This wasn't going as I'd planned it to. Instead, I was slowly and erotically being mind-fucked by the Horde King and was succumbing to his will effortlessly.

He pulled back, but kept his wings around us, keeping me cocooned in their silky warmth as his hand worked over my wet sleek heat, and the other held my face lifted to his. "Will you submit to me and allow me to fuck you?" he asked again.

"Do I have a choice?" I asked, spreading my legs further apart to give him more access. What the hell was wrong with me? I felt a single finger delve deep inside of me. I cried out and impaled my own body on it further, finding a rhythm as his mouth found mine and took control.

"So fucking wet, so slippery with need," he growled as he pulled his mouth away from mine and added yet another finger inside of me.

Something was wrong, because this felt too fucking right, and I wanted him inside of me unlike anything before him. Even more than I'd wanted Ryder. I wanted him to bend me over and fuck me until I screamed for more. "What are you doing to me?" I asked breathlessly as the beginning of an orgasm started to build.

"See me," he growled and claimed my lips again.

I shook my head at him as I held my eyes tightly closed, and continued to ride his hand as he added yet another finger inside of me, stretching me as his enormous cock pushed against my belly. When I was about to come he stopped; everything stopped. I was no longer chained to the ceiling, but lying on the bed with my legs spread wide, and the deadly creature loomed over me.

His brands were moving, his skin was now lustrous, and his wings blocked out the light from around us. "You smell good," he said as he sank between my legs and lowered his mouth to where my panties still covered me. He didn't taste me; instead he smelled the need which was soaking my panties.

"Tell me to fuck you, tell me to part this flesh and make you mine," he demanded. "Submit to me, and become mine."

I was supposed to say no, but my brain was shutting down and I had the sinking feeling in the pit of my stomach that I wasn't seeing everything that was here, that I was missing something in the room. "No," I cried as my body shook with the need to say yes. I wanted Ryder; why wasn't he here? I needed him to be here. "I want Ryder," I blurted out, which made the Horde King pause.

"You're mine now," he replied, dismissing my need as his fingers parted my panties and started moving inside of me again.

"I don't want you!" I cried, even as I pushed myself against his fingers with a need I couldn't explain. I should have kept the dagger. I should have followed through with the plan. How could I have not seen him using his powers on me? "I want only one man!" I screamed it, trying to make myself understand that I was doing something wrong by trying to come for the Horde King. The hunger was gnawing on me, and the events leading up to this were driving it deeper. I was trying to focus, trying to stave it off. In the end, I knew I'd cave.

This was all wrong, and when his wings came down to cover us once more, I could no longer care. I needed this creature inside of me. I wanted this need for him to go away. I kissed his mouth using my hands to hold him to me as I did so, since they were no longer tethered to the chains.

"I'm going to have you," he whispered as my clothes melted away with his will. His mouth latched onto my nipple as his magic worked the other one, his fingers sinking deep inside of me. They were hitting the spot, which was sending me toward the cliff that would send me off the edge.

"Nooooo, I want Ryder. I need Ryder." Why

wasn't he coming? He was my Knight in a fucking Fairy suit! He was supposed to storm the castle walls and protect me, to save me. I was his, damn it! Only his.

"See me!" he snapped, and drove his fingers inside of me until I was helpless but to lay there as he fucked me with them. His other hand held my chin to keep my face immovable.

"No!" I screamed as the impending orgasm threatened to explode.

I blinked as his form started changing, as if something was fighting for release. I strained to see what was there. My mind wanted me to ignore it. His face was moving, as if something else was inside of him. I wanted to close my eyes. I wanted him to make me explode. Most of all, I wanted to be somewhere else, and with someone *else*.

"See *me* damn it!"

"I see you," I screamed, wanting him to shut up and allow me to find release.

"Goddammit, Pet, *See* me!" he shouted as the walls shook around us.

The pending orgasm was forgotten as my entire body shook from his words. I blinked at the golden eyes that looked down at me in stunned silence. As if he was the one who was shocked at his revelation. Other than the wings, he was here. Ryder was here.

"Now you see *me*, Synthia," he whispered breathlessly.

My lips and fingers trembled as I reached up to stroke his skin, afraid I'd died from the Horde Kings attention, or turned FIZ, and this was where my mind had gone—to Ryder. I was in his arms and shaking with all the tension and fear I'd be feeling; it all came out at once.

I was touching him. "Are you real?" I whispered, afraid to say it too loudly for fear he would disappear.

"Fuck, you're so beautiful, and now you really are mine," he growled and took me to the mattress hard.

I pushed at him. "What the hell? Where's the Horde King? Did you kill him?" I asked, unsure how he'd accomplished this. Maybe I had passed out, and this was a dream. If it was, I never wanted to wake up.

"Syn," he growled, trying to kiss me.

I pushed at him. "Am I dead? Did he turn me FIZ? How is this possible?" I demanded.

"What if I told you I was him?" he asked, letting me up finally.

"No, because that would be a lie and you can't lie," I said.

"Syn," he whispered, running his hand over my naked leg.

"Ryder." I pleaded for him to tell me he wasn't the King. He just looked at me until I was left without a choice. I slapped him—hard. "You...mother fucker! How could you!?" I demanded, but he pushed me back down, and he was inside of me before he could answer.

I cried out as he stretched me further than he ever had before. My body throbbed with need as he drove himself in to my core. "Fuck, I need you, Pet, come for me, good girl, come!" he screamed in the multitude of voices that instantly had my body shaking from the electrical power that tore through the room.

I exploded around his shaft, painfully. My entire body shook with power as he released his need and fed me. He continued to pump his cock inside of me until the aftershocks of the orgasm subsided.

Oh my God.

This wasn't happening.

Fucking hell!

Oh my holy flipping buckets!

Chapter FOUR

I lay there staring at him, unable to look away from his beauty. Everything was coming back; all the hints, all the truths that had been staring me in the face. "You walked through the wards," I accused. I struggled out from under him and scooted to the other side of the enormous bed, never taking my eyes off of him.

"Child's play, Synthia. I had Eliran make an amulet that tricked the wards. There are a lot of creatures that the wards did not take into account. We knew the Demon was one of them."

"Ryder, I asked you straight up if you were the Horde King, and you said no," I whispered. I realized at that moment, he hadn't actually answered me any of those times with a solid no. He'd danced around the question.

His golden eyes watched me as everything that his words implied crashed in on me. He'd tortured my brother; he had been the one to set everything in motion that had sent me to the Humans, which resulted in them being killed. Because of him, it had always been him. He was the reason I'd lost my family, he was the one who had sent my entire life spiraling out of control—and I'd fallen in love with him.

"*You're* Alazander!"

"No, I'm not."

"Then who the hell are you really, Ryder? Please, tell me who the hell I have been fucking!"

I was pissed, and his lips that jerked up in the corners with a start of a smirk were not helping. I wanted to kiss him. I wanted to strangle him. Worst of all, I *wanted* him! It all pissed me off in the worst way.

"The Wild Hunt!?" I accused, throwing angry, sharp as daggers at him. I pulled the covers around my naked body, too shocked to do anything else.

"You were caught and fucked by me, the Horde King; always winner of his own event," he smirked wickedly. "I never lied to you, Synthia, if that is what you are wondering. I let you draw your own conclusions, and I wasn't, in fact, the Horde King until the day you were taken to the Blood Realm. That action forced my hand." He gave me a small smirk. "I told you that I would save you, Synthia."

"Why? How? This doesn't make sense! How could you be the Horde King, and yet *not* be him?"

"Because I ascended to the throne," he answered simply.

"That's it? You just jumped up on the throne, and the actual Horde King allowed this?" I gasped in surprise.

"Not exactly, Pet. That's a long story. How are you feeling?" He quickly changed the subject.

"Oh, I don't think so, you fucking spring it on me

that you're the Horde King, you made me freak the heck out at the idea of being given to the Horde—to *you*! I told you I planned on killing *you*! You couldn't have thrown me a little bone? No, because you're an asshole! You made me think I fucked the Horde King!"

"You *did* just fuck the Horde King, Synthia, and you weren't complaining," he said with a small smile.

"I am going to do more than complain in a moment," I gritted out. "Why couldn't you just tell me as soon as we got here? Why the act, and scaring me out of my mind? Spill it, Horde boy!"

"I am sorry for scaring you. Too much has happened over the past few days, and I didn't know how far you had been compromised," he said tenderly as he reached out and tried to cup my face. I flinched slightly away from him. "I had to know where you stood with me, Pet. I just didn't count on your hunger being so strong. I felt it, and I couldn't think past that to anything else."

"Tell me what happened," I said softly, and relaxed a little. He shifted his body and those wings into a more comfortable position against the pillows and looked at me sadly.

"I killed him. Too much had happened and it was escalating out of control with no end in sight. He pushed too far, and I was left with no choice but to kill him."

"Ryder." I felt sweat beading on my forehead. I knew he was not telling me everything. I needed to know more. "How does you killing the Horde King give you the right to claim his throne?" With Fae politics, nothing was that easy.

"Because I am...*was* his son, Synthia; Danu's Heir. Killing my father gave me his throne. I had not claimed it, because I didn't want anyone to know he was dead. I needed to buy as much time as I could to try and save Faery without my father's sins and Fae politics interfering with that goal. Now everything that I have delayed will come to my realm with a vengeance."

"Wait, so you didn't make the contract for me, the one to my parents?" The Horde King who had made that contract was the one who had irrevocably screwed up my life. Hope was thrumming through me, my heart was beating wildly.

"No, Synthia. I sent Ristan with the Horde emissaries to make that contract for you in the name of the Horde King. I'm not proud of the lengths I went through to secure it, but I'd have done much more to secure you."

"You cut my brother up. You knew it would break my parents' resolve to withstand your demands."

He gave a slight nod of his dark head. "His hands? That is the least of what my Father would have done, and your parents would have expected nothing less."

My heart was hammering wildly, his eyes watching my every thought that crossed my mind. On one hand, I was relieved to find out who he was, while on the other hand, everything I'd ever heard about the Horde King was running rampant through my mind.

He lifted his hands and ran them through his hair as if he was the one who was frustrated. "There is too much to tell you, and too little time. You are going to stay here and listen without interrupting me. Please. I'm going to sit beside you and I will do my best to explain everything. After I'm done, you can ask me the questions I can see burning in your eyes."

"Fine," I replied, pulling up the sheet around my naked body. I watched him lower his gaze with anticipation burning in his golden depths. He smirked and waved his fingers. I gave a small shudder of breath as I felt satin press and wrap around my skin. "Thank you," I whispered, and scooting back against the mountain of pillows piled against the elaborate headboard.

He moved closer, as if he was afraid I'd run away from him. I felt my skin tingle with the raw current I'd always felt when sitting or standing too close to him. He pulled the sheet from my body and smiled at the red satin bathrobe he'd glamoured for me.

"Red suits you, Blood Princess," he murmured as his fingers trailed over the naked flesh of my leg.

"I'm waiting," I replied, afraid to allow him to waste time with the questions burning on my tongue.

"Always so impatient," he said roughly. He moved closer to me and lay back against the pillows. His mammoth wings rustled and folded back neatly as he settled in comfortably beside me.

"Just over twenty two years ago, my father was killed by my hand. I am sure your parents and your brother told you how he was abusing the other Castes of Fae. What they may not have known is that he was abusing his own people first. Power can corrupt even the strongest of beings. In the beginning, my father was much like your adopted one. In my eyes he could do no wrong. He was everything to our people, and exactly the creature that Danu wanted him to be.

"Over time, something changed within him like a sickness. He started making demands of our own people, and eventually when he got bored of that, he took more. He took the daughters of our enemies, as well as our allies. *Gifts* he called them, and he spared those who gave them freely to him. He took what he wanted from those that would not, and levied huge consequences for those who defied him. He wanted something tangible to assure they knew he had the power. Any slight, real or imagined, from one of the Lords or other Kings would result in the abuse of their Gift." He exhaled slowly, as if the memory was more than he wanted to remember. His eyes took on a hued glow of amber and obsidian.

"My uncle, Kier, saw it happening, and tried to stop it. I think Alazander had been sick long before we caught sight of it in him. Not only did he abuse the female Gifts, he had been handing them off to others of the Horde to use at will. He did more than just use those he took from their families. He shattered many, and then they were handed off to his Elite Guard. We're not Human, and I'm not proud of my father, or what I did at his bidding. I used those females; willingly or not, I took them. I did what he wanted, what he expected of his sons. I've done things that, looking back, make me sick, but I enjoyed it at the time. I was raised to be of the Horde, and that meant I was raised to be hard, fierce, merciless, and take what I wanted."

Something in his eyes told me that he hadn't enjoyed what he'd done. He wasn't as much of a victim as the poor women had been, but he was still guilt-ridden from what he'd assisted his father in doing.

When I refused to comment on it, he continued. "I was there when your grandfather was betrayed, and killed," he said softly. "I was there when he killed Anise and put that idiot Dresden on the throne. I have always been at his right hand and led his campaigns. I was the one who led the Elite Guard you saw today."

I stared at him, dumfounded. "How old are you?" I whispered.

"I have lived over a thousand of your years," he replied steadily. I sucked in air as I was trying to wrap my mind around it. "I have always told you that I am not proud of many of the things I have done, and I have done some very bad things, Synthia. Many of my regrets were for what I stood by and allowed.

"Kier was often at our court and he was a sore spot for my father. We had become affected by the plague that was sweeping through the Horde, Blood, and Dark kingdoms. We had been working with Kier to find who was responsible for what was happening to Faery, and trying to find a way to stop it. Kier had also been trying to get his sister released from Alazander and back to the Dark Kingdom for years as my father's madness had escalated. Adding to this volatile situation was Danu. She was not pleased with his excesses and abuse of the Fae people and had been relentless in the visions of what would happen if we did not intervene.

"So, Kier and I, along with the Elite Guard, had been formulating a coup behind Alazander's back. Not exactly an easy thing to do, considering the magnitude of his powers. It boiled over one day when my mother put voice to her concerns during one of Kier's visits. My father abused her in front of an entire assembly of the Horde. Most thought nothing of it, since Alazander was known for taking his wives and concubines wherever he deemed fit. Dristan could take no more and tried to intervene. Alazander turned his attention from my mother to my brother."

I swallowed, slowly placing pieces together. My eyes flickered up to his, and caught him lost in the memory of his past.

"It was as if the centuries of insanity had all escalated to this moment. He'd done so much damage to everything, most of our allies had turned on us. He'd killed so many innocents. He was killing us, and even though we were the strongest of the Castes, sooner or later, fate would catch up with us. I was the only one who could kill him. Up until then, I couldn't do it. I had faltered, right up until that day." He exhaled a shattered breath and shook his head. "He pierced Dristan through the chest with one of his wing talons. Dristan had chosen death rather than to witness more of my father's sickness; he knew attacking the Horde King, even in defense of our mother, was suicide. We all knew what my father would do next. I killed him then. I was unable to stop the beast inside of me from coming out when I'd seen what he had done to my mother and Dristan. But, in killing the reigning Horde King, I was fated to take his place on the throne."

I swallowed and tried to picture the men they had been, and the ones they had become. "He was family, Ryder. You chose to save your brother, but at a price to yourself. I would have done the same thing had I been in your place."

His mouth slashed into an angry line, and his eyes turned from amber, to complete obsidian. "I don't think you would have. You, unlike me, would have looked for a way out of it without killing your own father."

"He took the choice from you when he struck at them. You made the right choice."

"For who? Dristan? My mother? For Danu? For Faery? I did not *want* to take the throne!!"

"But you weren't the Horde King before tonight?"

I asked carefully.

"No, there was too much that I had to accomplish, that I could not do as the Horde King with all that the title entails. Those in attendance that night were sworn to a blood oath not to reveal what had happened. To perpetuate what needed to be done to save Faery, Kier adopted me as one of his sons so that we could misdirect our enemies and find the heirs and relics of the prophecy. It allowed me to hide in plain sight without being challenged, or lied to by those who would want to challenge or cause the Horde King issues."

"That's how you were able to say you were Kier's son," I said with a wince. "You're not Adam's brother; you're his cousin."

"I am. My mother is Kier's only sister. He saved us, all of us. If he hadn't been willing to help, my father or the Mages would have eventually killed us all. Ristan had already been having visions of what was needed to fix the damage my father and the Mages had wrought on this world. Part of the prophecy included atonement for the damage done by my father, but something like that has to be undertaken very carefully so the other Castes don't sense weakness and attack. Another part of the prophecy is the recovery of the relics and the union of the Light and Dark Heirs and their offspring.

"So, why me? I don't understand why you asked for me."

"You are part of the last piece of the prophecy that we did not discuss with you before. The one that concerned the union of the Horde and Blood Heirs. You're an Heir, or you will be. Danu picked you," he whispered as his hand found mine and swallowed it in his much larger hand. "Together we will give life to an Heir of both Horde and Blood, one who will help heal the lands."

"Hmm-hmm, sure. Just like I was supposed to with Adam? Anyone ever consider the idea that maybe Danu ate a batch of funky brownies and decided to send Ristan some very random, very kinky dreams? Or, maybe Ristan ate the brownies? It's plausible with that Demon."

"I don't think Danu eats funky brownies, as you call them."

"Wishful thinking on my part," I said with a small shrugged my shoulders. "I'd really like to meet this Danu, and give her a solid piece of my mind. I also want to know why all her visions about me include making babies."

He shook his head and smiled sadly at me. "I don't know why she had to make things as complicated as she has. I know she cannot directly help us so she sent the prophecy to try in her own way to help. I do know that her anger with my father knew no bounds and we have been trying to heal the rift with her since his death."

"So why did you cut up my brother?" There it was, the final piece I could not reconcile him doing.

"I wish I did not have to go that route, but it is a tactic my father would have used to get his way. I couldn't just go to your parents and tell them that I'd killed the reigning Horde King as I asked for you, not without them trying to attack us outright to test my strength, so I sent the emissaries in my father's name. When that did not work, I used Liam. Up until that point, I had nothing to do with him and I had been trying to figure out how to let him go, as I had with many of the other prisoners that my father had collected. The tactic worked; your parents accepted my offer and Liam was released," he said as he took another breath and continued on.

"Everything was going according to plan. We were on the trail of who was harming Faery, we had two of four Heirs identified, and then your parents did the unexpected and reneged on the deal by stealing you away and hiding you. Ristan's vision's never changed, so we knew through him that the Blood Heir was still out there, alive. I knew that if I had been your father, I'd have sent you to where no other Fae would. They sent you to the Humans. The Guild was unexpected, though, and smart.

"I had to pressure them to keep the contract. By sending small groups of the Horde to the borders and attacking, I managed it with little to no bloodshed. I could have asked for Liam back, I was within my rights, but I figured enough damage had been done to him already."

"Wait a minute. You planned on adding me to your harem?"

"If you mean the Women's Pavilion, then yes," he replied smoothly.

"You still have a harem…?"

"Yes, and I won't be getting rid of it either, Synthia."

I felt my stomach hit the floor like a ton of bricks.

"Now you know how and why I let everyone assume I was the Dark Heir. It allowed me to move around with the backing of the Dark King and find the relics, as well as you and the other Heirs that had disappeared by that time, without revealing who and what I am," he smiled as his eyes sparkled with mischief, as if he hadn't just said he was keeping a harem of women. "Strange how destiny works; you left Faery to escape me, and you landed in my lap, anyway."

"You planned on keeping me, knowing you had to find the Blood Heir and get her pregnant?" I asked slowly. At this, he looked mildly confused. "You're an asshole!"

"That doesn't matter, Synthia. I found you, and it's you I have to create an Heir with."

"And you don't see a problem with this?" I asked, sitting up to move away from him. I needed distance.

"No, I don't. It's worked out perfectly and so much makes sense now."

"Kiss my ass, Fairy! I'm not having your baby just because you want me to, or because some stupid, funky brownie eating deity saw something. Obviously she has no freaking idea of what the hell she sees either, because less than forty-eight hours ago, I was supposed to be having Adam's baby to save your world! You have a harem of women, go fuck them and leave me out of it!" I was fighting tears. He had a harem of women somewhere in this place, he was the flipping Horde King, and he'd said nothing about loving me, only the damn need to save his fucking Fairy lands!

"You're having my child," he growled, as he moved off of the bed and glamoured on silky blank pants. His wings seemed to expand with the slightest movement.

"No. I'm. Not!"

"Yes you are, you're already pregnant, Synthia."

"No, that's something I would notice!"

"The reason you became sick when you were living in your guardian's home is because you were pregnant with my child. A Horde Heir, the wards sensed it. They were trying to protect you from the child we made."

"You're lying," I screamed.

This wasn't happening!

"It's happening, whether either of us wants a child now or not. I would have preferred children later, but this seems to be how Danu wanted it all to work. I am sorry, but you will have to adjust to this quickly."

"Me? Me!? Take me home, Ryder. Is that even your name?" I didn't know what to think anymore, or what to believe. He'd played with words so much that I wasn't sure I could trust him anymore.

He laughed regretfully and shook his head as he lifted it to face me. His wings expanded, and the room sizzled with his immense power. He strode forward with purpose, but I held my ground.

"I have a few things to attend to and will be back shortly. I suggest you get prepared for an exam from Eliran while I am gone."

I watched as he sifted out, and left me sitting in the huge elegant bedroom of the Horde King, alone. I brought my shaking hands to my stomach and felt the flat line of my abdomen. A baby? I wasn't ready for a baby, and I wasn't ready to be set aside in a flipping harem and forgotten about as all the other females had been. I had to get the fuck out of this place, soon.

Chapter FIVE

Eliran finished his exam with Ryder present; everything looked fine as far as he could tell this early in the pregnancy. It left me numb that I was actually pregnant. I was freaking pregnant! Ryder hadn't been playing with words. Eliran had shown me the blood work and had even done the test with me standing beside him watching his every move.

I sat on the exam table, numb, unable to put into words what I felt. Sheer panic was gnawing at my insides as I pictured my future here with Ryder and his entire harem of women. Where did I fit in? Ryder was the freaking Horde King, and I was a flipping concubine. No, correction, I was his pregnant concubine!

I was willing to give this a shot. I was not, however, willing to become just another female pining after his Highn-ass to visit me in said harem. Nope, was not happening. I turned to find him watching me, his eyes back to the beautiful golden color that haunted my dreams.

I wanted to throw myself in his arms and listen as he told me everything was going to be ok. But, this was real life...or, more to the point, *my* life and shit like that never happened. I was doomed by a destiny that had my entire life planned out for me.

"So, what do we do now?" I asked, trying to get out from inside of my mind where shit was getting deep.

"You're having my child, period," Ryder snapped heatedly.

"I didn't say I wasn't, Fairy. I asked what now; how do we make the baby strong enough that it is accepted by the land?" I asked, letting the fear I had felt about being with Adam and producing his child finally out.

Ryder's face went from cold to worried in the flash of an eye. He hadn't considered this? So much for thinking he could figure this one out. "It's my child," he replied simply, as if because the child was his, it would live.

"The children of Faery are dying; the sickness is hitting the strongest Caste first…which is Horde, right?"

"We will figure it out together, Synthia. It's my child; do you think I'd allow anything to happen to you or my child?" he growled.

"I didn't say that!" I said defensively. "I want to know how to ensure our child isn't one of the many dying."

"Eliran, get everything you need for this pregnancy. Take Ristan with you, and go find whatever it is you will need to take care of Synthia and *our* babe."

My heart flipped and did a little jig as it hit the floor with my reality check…and bounced away. This was really happening. I was having Ryder's child…

correction, I was having the Horde King's love child.

"I'll be back as soon as I can," Eliran said and nodded to Ryder before he turned and sifted from the room.

There was total silence in the room now. All I could do was sit and stare at Ryder. Gone were his wings and Horde looks. He looked as he had in my world, once again. It was hard not to throw myself at him and thank whoever had gotten us here. Because here was without Alazander, and here was better than what I could have hoped. No matter how fucked up *here* was, I was still with him.

"Come, I'll take you to where you will be staying. I have things that can't be put off any longer now that I am King of the Horde," he said gently as he reached out a hand for me to join him.

"Ryder, tell me it's going to be okay. Tell me you want this," I whispered unable to fight the feeling of needing him anymore.

He walked slowly to me and pulled me from the table until he held me against himself firmly. His body was hot and hard but comforting as his heat stole the chill from my bones. He tilted my head until I was looking at him. His mouth lowered to claim mine, his kiss searching and demanding.

One second we were in the exam room of Eliran's small clinic, and the next I was in his arms and back in his elegant bedroom. He broke the kiss after a few moments and I had to remember how to breathe. Kissing him here in Faery, without him hiding his powers, was electric.

"I want to kiss you until your lips are sore, and I want to whisper dirty words into your pretty little ears, Synthia, because it makes my cock so fucking hard, and it turns me on to know you're hearing it and anticipating it." He kissed my neck softly. "I am King now. I am not sure I can be what you need me to be. I am King first and foremost here," he pulled back and looked at me, smiling gently. "We will be okay now, nothing will ever harm you. Nothing will ever hurt you again. I promise you this."

"What if you're what hurts me? And where am I being sent?" I asked.

"I don't want to hurt you either, Pet. For your protection, I would prefer you stay in the Pavilion while I hold court to deal with quarrels between the Castes of the Horde. For now, I would like for you to take over a room that is part of my chambers."

~~*

I was shown to a room that adjoined his and was decorated in gentle hues of blue. The bed was huge, but then again, I'd come to expect that where the Fae were concerned. The canopy had sky-blue silk drapes hanging from it. It looked like something from a time long ago.

Four women stood at the far side of the bed with their eyes lowered to the floor. They were dressed in thin sundresses, and cotton shoes covered their feet. I didn't say anything as Ryder stood beside me, silently allowing me to take in the room.

"Hello," I said, breaking the silence and tension in the room.

"Synthia, this is Darynda," Ryder said as an auburn haired beauty bowed her head even lower. "She will be in charge of your care. Her father is noble, but not of the royal family; it is our equivalent of the old peer system that was used in your world. To serve the royal family is considered an honor, and I think she would do well with you."

I turned my head in his direction and hiked up an eyebrow. Yup, these guys lived in the dark ages. "And they do this willingly?" I asked. Call me old-fashioned, or even new-fashioned, because slavery was just that, and I wasn't keen on it in any form.

"Ask them," Ryder replied, instead of answering.

Darynda lifted brilliant blue and grey eyes and gave a friendly smile. I took an instant liking to her. She was a little shorter than I was, but her eyes showed a spark that wasn't obvious in her demeanor. I knew that spark, because I had it in spades.

"Do you serve willingly?" I asked, since she hadn't answered the question.

"We all do. This is an honor and a mark of respect that we show our families by being chosen, and serving," Darynda said and dropped into a curtsey. She then introduced the other women who stood behind her.

Keeley had to be a Brownie; I could tell by the way her giant hazel eyes darted around the room looking for anything out of place; not to mention, she looked no bigger than a twelve year old, much like the Brownie at Ryder's mansion had. Her hair was short and chestnut brown with light blonde highlights that were scattered throughout it. Faelyn was a Pixie, and she stood with an awkwardness developed from flying more than walking. The Pixie had bright blue eyes in the shape of a saucer, and blonde hair with pink tips that looked like she'd dipped them in dye recently, judging from the brightness of the color. Her wings twitched nervously.

Meriel looked to be Fae, but I couldn't judge from her appearance which Caste she belonged to. Her black hair had green and blue highlights to it, and she had a sensuality about her that seemed to surpass many of the Fae women I had met to date. Her green and gray eyes seemed to be tracking Ryder, and I wasn't quite sure of what to make of that.

They seemed willing to be here, and happy about it even. I was still reeling from the news that I was pregnant, and probably wouldn't be the best company at the moment. I actually felt sorry for them having to serve me.

"I'll leave you to get settled in, Pet. If you need anything, they will get it for you. You're not to leave this room without an escort, do you understand?"

"Whatever," I said, lowering my eyes.

"I'll be back tonight. Sinjinn will be close by; if you need me, just tell him. Otherwise, the only part of the castle you are allowed in is the pavilion for now."

I watched him sift from the room before turning my eyes back to the four women who all stood silently, staring at me. We stood awkwardly taking each other in, before the one that had been called Darynda started up a conversation with me.

"So, you are what all the noise is about?" she asked in a smooth voice.

"I guess," I said, not wanting to get into why I was here. I was still in shock and reeling over what had just been dropped in my lap.

"Okay, all we know is that you seem to have the castle in an uproar, and we were wondering why?" she asked as she tilted her head and smiled.

"Because I'm the Blood Princess would be my guess," I replied. At the expulsion of breaths, I figured they knew what that meant to the Horde and Faery. They broke into excited chatter until the door of the room was opened, and Claire popped her head in.

She'd been friendly on our last meeting, and even under the circumstances, I'd played nice with her. Of course, last time she probably thought I'd just been someone else to feed Ryder.

She walked in looking spectacular, her long frame decked out in a seafoam green silk dress that was far more lavish than anything I had ever seen her dressed in before. Her eyes threw angry sparks as she looked me over, which caught me off guard. "I was sent up to explain your position here." The look on her face said she wasn't happy about it at all.

"And what is it that is expected of me?" I asked, giving her the benefit of the doubt.

"You're *his* whore, of course. You serve his needs, and as his concubine, you do anything he wants. You will be moved to the pavilion soon, where you will be expected to service the men who he deems worthy of fucking you. Now I know you think you are special to him, but we all were at one time. His passion is fleeting, and we all play our parts here."

"Is that all?" If he thought he could put me in the harem to feed his elite guard, he had another thing coming.

"Listen, you are nothing new to us. You think you are so fucking special. You're nothing, less than nothing, really. We are taking bets; you know what bets are right? You should, since it's a Human term. Many of the women in the pavilion give you a week of holding his attention before he moves on to someone of the Horde."

"Considering I've held his attention for a few months now, and that he's the one who brought me here...put me down for six months." I smiled coldly. She wanted to be a total bitch? Bring it, I could play this game. "Now if you would excuse me, I'd like a bath."

"I don't think so!" she screeched, losing all sense of playing it cool. "He won't be coming for you tonight. He's made other plans." She hissed but sheathed her claws. "He's made plans that include me tonight."

I felt bile rise to the back of my throat. "Then that is his choice. You think it bothers me?" It did, and I was doing my best to act nonchalant.

"Watch your back. You are not going to make many friends here, Witch."

"I'm not just a Witch anymore. Haven't you heard? Turns out I'm the Blood Princess, Claire. I didn't ask to be here; Ryder made a contract with my parents for me. It's a simple matter for him to fix, since he is the only one who can undo it."

"Wrong; here, you are only a meal for the newly crowned Horde King," she argued.

"Whatever," I quipped and turned to my helper gals.

"He was with me last night, gaining strength to travel to the Blood Realm," she cooed with a nasty taint to her sweet tone.

Ouch!

"He fed from you?" I asked, trying my best to hide the hurt that was even now burning in my chest.

"Yes, and he was *very* hungry," she said, watching me as I turned around to face her.

"You slept with him?" Yes, I was a sucker for punishment.

"How else does one feed?" she replied coyly.

"He's the King, it's his choice," I replied, trying to keep my face from betraying my feelings.

I'd slept with Ryder right after he'd been with Claire, but then he'd come for me and in doing so, he would have needed to be strong and ready to fight if presented with a worst case scenario.

I felt sick to my stomach; worse, I felt like I was going to...I threw up all over the bed with Claire watching me. She cringed and recoiled as if I'd thrown up on her. Fucking Fairy was dead! This was his fault, his stupid doing.

He'd gotten me knocked up!

This was going to go badly.

Chapter SIX

I'd retched until I was dry heaving. Someone had cleaned up and another had wiped my face with a cold cloth. They tucked me into the fresh bedding, and I could hear whispers from the doorway. Hours went by, and when Ryder didn't come to get me, despair kicked up its ugly head. Why hadn't he come to get me?

Eventually, I'd fallen asleep as comforting hands soothed my hair like my mother had done many times when I'd been a child. It was comforting, but when I'd woken up, only Eliran was in the room with me.

"You were sick again," he stated the obvious.

"You think?" I replied harshly and instantly regretted it. "I'm sorry, Eliran."

"It concerns me that you are still getting sick. You are fully Fae now. You should be fine. Ryder seems to think that the first few times had to do with the wards inside your Human abode."

"Home; it was my home, Eliran," I whispered.

"Right, well, since you are newly out of Transition,

we need to keep a close eye on your pregnancy. The first two months are the equivalent to a Human's first trimester of pregnancy. If you were to miscarry, this would be the time that it would happen."

"Any idea why I am throwing up so much now that I am no longer in a house warded against the Horde?" I asked, finding myself concerned. I hadn't wanted to be a mother, hadn't even wanted to think about it. I may not have wanted it, but the thought of losing it brought tears to my eyes.

It was amazing how soon you could become attached to something you hadn't wanted. I felt the tears flooding my eyes and tried to stop them, but failed.

"Synthia, you shouldn't cry. I promise to do everything in my power to ensure that you and the baby are both healthy and fine."

"I don't even know why I'm crying," I replied honestly.

He smiled softly. "It's the hormones. Normally they wouldn't be this bad, as you haven't been through your second heat cycle yet. The hormones can be worse in a newly Transitioned Fae. I tried to explain that to Kier as well, but he thought it better we not include that. You had enough pressure already on your slim shoulders. Fae pregnancy in the first heat cycle is rare, and yet we'd held hope that you would be different. You are, lucky for us."

"I thought the plan was for me and Adam to have a child right away?"

"Plans usually are grand when they start out. We only hoped you would be able to, Synthia; hope is all we have left. You are different, though, as you can see.

It is very possible that you could have done exactly as they had planned for you and young Adam. The only downside is that you are a newborn in our world and your newly found senses will be overwhelming for a while."

"Great; so basically, I'm going to become a freaking water faucet!" I asked, drying the tears—or trying to. Poor Eliran patted my hand and made promises to return later. He looked a little uncomfortable and almost tripped over himself to get out of the room and away from me, and I didn't blame him. I felt unlike myself, and now at least I had a reason for why I felt the way I did.

I'm not sure how much time had passed when Ristan came in slowly, as if he were afraid of what he would find. I looked up with puffy red eyes and started crying again.

"Well shit, Flower. Never took you for the sissy type," he said, as he sat beside me on the bed and pulled me close to his shoulder. His dark blue button down shirt got an immediate soaking. At least he looked the same; the only thing different was a gold medallion on a thin chain around his neck that had the same design that was on the mark Ryder had given to me of the two dragons on the Celtic cross. This made me cry harder.

"It's his fault!" I cried.

"Takes two to play *hide the snake in the cave*," he replied.

"Hide the snake in the cave!?" I blinked, before I started laughing.

"That's my girl," he said with his shoulders shaking from suppressed laughter.

"This is crazy, Ristan. I didn't ask for any of this. I'm not ready to be a mom," I said, wiping at my eyes.

"I don't think anyone is ever ready. You will be used to the idea when the child comes. He will be very protected, and cherished."

"Who says it's not a girl?" I asked, pulling away from his shoulder.

"The vision," he said.

"Was it the same one with me having Adam's baby? Yeah right, like I'm going to buy that crap. No offense."

He laughed and shook his head. "Sometimes I don't know whether Danu hates me, or if she just likes screwing with my head. Either way, she's a bitch. If I got a choice in the visions, I'd have you married and in my bed so fast your sexy little puffy eyes would roll." He wiggled his eyebrows and kissed my cheek. "Now, Flower, no more chasing off the boys with tears. You're so much more badass than tears; at least send 'em running from punches."

"Ryder didn't come for me. He said he would last night," I replied ignoring his comment.

"He was otherwise busy. He has a lot to do, now that he is King," he explained.

"He promised, and Claire said they had plans together?"

"That's doubtful since he was with me, and we were doing Court business that ran much longer than it should have as far as I am concerned."

"So Claire can lie?" I asked, wondering why she could and I couldn't.

"No, but she's a lot older and excels at word play."

"Is Ryder going to grow tired of me?" I wasn't sure why I'd asked, but I had a feeling Ristan wouldn't lie to me.

Ristan turned to look at me closely. "Is that what you think? He went fucking crazy when you were taken. He went berserk and took the throne when we could have easily gotten you away from the Blood Realm, but he couldn't wait to get you back. He wouldn't even give us a day to make a plan and see it out. You really think he's going to just lock you in the pavilion and take someone else?"

"He was ready to take his throne, anyway. You guys were coming back here to do just that. I'm blonde, Ristan, not an idiot."

"You're smart, Flower. Never said you weren't. Ryder's been putting off claiming that throne for more than twenty years. No, once he knew where you were, he called the full assembly of the Horde and marched right up to the throne. He manifested the crown of the Horde King and announced that Alazander was dead. We plan on something more formal down the road, but he was in too much of a hurry to do more than an announcement right then. Alazander was a bastard. This isn't something he wanted to do, ever. Keep that in mind for the next few weeks. He has a hard road to walk right now. Everyone will be challenging his right to take the throne, even with him being the Heir of the Horde. It is one of the reasons for the *shock and awe* display yesterday. We couldn't give them any time to think for one moment that he wasn't Alazander. As it was, your brother was figuring it out when Ryder decided it was time to leave the party. If for one moment your father thought that the Horde King wasn't Alazander. It would have been all over, and our departure would have been far bloodier."

"Does Ryder look that much like Alazander?"

"In Fae form, not really, but in the Horde King form they look very similar to one another. Over the last few centuries, Alazander was rarely *not* in the form of the Horde King. Those that had been up close and personal with him would be able to see the differences, but not many lived to tell of it."

"Seriously, you think they would have challenged him?" I asked, unsure how I would have felt about it since I'd thought he was Alazander at the time, too.

"Absolutely. Alazander terrified this world, but one of his sons would be another matter entirely. Any Fae Lord worth his salt would be compelled to test him, much less your father who had been battling Alazander for centuries."

"Ryder would kick ass while chewing bubblegum, Ristan. I've never met anyone with a head made of rocks like his. Shit, he could probably just head-butt them with that box of rocks he has and be just fine."

"Oh he would, but some things are worth a good ass kicking," Ristan said with an evil smirk on his face.

"He'd kick your ass, Demon."

"But it would be so worth it," Ristan smiled and winked at me.

Ristan wiggled his finger, and the entire room grew thick with magic as he turned it from blue, to more appealing shades. Turquoise sheets now matched the bed's canopy, and a white couch with matching turquoise pillows lined the far wall. There was a huge claw-footed tub that dominated one corner of the room. No dressers here, not when you could glamour on clothing…not that I could do it well yet.

"That's better; the other was too depressing. Come with me; there's someone I want you to meet. She was much like you when she came here," he said, getting up and pulling me out from under the warm covers. He stopped and looked at my silk robe for a moment. He smiled slyly, and pantomimed his fingers into a finger gun, took aim, and as he said "Pow," the robe changed to a red silky top and pant set with soft leather slippers that matched in color. He blew on his fingers as I laughed at him and his crazy antics.

"Thanks." I grinned at him.

"Don't thank me. I wanted the naughty little school girl outfit, but this is more appropriate." He smirked and held out his hand. I took it, and we sifted into the pavilion.

We walked through the pavilion and Ristan pointed out anything he thought I might like to explore, like gardens and pools. There was a bustle of activity here and so many creatures I had never seen before. Dryads, sprites—all female, and the Demon seemed to know every one of them as he had to keep stopping to give a little kiss or some sort of affection to the giggling women as we walked. At one point a faun with dainty hooved feet and fur up to her small waist—she had nothing covering her chest—kept pace with us. She batted big brown eyes at Ristan invitingly before running her finger over her lips seductively. Her breasts were lush and hardened as she made an inhuman noise at him before she turned and scampered away.

I turned my eyes to Ristan and shook my head. "Is there anything you won't do, Demon? She has freaking *hooves!*"

"Hey, a Demon has to catch his dinner somehow, and don't let her fur deter you. She's a wild cat in the sack," he teased good-naturedly.

I held up my hands and shook my head. "Oh please, no details! Keep it to yourself," I joked.

"Hey, I get it where the getting is good." He wiggled his brows as he laughed. "Dacey and I were just playing with you; however you can't judge anything around here. Most of the ladies have other shapes they take." His face saddened for a moment. "This is such a different place than what it used to be." He sighed.

"How so?" I asked, wondering what it could have been like to put that hurt in his eyes.

"Flower, when Alazander ruled this world, this was a place of sheer terror. We have done what we can to fix the damage, but some hurts will never heal," he said quietly, with a distant look of melancholy.

"You're speaking of the Gifts?" I wasn't sure how much I wanted to know about what had happened here.

He nodded slowly in answer. "The Gifts, wives, and his concubines. Ryder released them all upon Alazander's death; however many could not return to their homes. Some because of the fear of how their families would treat them and some because of the relationships they had found here. This is a sanctuary as much as anything else these days. Please keep this in mind when you think of this place. It's more than a harem as you have called it, Synthia. To these women, being removed would crush them more than they already are." His swirling eyes begged for understanding. In all of my imaginings of the harem, this was the last thing I had expected.

Ristan stopped inside one of the brightly lit rooms

and motioned for me to follow him in. There was a beautiful petite woman with long, inky black hair seated on the bed. It looked like she had been reading but her silver and black patterned eyes narrowed on me when I stepped through the door to stand beside Ristan. She and Ristan shared a strong resemblance, minus the missing brands on her arms.

"Alannah," Ristan nodded to the woman.

"Hello," I said, not sure of what was expected from me.

"Who is this lovely being, Ristan?"

"This is my Flower; isn't she beautiful?" he asked the woman.

"Very. She's Blood Fae, though; very touchy, that bunch."

"Syn is very touchy," Ristan said, wiggling his brows at me.

"Stuff it, Demon," I grumbled and smiled as the woman broke into a beautiful smile that made her face look even younger.

"She's witty. Will you marry her?" Alannah teased lightly.

"You know I can't, and I think she might take offense to me offering," he said and moved to shoo me from the room.

"She would be your equal," Alannah said with a look of mischief in her eyes.

"She is new to the Horde Kingdom. I thought she should meet you."

"Is that so? No, I don't think so," she said, lifting

her eyes back to me. "You brought her here to smooth her transition from the Human world into the pavilion. If you wish for her to become accustomed to this place, keep that snake from her nest. Claire is itching for power, and she isn't going to stop being a thorn," Alannah said softly with a knowing look.

"Alannah, Synthia is skilled in warfare and would wipe the floor with Claire's pretty face. She shouldn't be worried on that front. She needs friends, and you would make a great ally."

"Is that so? And why not bring this blossoming beauty to Ciara?"

"Because she's a bad influence on everyone," Ristan said as he ran his hand over his face. "That girl is not sane."

We stayed and chatted for about a half an hour about inconsequential things, and with a new friend firmly in place, we left the pavilion. I had to admit that the Demon was trying his best to cheer me up and help me feel more comfortable in this new world I had landed in. A Demoness in the pavilion had me curious in light of all that I had seen today.

"Was she brought here for you?" I blurted softly, not sure how he would respond with this place's history. He started laughing.

"Not intentionally," he chuckled.

"Ristan, dating from inside of the harem, you slut," I quipped, but continued. "Shock me with that deviant behavior, Demon," I joked.

He snorted and shook his head. "Don't go making matches for me, Flower. I'm too busy with Danu inside my head to make any attachments; I like playing *catch and release* for now."

Chapter
SEVEN

I was lying in bed, considering ways of killing Ryder for not coming for me when he said he would, when he finally showed up. He sifted in, threw off his cloak, and eyed the giant tub. I watched in silence as he waved his hand and the tub filled with spicy scented water. It occupied the room as much as the man did.

I felt like I lost my courage and everything I wanted to say as his jeans melted away and he slipped beneath the bubbled surface. His arms hung over the sides, and the once huge tub looked much smaller, filled to the brim with Ryder. His head was resting back against the rim and his eyes were closed.

I wanted to throttle him for looking so sexy when I was so upset that he hadn't bothered to show up when he'd promised me he would. Naked Ryder was a catastrophe for my mental state. I went from knowing how to talk, to a brainless sex crazed being.

"Eliran said you were sick earlier. Are you better?" he asked without opening his eyes.

"I'm no longer sick, just pissed that you didn't come get me as you had said you would."

His head came up, and his eyes landed on me. They were no longer the golden color of a few moments before. Something within his eyes stared at me, hungrily. "Why are you pissed now?"

"You promised to come and get me and then left me here!" I growled.

"It wasn't by choice, Pet."

"Okay, how about…you said you would get me, and bring me to your room. Instead, you left me with Claire!" I grumbled.

"I sent Claire and Ristan to you to explain things; didn't he let you know what happened?"

"Oh, Claire explained things alright, and the Demon didn't show up until today," I snapped angrily. His eyes opened slightly and slid to me.

"If you're not sick, get in this tub with me."

"You don't get to order me around, Fairy!" I felt hot tears burning behind my eyes. I wasn't sure where we stood, or if he even wanted us. I knew he wanted the baby to save his precious Faery, but that wasn't the same as wanting it, or *me* for that matter.

"It wasn't an order, it was a request," he said, clapping his hand over his eyes. He looked as tired as I currently felt. The tour with Ristan had taken a lot out of me, even though we hadn't done more than walk and talk for hours.

"Fine," I growled, irritated by the entire situation. I stripped out of my clothes, stomped over to the tub and got in on the other side. The water was warm and welcoming, and his presence gave it an added level of comfort.

His big hands pulled me from where I'd sat across from him, until he'd nestled me in his arms, my back snuggled against his chest. I rested my head against his wide chest and allowed some of the tension to leave my mind.

"Ask it, Synthia," Ryder whispered against my ear.

"Ask what?"

"Ask the question that is burning on your tongue."

"Why me, Ryder, why not someone else who would want you back," I spit it out before I could lose my courage.

"Because I wanted you, Pet. It is as simple as that. Even if I had not signed that contract, you would still be mine. I planned on waiting until you were ready, but I still would have taken you from Adam. One way or another, I'd have come for you. Fate pushed us together, but destiny knew we belonged together. Now you just have to accept it," he continued.

"You expect me to become just another woman in your harem?" I asked, as a single tear slid down my cheek.

"I don't think of you as just another anything. I won't send them away; they are my responsibility and they belong here with the Horde. I need to have a care for what their families have been granted and rewarded in return for them. Those are contracts I won't cross," he said guardedly.

I shook my head and moved to pull away from him, but his arms pulled me back. "I feel like I'm just another pretty thing for the collection."

"That's not true, and you know it. I have had

them for many years, and they live comfortably in the pavilion. I won't uproot their lives for any reason. Don't ask me to, Pet."

After speaking with Ristan earlier, I understood where he was coming from; I just wasn't sure where it left me, or how I felt about it. I needed to change the subject, so I did. "Tell me about the beast, Ryder," I whispered, watching him closely.

"He's a part of me. Like a split personality mixed with my own. We are one; I'm his host. All of the Fae get brands when they Transition, but only a select few inherit a beast as well when they come into their full powers. Mine just happens to be stronger and uglier than most others. The form of the Horde King is what you see when he and I merge and become one. The first time we took that form, was when I became Danu's chosen Heir. Until your presentation, that form had only been seen by the Horde the day I killed my father." A small smile tugged at his lips.

"What does he look like when it is just him? Do you know, or do you have to be in front of a mirror?" I teased softly.

"He is whatever he wants to be. He is the spirit of all of the creatures of the Horde and can be any of them if he so chooses it."

"So your beast took me and did this?" I indicated my stomach as a whole. "Why? Did he know who I was?" I climbed out of the tub, because I knew where my questions were heading, and if he couldn't answer the next one correctly, I wanted to be out of reaching distance.

"No, he just refused to let you go, or belong to another man. By impregnating you, he did what I couldn't at the time. He claimed you as ours for eternity by planting the seeds."

I nodded and continued with my original line of questioning. "Do you want this baby—our baby?"

"The child is needed to save this world. He was smart in claiming you and ensuring you were ours with the child. We can now move forward with what else is needed to save Faery," he replied carefully, his midnight eyes watching me.

"Do you want this baby?" I asked again.

"To save Faery, yes, I do," he continued evasively.

"Fairy, answer the question! Do you want our baby?"

"If it comes with his beautiful mother, yes I want him."

Relief flooded through me; at least he wanted it. "Did you fuck Claire?"

His head snapped up, and he glared at me. "Not since I told you that I would only feed from you," he answered.

"Have you fucked her since you took the throne, Ryder?" I fixed the question. I was getting better at the flipping Fairy word games.

"I have not fucked her since the day you watched me take her over my desk. I told you that if I fed, it would be from you. I fed from the pavilion as a whole. I fed from their emotions, from their fears, and their hopes. Is that what you wanted to know? I had to feed to save *you*." He was smiling now, like he thought I was cute or something.

"Funny how saving me wasn't even saving me,

considering you were the one I needed saving from…"

"I told you I would always keep you safe. I also promised you I was coming to save you from the big bad Horde King. I just didn't explain to you the details of how I would manage to do it."

"Yeah, about that, how could you say that when you *were* the Horde King?"

"As I told you, I wasn't at the time. I found you in your dream right before I took the throne."

"You are such an ass," I grumbled as I got out and quickly put on the sundress I'd discarded earlier.

I was turning to head back for the bed when he pulled me back into the bath with him. I sloshed the water as I swung my arms trying to catch my balance.

"Stop fighting me, Synthia. You make the beast want to come out and play with his new toy."

I quickly stopped and looked down at the now ruined sundress. I tried to make it disappear as he normally did, but it stayed on. He whispered against my ear, and it dissolved as if the water had consumed it.

"Much better," he whispered as his arms wrapped around me and slid down until they rested on my lower belly. "We made life," he growled huskily.

"Yes, we made life with the help of your beast."

He snorted, and I laughed. It was strange feeling his hands on my womb, on the child we'd created, even if the beast was strutting his shit around inside of Ryder. I leaned my head against him and relaxed, ignoring everything else that was going on. Here, right now, it was just the four of us: Ryder, his beast, our child, and me. Shit, this tub was crowded.

"Answer me this, what is it that Ristan saw that made you design the contract to take me from my parents?"

He exhaled, and I shivered even though the water was holding the perfect temperature. I turned my head until it rested against his shoulder, and our breaths mingled.

"He saw us having a child, one that would be of the two strongest Castes of Fae. A child that would eventually heal the damage done to this world by my father. But he also saw the alliance we would make that would begin healing the damage my father had inflicted across this world." He paused and pinched my nipple until it puckered into a hard pebble beneath his touch. "For most of my life I watched my father ruin everything he had touched. I plan on fixing it, but in order to do so, I may have to do things that you won't like."

"Like?"

"I'm the Horde King, Synthia; we earn our way by being brutal. If I don't show them my strength, I will be challenged incessantly by every King and lord that believes he is stronger."

"I had a feeling about that; I don't understand where I fit in, Ryder," I said honestly. This was the root of what was bothering me. He pulled me closer and nuzzled his nose in the soft column of my neck.

"You fit in right here," he rumbled softly as he wrapped his arms around me. "Everything else we will figure out as it comes."

The rest of the night went by slowly. There was no sex, no rushing through it with fighting, and no words were used. We just lay together in the bed, holding each other as if nothing else mattered. It was refreshing, and even though I had a million questions to ask him, I ignored it. Tonight, I would accept his comfort.

Chapter
EIGHT

The next morning I awoke to an empty bed. Ryder had left either sometime in the night or early in the morning. I ran my hand over the pillow where his head had been, the indent from it still visible, as well as the heat from his body. I groaned.

These freaking hormones were something else. I felt like my emotions were starting to come unhinged, but at least now I had a reason for them to be this over-active. I'd been through hell, and at least now there was a light at the end of the tunnel. I was safe, and while my situation was not ideal, I could manage it.

It was odd. I felt like I could breathe better now that I knew he was the reason I'd been through hell. If he was what this had all been for, I was willing to make it work between us. I needed to find a foothold and figure out how to break through his hard exterior. I just had to find a crack in it and force my way through. It wasn't like I could walk away now. I was in too deep and pregnant with his child. No, leaving wasn't an option right now, even though I missed being in the Human world.

I missed home and Alden. I missed the cemetery

and the midnight dances inside of it. I missed Adam and Larissa.

I had been through so much in such a short time, and was learning who I was and what I was. I knew my feelings for him, but even with knowing, it still baffled me how I'd come to love him in so little time. I loved him, even after everything he'd done. But life was funny. I'd figured out what I wanted. Go figure, I wanted the one man who drove me batshit crazy and over the edge in one single word.

Man, I was emotionally screwed. I was crazy to think I could stay here with him and his harem of women that he'd already said he wouldn't give up. And then there was Claire, who obviously hated my guts; not that I blamed her, since I'd be pissed if someone took Ryder away from me, too.

I had a choice to make, and it couldn't be made inside this room. I sat up and looked at the door to where one hot Demon stood smiling with a gorgeous red cocktail dress held up to his frame. "I'd go with blue. It would make your hair stand out and show off the highlights," I said smiling.

"Ahh, what if I like red?" He grinned.

Go figure, my one friend in this place was the Demon I'd planned to hate. There it was again, another thing I'd failed to do. I'd planned on hating Ryder, yet every time he touched me, I caved like some weak-knee school girl.

I was weak around him, and I needed to be strong right now. My entire life was depending on it—and I was immortal! Well, almost immortal, but close enough.

I started to get up, but Ristan held up his hand

to stop me. "Let me get your handmaidens; you now have five. Zara will be joining the ones you already met. Ryder left specific orders of what was to be done today. You will be presented to the Horde, and blessed for the child you carry. It was a custom Alazander abandoned, not sure why, but it used to be that all of the Kings wives or concubines were blessed this way during their pregnancies to ensure the health of the child and prosperity for the Horde. Ryder is hoping to pick up most of the things our people lost because of him. Prepared to be pampered, my blossoming Flower."

Pampered?

Pampered.

And by pampered, he'd meant I was being given a spa day. I had Keely the Brownie working my hair, tying it up for the bath, while Faelyn the Pixie fought me for the sweetly scented soap. I won, of course, and eventually she stood back and allowed me to wash myself. Cherry blossom petals filled the wide tub, and were beautiful, but considering I had five girls falling over me while trying to help me, I couldn't enjoy them.

After the debacle of the bath, I was pulled from the water and stood naked in front of a mirror. I growled at this, and shook my head. I was shoved into a chair someone had brought out, or maybe glamoured (I was too busy watching them hustle and fuss over my appearance to pay attention), and my hair was braided after it had been slicked in some kind of cherry scented gel by Faelyn, and styled into a beautiful updo. Meriel busied herself on my hands with a manicure while Keeley was working pedicure magic. Now, more than ever, I was missing my OPI collection.

Make-up was applied by Darynda, who winked at

me mischievously as she told me this was her magical talent. She was the equivalent to a make-up artist. When she was done, I had black kohl on my eyes, which made the blue and purple of them pop brightly. She'd applied a light blue shadow and a touch of violet to my eyes which was subtle and yet beautiful.

The women all ignored my continual silence or lack of opinion and continued prepping me; Meriel smiled and wrinkled her nose as she glamoured on a light blue top that left my sides exposed. Darynda glamoured on a skirt that closely matched the top, but covered me to my ankles, minus the slits down the side.

"Jewelry; she's going to need armbands," said the Pixie, who looked like she couldn't be more than sixteen. I watched as they all chatted happily and argued like old friends over which arm pieces would suit me better.

The necklace that Ryder had my mother put on me when I was presented to him wasn't coming off anytime soon, and I now knew that it bore a medallion that was the same as Ristan's. To compliment it, the necklace they chose was simple and slipped under the other like an extension; the metal of the chain was old and looked almost vintage or antique. Diamonds the size of almonds hung at the tip, which accentuated my breasts.

Platinum bands were slipped onto my biceps that held the head of a dragon with rubies for the eye. I watched as yet another cuff was placed above it, these ones were gold and the dragon's eye was a brilliant diamond.

They stood back when that was finished and I waited for them to discover I was still missing shoes. Eventually, Darynda smiled and said it.

"She needs something on her feet. Something simple but beautiful," she mused as she tilted her head and her lips lifted in the corners. "She also needs to learn how to smile more."

"Darynda," Zara said as she walked into the room.

"Well, she does," Darynda said, smiling triumphantly as she fluffed her shoulder-length auburn curls.

"Does she have a name? Maybe you should use it," Zara said with an authoritative tone.

"You can all call me Synthia, and yes, I'd very much like something to cover my feet," I said, stopping the argument in its tracks if that was where it was heading. I was nervous enough, and having them bickering would only make my nerves get worse.

Darynda clapped her hands and a gold box appeared. She smiled triumphantly and dug through the box instead of just glamouring on shoes. She held up jeweled sandals that looked anything but comfortable. I held out my hand and accepted them anyway. I had other things to do today besides playing dress up.

The shoes were surprisingly comfortable, and the jewels, even though they looked rough, didn't scratch my skin at all. They'd been smoothed until they were soft on the tender skin of the foot. I turned and gave myself a quick once-over in the mirror. Holy freaking Fairy buckets, these girls were good.

I looked like a princess!

I mean, I was a princess...which was weird to say, not that I had *out* loud very much, but still, I actually looked the part now.

"Is it true that you hate Fae?" Keely asked, and got a stern shushing from Meriel.

"Who told you that?" I asked, as I ignoring Mariel's hisses to be quite.

"Claire said that you hated Fae, and made a living off killing us."

"Did she now? I used to hate everything Fae, but only because I watched the people who raised me get slaughtered by them. They killed my family, and yes, I have killed Fae before. In fact, I killed a few just last week. I was raised by Humans. I actually thought I was a Human until Ryder brought me to Faery for the Wild Hunt."

"Do you still hate us?" Darynda asked, coming into the conversation.

"I'd have to hate myself in order to do that. No, I now understand that not all Fae are bad, just like all Humans are not good. I can't blame an entire species for what happened to my parents. But, I also think you shouldn't listen to rumors."

"Claire said you took Ryder from her; she also said that you think you are above us. I personally like to give people the benefit of the doubt. I'm not one to judge a book by its cover, or listen to idle gossip from jealous women either."

"Well, I think you should stop while you are ahead. Claire doesn't like me; I get it. She obviously went above and beyond to feed the rumor mills with crap. I'm not going to indulge her in a battle of wits, because to me it seems she is missing hers and that wouldn't be a fair fight, now would it?" I asked, meeting Darynda's blue and green eyes with a grin.

"Wow, she wasn't kidding when she said you

didn't play with words."

"Probably the only thing she told you that was the truth. I hate word games, and I couldn't care less who hates me over some lame ass rumor started by a bitter ex. So you were right to ask me, and I have nothing against the Fae in *this* world. "

"Claire isn't bitter. She's enraged and rightly so since you have been moved into what is supposed to be reserved for the Queen of the Horde. Her sister is contracted to marry Ryder, this would traditionally be *her* room," Zara blurted.

My head snapped around to stare at her. "Ryder plans on marrying?" I felt my blood pressure spike and my anger rise as I waited for the answer.

"He's the King of the Horde; of course he will marry," Darynda said carefully as if she wasn't sure she should be discussing it with me.

"Claire's sister?"

"Well, her half-sister. Ryder's father made the contract, but he signed it. He has been engaged to her for years, but it's uncertain how long before Cornelius demands they marry. Claire says it should be soon."

"I thought the Fae married for gain."

"And Claire's family is the largest and most powerful in the realm, minus Ryder's own family. He accepted Claire into the pavilion because she was gifted, but Abiageal is the oldest. The Horde normally stays within the Horde for the first marriage."

"So Ryder will marry within the Horde?" I felt sick to my stomach.

"Well, yes. It's been the custom of the Horde for

as long as history has been recorded."

"I thought that Ryder's mother was the first wife, and she was a Dark Fae," I said softly, trying to rein in my emotions at this sucker punch.

"She became the first wife when Alazander's first wife died," Faelyn supplied helpfully. I could only guess at that, based on the stories I had heard about him, he probably killed her.

I felt my heart sink to my toes. Ryder never said he'd marry me; he did say that if I hadn't been the Light Heir, he'd keep me. I searched my memory for anything that he'd said that could have hinted at more between us then just being his concubine. I knew there wasn't. Just that he'd keep me. Ryder had probably known all along that he wouldn't marry me, or had things changed now that he knew I was the Blood Princess, and I was supposed to be Danu's Heir? Didn't that change things?

One thing was fore sure; I wouldn't stand around and watch the man I love marry someone else. I'd have to make him love me, or leave him and hope he let me go.

Chapter NINE

Dristan, Sevrin, and Savlian arrived, dressed in the form fitting uniforms of the Elite Guard—sans headgear, and escorted us as a group to the crowded hall that was already filled with the waiting Horde. The room was unlike any other I'd seen so far in the palace, and had been decorated in crimson and black. A gigantic tapestry covered one wall with the same design of the two Celtic dragons that had once adorned my hip and Ristan's medallion, only the dragons on the tapestry looked more fierce and deadly.

My eyes wandered over to the back of the hall where the dais was and saw Ryder. His eyes watched me as I approached with the others. He was once again in King mode, his huge wings eclipsing the sun's light that shined through the enormous stained glass window behind him. If it hadn't been for the light coming in from the other windows, he would have been swallowed in the shadows they created.

The throne on which Ryder sat, looked wickedly cool. The immense seat was created of black oak with skulls and bones embedded in it. I narrowed my eyes, and with a sinking feeling in the pit of my stomach, I realized that the bones were real. The arms of the throne were each finished with a skull on which his hands rested. Ewww...

To his right and slightly behind the throne, stood Ristan; Zahruk stood to his left. Both wore the black body armor of the Elite Guard. It was looking like all of Ryder's men that had accompanied him in the Human world were part of the unit as I spotted them standing at attention at strategic posts behind Ryder.

Ryder looked to be in full control of the entire Horde; a proud beast, destined to rule them all. I shook myself from my inner thoughts as the group around me came to a full stop. We stood there until Ryder nodded, and all of the women in the room dropped to their knees and bowed their heads. Like sheep. Every male remained standing, which I thought was odd. I was the last to kneel, and only when I'd held Ryder's eyes for a few moments before I silently, and effortlessly dropped to the floor.

I felt like a stupid sheep, as if by going down, I was somehow admitting that I was his. As if! I only did it because I didn't want to cause a scene in front of the entire Horde. Ristan had mentioned why we were here, and Darynda had assured me that I couldn't just skip it. It wasn't until Ryder stood and held his hand out that I got the first inkling of what was going to happen.

"Synthia, stand and come to me," Ryder said in his multi-layered voice.

I shook my head, but even as I did so, I was working on standing up.

"This is the Blood Princess, and also the mother to my first born child. She holds the key to Faery in her womb. Ristan has seen our child, the one who will begin the healing of our world," Ryder said, and the room exploded with cheering Horde creatures. "I'll have a vow from my kingdom to protect her from harm, and your protection of my child, Danu's heir."

The entire assembly said, "Aye," as one. When I reached where Ryder was standing, we were joined by most of his men and some I hadn't seen before as they moved into protective positions. When Ryder held out his hand, I hesitated, but placed mine in his much larger one. He pulled me close, and crushed his mouth against mine. The room once again broke into loud cheers.

"Bow to your people, Synthia," he whispered, and I quickly gave a clumsy curtsey to those gawking as I turned to face them. Yes, I was hopelessly fucked.

I watched as they bowed back, and then I was pulled back around and tucked beneath Ryder's arm as he once again took the throne, with me in his lap. Cheers erupted as Ryder held up my hand, but I pulled it from him and glared openly at him which seemed to impress the Horde all the more.

"She is off limits to every male here; she is mine."

His eyes scanned my face, and I realized with perfect clarity that Ryder was the only thing keeping me protected in this place of monsters. He could read my expression, if his eyes softening were anything to go off. I watched as he lowered his gaze to my midsection, which was perfectly flat. They came back up to meet mine, filled with triumph and heat that I hadn't expected to see in them while standing in front of the entire assembly.

The women stood, and music filled the room. Men moved about, bowing to females. It was as if I was watching an ancient scene of nobility play out before my eyes. There were wicked smiles on the faces of all of those present. I swallowed the urge to run, as men's eyes turned toward us in lust. As if the entire room expected Ryder to take me right in front of them. I narrowed my eyes on them. That shit was so not happening.

"You feel good in my lap, Pet," Ryder whispered softly against my ear. "How are you feeling?"

"I'm fine," I replied, turning to lean my head against his cheek.

He jerked his face away from me and spoke low and sharply in my ear. "I can't afford to show a weakness, Synthia. It might look safe here, but there are those who would use you to get to me if they thought I was emotionally attached to you." I stared at him, stunned. Talk about sending mixed signals!

"Sometimes I wonder why you fight so hard to save this place. Why fight for something that isn't safe? You fight to fix the world, yet you can't even trust those within your own walls?"

"There are few I trust with my life. I fight because I love Faery; it's my home. If something was happening to your world, Synthia, you would fight for it. You are a born warrior; we are more alike than you know."

I fell silent, considering his words. He was right. I'd fight to save the earth and everyone in it. I turned my head to find Claire glaring at us from across the room. She hated me, and it ran deep and ugly inside of her. She was a problem I needed to fix before I got too fat to do so.

~~*

We were dismissed from the throne room just a little while later, and Ryder went to a room just off to the side and behind the dais where his throne was. It must have been an office or meeting room, as Zahruk and Ristan followed him. I was invited to the pavilion by Claire, but I skipped it and walked back to the room I'd been given. There was no way in hell that I was going to sit with Ryder's harem and have lunch. It didn't even make sense why they would have a lunch since Fae fed from emotions...not food. Maybe she planned on trying to make me miserable and feed off that.

I'd been so lost in my own thoughts, that I hadn't even noticed the five handmaidens following me back to my room. Why hadn't they gone to eat like the rest of the sheep in this place? I turned and eyed them, none of them looked happy with my decision to skip the meal. Sinjinn, Aodhan, and Dristan were following close behind the handmaidens.

"You guys don't eat the food?" I asked.

"We serve you. Where you go, we go," Darynda explained.

"So if I jump off a bridge, you'd join me?" *Sheep... line up for the slaughter.*

"A bridge?" she asked with a confused look on her face.

"A bridge," I said, and when it didn't seem to register on her face, I explained it.

"Why would you wish to jump from a bridge?" she questioned, still confused.

"Never mind," I said, and started walking down the hall in the direction of the room I was staying in.

They continued to follow me down the hallway and up the long, winding staircase, and even though Sinjinn had offered to sift me up, I needed the exercise. I'd gotten little to none since coming here, and even though I was pregnant, I was staying in shape.

"I wanted to be alone," I said over my shoulder as I took the steps beside Sinjinn, and the women who were behind didn't fall back, instead they rushed to keep up with me.

"That we cannot do, Princess. It is our duty to see you are well and cared for," Darynda said calmly with a pointed look. When I refused to comment she crossed her arms and continued to follow me. I was pretty sure she'd tap her foot impatiently if she wasn't walking at a brisk pace just to keep up with me.

"You want me to be fine? Leave me alone for a minute. In the last few weeks I have watched my best friend be murdered right in front of me, I found out I wasn't Human, I have been stabbed by Zahruk, almost blown up, given to the Dark Heir as his fiancée, kidnapped, met my Fairy fucking family, and now I'm a whore for the fucking Horde King! You want me to be okay? Then get the fuck back for five minutes!" I was shaking, which only made me increase my speed as I fisted my hands at my sides.

The horrified looks on their faces made me feel like an ass, but I just needed a moment to breathe—alone. I needed to make a plan, and to do that, I needed to be alone. They didn't leave; they stayed right freaking behind me.

"I'm sorry you have been through so much, but we did not do this to you. We are here to serve you, to make this easier on you," she whispered.

"I'm sorry I freaked out, but sometimes the silence helps," I replied softly with regret sinking in. She was innocent, and didn't deserve my anger.

She smiled and nodded as she and the rest of the

gals dropped back to give me a bit of space. Zara started whispering to the other girls as if I wasn't even there.

"She's a bust. The King will not enjoy her anymore. She already bears his child. He will move onto another concubine to strengthen his line," she murmured as the others tried to shush her.

"You don't know that," Darynda whispered softly, and I found myself liking her even more. In this place, some of the women seemed a bit catty, but Darynda seemed to say what was on her mind, even if it was dead wrong.

"She's already pregnant. It's not like he will keep her in the Queen's rooms now. I requested this position so I could be close to the King," Zara muttered behind me as we continued toward the room she thought I was about to be removed from.

"Claire speaks out of turn when she should hold her tongue. She's bitter and ruthless as she hides behind a sweet face. We all know that. She twisted her words just to go with the men to the Human world. She's spoiled, is what she is, and you would be wise to stop holding too tightly to her skirts. She has no intention of helping you. She wants the King even though he's meant for her sister in marriage. She was gifted, and has been trying to be chosen as second wife or first concubine. Does that sound sane to you?" Darynda whispered heatedly.

"Synthia seems nice to me, and she isn't rude and demanding. We may end up back in the pavilion, but at least we won't be getting our faces slapped for choosing the wrong color dress for Claire. Really, Zara, think about it. How far are you willing to take this little torch you carry for Claire?" Meriel joined the whispered debate in my defense.

"I think Claire speaks true, and I for one plan on making it to his bed. I'm not meant to be a handmaiden. I was born to be so much more," Zara retorted. I rolled my eyes and wasn't sure if I felt sorrier for myself or for the poor guys escorting who had to listen to this crap.

"He hasn't even turned his eye to any woman since he brought her here! Do you really think he is going to just boot her back to the pavilion? If his plan was only to secure a babe in her belly, his job is already done. Has been done for a while! Yet she's still in that room," Keeley softly added, her voice almost inaudible.

"Claire will have her out of that room before her sister steps foot in this place. She won't stand for this wench to be in that room. It belongs to her sister!" Zara's voice raised a little at this, as the other four tried desperately to shush her quickly.

I turned and looked at Sinjinn, who was watching me closely. I lowered my eyes and walked briskly down the hall, noting that everyone was keeping up with me regardless of how fast I was walking.

"Claire is filling your head with nonsense. Synthia is the Blood Princess, not some wench. If I were you, I'd thank the Goddess you have an easy concubine who seems to be pleasant enough to say thank you!" Darynda continued softly.

"Everyone keeps saying how powerful she is, and yet she can't even use glamour. She can't even cast magic. You really think she can stand up against Claire?" Zara sniped, raising her tone.

"Have you ever considered that maybe it's because she's very powerful? How many concubines have you seen come into the pavilion with that mark on them?

None! He doesn't put his mark on anyone other than his Elite Guards. Yet she has it on. Did you ever stop to think that maybe she is too powerful to control without it?" Darynda mused. I sped up a little as I could now see the door to my room.

"I don't care who the hell you think she is, or how powerful she is. Soon she will be nothing but a fat, useless cow! He will toss her aside for concubines he can feed from. His appetite has to be enormous and I plan to be included with them. In order to do that, I need to serve someone who holds his damn interest!" Zara hissed over the other feeble shushes.

She did not just go *there*!

I spun around so quickly that no one else stopped as I walked back toward the negative Nancy who was too stupid to take the advice they were giving her. "Say it to my face!" I growled. She turned as white as freshly fallen snow. "That's what I thought. You wanna be with someone who can get close to Ryder so you can crawl in his bed? Go find someone else. I don't want some little brainless twit who can only talk shit to my back serving me. Sinjinn," I called his name and he stepped up to my shoulder and gently placed his hand on it to reassure me. He looked relieved that I was putting an end to this.

"Zara, get to the pavilion. Synthia doesn't wish you to serve in her entourage anymore. You may no longer serve the Princess, or any of the high-standing concubines. I have seen her fight, and if I were you, I'd run. Synthia is definitely collared because she is very powerful and very special to the King."

"You can't!" she sputtered as she started to get hysterical. Sinjinn and the other men grimaced at the sight. I wasn't one to indulge spoiled little bitches and their fits.

I reached out and slapped her cheek—hard. "Sorry," I grinned and tilted my head at her, "I was afraid you'd pass out and shit. Wouldn't want that now, would we?"

"You bitch! I'll kill you!" She shrieked.

"Okay, well I planned to do this the *sane* way. But if you insist," I growled, balling my hands into tight fists.

"Dristan, see that Zara is sent home to her father. Make it known she threatened the King's favorite pregnant concubine's life," Sinjinn interrupted, but he looked like he was either fighting off the urge to strangle her or laugh; could have been both.

The other handmaidens stared with wide eyes and mouths that hung to the floor as Dristan genially moved to take Zara away. And then I felt it, the electrical current that was always around when Ryder was close. I turned and met his midnight eyes. "Fuck you, Fairy; find a different snack. I'm off limits at the moment," I growled irritably, and walked into my room and slammed the door so hard the wood groaned in protest.

I didn't wait to see if he would follow me. I kicked off my pretty shoes and climbed into the bed, pulling the covers over my head, and cried. I was tired of feeling like an outsider, and the hormones were on full overload at the moment. I didn't need him pulling me into his arms, and making me cry harder.

Chapter TEN

I was dreaming, and Ryder was there doing sinfully delicious things to me while I allowed it. I moaned against his mouth and shivered as he glamoured my clothes away. I bit my bottom lip as a cry struggled to break from them.

Heat was thrumming through me, my entire body coming alive with it. Silk brushed against my back as he caressed me everywhere else. I could feel the raw current from him and smell his rich, unique spices. I whispered encouragements and begged him for more.

I felt him sliding down my body until he sat between my legs and then pressure consumed my mind. His hands parted my legs, and the heat of his breath fanned my sensitive flesh. I blinked and tried to sit up, but he pulled my legs further apart. I shook my head with the realization that this wasn't a dream.

His lips and tongue pulled and suckled on my pussy, and I cried out as my entire body jerked from the pleasure of it. "Ryder, no," I cried, already trying to push him away, even if it was a futile effort. His big hands came up to capture mine, and he held them firmly against my belly as his mouth continued to devour me. "No," I said again as I lifted my hips for more.

I didn't want this.

God, it felt so good.

Ryder's mouth continued to feast greedily from my core, until I began to moan uncontrollably from it. His hands roamed against my flesh, and I went soft against his touch. "Ryder," I whimpered, still groggy from sleep, but he ignored my plea and continued to use his tongue savagely, leaving nothing untouched. He made slurping noises and groans of pleasure as he sucked my clit into his mouth and roved his tongue over it hard, slow, and erotically. He was a fucking God in bed. It was as simple as that. The anger faded away even as I tried to remember why I was mad. He growled against my slick flesh as his hands came up to slide under and cupped my ass to give him better access.

My body arched for more of his possession, my head tilted back on the softness of the pillows as his mouth made love to my core. I lifted my hips to give him better access, demanding he continue; not that I needed to, not that he would leave me like this. I moaned and panted with need. He was slow, steady, and determined to draw the orgasm from me.

He said nothing, just continued to ravish my pussy until he got what he wanted from it. He moaned as his tongue and lips sucked against the slick wetness he'd just created as my body quivered and jerked while tremors of pleasure shot through me. I was still shaking from the powerful orgasm as he moved up until he was poised and ready to enter me. His eyes met and held mine, captured by the heat burning from within his, and he kept my eyes locked with his in a silent promise of more pleasure as he slid his cock inside of me slowly.

He fed me inch after blissful inch of his hardness. He moved slowly as he rotated his hips, fucking me gently, jerking his body to the hilt, buried inside of my warmth with his eyes never leaving mine. Each thrust took me closer to the edge of sanity as he drove his engorged cock inside of me again and again.

"I love being inside of you, Synthia."

"Ryder," I whimpered as the pending orgasm built to a dangerous level inside of me. He was controlling it, holding it just out of reach.

Our breathing was heavy, but it didn't matter. Nothing mattered but the primal need to find release together. He lowered his mouth, and claimed my lips in a hungry, demanding kiss that stole my breath away, as he fed me his own back.

When he pulled away, I cried out from the loss of his mouth and met his eyes, which now glowed with hunger. His mouth lifted into a wicked grin as his hips continued to move slowly, deliciously, while he brought me to the brink, only to stop when I was close to going over the cliff he was holding me on.

"You need to come, don't you, Pet? Fuck, you're so wet and sweet. I could eat this sweet pussy for days," he grunted and pulled out to do just that, but first he took his time getting down there.

He yanked my legs until I was spread apart for him to feed. He smiled and kissed my neck before moving lower to kiss and nip gently with his teeth on the left nipple, and then the right, sucking them into his mouth and flicking them as he had done with my clit earlier.

He lifted his head and smiled with my nipple still held between his teeth before he dropped one leg and used his now-free hand to run it over the heat of my junction. I kept hold of his eyes, and watched as he ran his tongue slowly in swirling patterns over my naked skin. The heat from his blistering mouth sending my brain into a frenzy of need that he controlled, effortlessly.

His fingers entered me, spreading me, fucking me. I closed my eyes, unable to keep them open any longer. "Open them. I want you to watch me make you come, Synthia. I want to see when desire floods through them, when the passion takes control and you give yourself over to me."

"Why are you doing this to me?" I cried, still riding his fingers.

"I'm fucking you," he ground out through the lust, which made his voice low and seductive. "I love your sweetness, love to be inside of it. You are *mine* now, Synthia, forever," he whispered, before he moved back up my body as he held my legs spread. "Now, come for me," he ordered.

He entered hard this time, and held nothing back as he pounded himself inside of me. His magic exploded over my flesh and the moment it did, I exploded with it. My body shook from the sheer magnitude of the orgasm. I screamed his name over and over as he continued to fuck me until his own release electrified and spread warmth through me.

He turned onto his side and pulled me flush against his body, our breathing labored and torn as we both fought to control it. He didn't say anything, and the feeding that he'd just given me made my eyes grow heavy with sleep. Tonight, I would allow his comfort; tomorrow, I would barbeque his ass.

As I drifted off to sleep, I felt his soft kiss as he

rained them down on my forehead. His soft words were whispered in the ancient language that I was starting to think was part of the Horde language, and something about them tugged at my heart strings.

Chapter ELEVEN

I awoke to Ryder kissing me, his eyes smiling as he ravished my mouth. I moaned and pushed with my hands against his chest, trying to push him away. Not that it was working, or that I had any chance in hell of managing it. I felt his mouth curve into a smile as his hand easily captured mine and trapped them above my head.

He didn't enter me, even though I could feel his hardness against my hip. He had taken the form I was more familiar with as he had last night, which only made what he was doing harder to resist. I pulled my mouth away from his, but he followed me and caught it easily with his, and growled his disapproval.

When he finally pulled away, he refused to allow me to use my hands. Instead, he kept them pinned above my head as his free hand stroked my stomach. I stopped moving away from him the moment his fingers grazed the skin above my navel tenderly. "Ryder," I whimpered. His eyes met mine, as his fingers continued to explore my flat abdomen.

"You will give me the strongest, most stubborn son that the Horde has ever known," he mumbled before his head lowered and kissed the flatness of my belly. "I won't stop with one child. You will be the mother of all of my sons and daughters."

"And when you marry Abiageal?" I asked, watching his reaction.

"She will be my wife, but you will still be the woman I go to sleep with and the one I wake up with. Nothing will change that."

"Are you serious?" I snapped.

"I'm the Horde King, Synthia. They expect me to follow through with that. It's a normal custom for the Horde King to take a bride from within the Horde. This was a contract my father made, and at the time I thought I could go through with it. Then I met you. You changed everything, but it's not a simple thing to undo. It's a binding contract, one I signed."

"Then I hope you are happy, but don't expect me to play happy whore for you. I am *not* willing to do that; not even for you, Ryder."

"It's not like I want her. I want you, Synthia Raine McKenna. She will go to the pavilion, like the others before her after I have done my duty," he mumbled and released his hold on my hands.

I sat up and scooted away from him as quickly as I could. "You think I care if you want her? It won't matter at that point, because I won't be here. Your duty will include bedding her. I'm not an idiot, Fairy. I know the old customs, and I know that most come from the Fae. You will have to," I stopped as my throat thickened with the words. "You will have to take her to your bed. That's not something I can just look past. My feelings might make me sound stupid to you, but I can't change them."

"So you'd take my child and leave?" he asked in

a deadly tone.

"Without a doubt," I sneered.

"I could chain you to my bed," he whispered as his golden eyes lifted to meet mine.

I flinched from the heat in them. Why couldn't he see how wrong it was that he wanted to keep me *and* a wife? I knew he was old, and that in this world it was common, but why couldn't he see it from my eyes? "Ryder, you can chain me all you like. In the end, I will leave you. Either by checking out mentally or physically; I won't stay if you marry someone else; don't ask me to."

"And you'd stay if I refused to marry her?"

"Maybe," I said. *Yes, I'd fight to stay with him with every fiber of my very being.*

"Yes or no, not that it matters. You are having my child. Leaving isn't an option at this point."

"I'm having our child; ours. He's inside of *me*, not you. You are so wrong if you think you can pull what you did yesterday in the front of your Horde on me again. You don't get to do this to me. Not when my entire life was shaped because of a choice you made before I was born. You stole my life, Ryder. If you hadn't demanded a contract, I would never have left Faery, and my parents would be still alive and would never have had to go through what they did."

"If I hadn't made that fucking contract, you'd be a very different girl than you are now. You'd have been mine either way. Danu chose *you* for this. She thinks you're something special. She thinks our child can fix this world, and when I find the relics, I hope she's right," he hissed.

"But you don't think I'm special?" I asked, crossing my arms, uncaring that I was naked. Besides, it wasn't like he hadn't seen it all many times.

"I think you're a scared little girl who doesn't know what the fuck she wants. You have no home, you have no friends, and you have no one who is willing to walk in here and fight me for you. And trust me, Syn, Adam and Adrian are not that stupid nor would Vlad or Kier allow for them to come here and challenge me."

My chest and throat burned from unshed tears. I closed my eyes and felt one drop. I shook my head and looked up into his gorgeous face. This was my Knight in shining armor, this was my savior. Right, I was such an idiot. "Feel better? Does it make you feel better to point out that I have no one left? No fucking options?"

"Syn," he said, sliding his fingers through his hair.

"Get out," I seethed, straightening my spine and reinforcing my courage. He might be the Horde King, but I was the Blood Princess, and I wasn't some weak ass bitch who would cave to this. I may not have what I had a few months ago, but he was wrong. I had options. I wasn't down and out yet.

"Synthia," he warned.

"Get the fuck out, Fairy! Get out! Get out!" I half screamed, half cried as the feeling of everything crashed down on me. I felt pain shoot through my midsection as if the fires of hell were tearing through me. I hit the floor hard and landed on my knees before I bent over and everything went black.

~ *Ryder* *~*

"What is wrong with her?" I demand and watch as

Eliran shakes his head.

"No idea. You said she screamed and then fell?" he asks, and his eyes fly to mine as if he can sense my guilt.

"We were arguing," I divulge, and listen as Ristan snorts.

"Dizziness and fainting are very common symptoms during pregnancy. She looks stable, but I'd like to keep her down here for tonight," Eliran continues.

"No. If you want to monitor her, you will do so from my chambers. She is emotionally unstable. I'd rather you keep an eye on her from a distance. She needs to feel like she has some control of her life. I took her from her world, and according to Sinjinn, she's already made one enemy he had to send packing for threatening her life."

"Synthia doesn't make enemies without good reason, Ryder. Did you question why the girl verbally attacked her?" Ristan muses and meets my eyes as if he knows Synthia better than I do. As if. I know every fucking curve, every inch of her beauty personally.

"She said something Syn didn't agree with. The girl was removed, but the fact that Synthia's not adapting to her place here is not acceptable. I won't let her walk away from me." I meet his eyes, daring him to argue.

"And the child?" I finally ask, after noting everyone is staring at me.

"It's fine as far as I can tell. I retrieved medicine for the nausea and vitamins to ensure that she and the babe stay healthy. My only concern is that she wasn't all of the way out of Transition when she conceived and is still not fully immortal. She's delicate, no matter how strong she seems right now. She needs to take it easy until the child is firmly planted in her womb."

"How in the fuck do we manage that when she's walking around hitting people? She's not like the other women here; she's explosive."

"When she is around you," Ristan points out, not even pretending to care that I am even now glaring murder in his direction. "She was fine when I was with her, Ryder. She's been through hell and not even you can deny that. She has plenty of reasons to hate us, and yet she doesn't. Nor have I *seen* her hating us. You, well she tries very hard to hate and yet she caves to your whims. You may not want to hear this, but I'm going to tell you anyway. Stay away from her unless you plan on apologizing for whatever shit you probably dropped into her lap. Give her time to breath, to heal, and for your child to be secured in her belly. I'm just saying give her time to acclimate."

"You don't think I have fucking tried? I let her walk away to marry someone else! I've given her up once, Ristan. I will never do it again."

"I'm not saying to let her go. You couldn't, anyway. She's carrying your child. I'm saying that if you want her to be willing to stay, give her time to adjust. Two months ago she was a Human with normal…well, she was a Witch, but my point is, she had normal problems. She knew what she was, and what she had to do. She was active and needed. Now, she is trapped in a pretty cage and the only thing she has to do with her time is to sit around and think. We took a fucking assassin and we cut off her arms. Took her swords. We took her purpose from her, and gave her what? This is Synthia we are talking about. She's a fighter, Ryder, and everything she has ever known is gone. It's all changing at a rapid rate, and she's coping by lashing out…not to mention she's got some raging hormones that are taking over. Just ask Eliran." He motions to the healer, who nods his head solemnly.

"I can handle hormones."

"You sure about that?"

"Yes," I grind out through clenched teeth.

"You're doing a shit job with it so far. Where were you when she was crying?"

"She was crying?" I bark and glare.

"For no reason; absolutely no reason, just crying her pretty little heart out on my sleeve. Shit Ryder, of course there was a reason. Claire had been there playing with her mind, and you didn't ask me to check on her until you were well overdue. Don't tell her you will be there unless you know for damn sure you will be. Look at this through her eyes, or at least try to. She needs time to adjust to everything here, and she's been sick on top of that. One minute she was this bad ass warrior, and the next she's just supposed to lay down her weapons and become a mother? That shit is just not going to happen overnight; it takes time."

"Syn is going to be a mother soon. She doesn't need to fight anymore! Doesn't she know I'll fight for her? And why the fuck does she only cry around you, Demon? What the fuck did you do to her?" I growl, allowing the beast to show from within.

"I was there too, Ryder. She was experiencing an overload of hormones. It's very common early in pregnancy, as is the nausea. Her body is changing and so far she's doing an amazing job of handling it. Crying and being emotional is normal," Eliran adds.

"And the pain she just had? Was that fucking

normal?" I glower and watch as he takes a step back.

"No, but she's pregnant with the son of the Horde King, Ryder. *Your* son. She's young and that child was conceived before she was ready to become pregnant. If she'd become pregnant after she'd been done with Transition, this wouldn't be happening. Any way we look at it she's in for a rocky road. The best thing for her right now is to take it easy and allow your child to reach the second trimester of this pregnancy. I have to look in on another patient. When you get her settled and she is conscious, I will look in on her."

"You do that, Eliran. Just keep in mind that the fate of Faery may rest inside her womb. She is your number one patient until she delivers that child safely. I suggest you be ready for when the time comes, and be prepared for everything that could go wrong, just in case it does."

The fucking beast inside of me wants out. He wants full control and fighting him off is getting harder with every passing moment. He wants to take Synthia, to show her what he is. Never fucking happy, he wasn't even happy that I allowed him to show her only a sliver of his passion when she first came here. He wants more, so much more.

She's ours, and not even that has made him happy. He wants to feed from her, to fuck her until she feels owned. She isn't that kind of woman. She can't be owned. Not by him, not by me. Even though I want to dominate and control her, I already know what the end result would be. She's a warrior, and she needs to be treated as such, not as he would have me do. She's our equal, our match—we need to tread carefully now, or risk the chance of losing her forever. That's not something I can allow to happen.

I watch Eliran leave the room; his shoulders slump

as he shakes his head. I'm an asshole, I get it. My world doesn't exist without her in it. I'd easily give in to the beast and become what he is asking for. I'd kill anyone who opposes me, and repeat history. She's my fucking anchor, and no one will take her from me again, not even to save this world.

"Ryder, she's going to be okay. I've seen her with the child in her arms," Ristan says softly.

"With Adam, not me. Bring the Dark Heir here. Maybe he can bring her around."

"How about we bring Vlad and Adrian, too? Maybe if we surround her with what she needs, she will just fall on your dick," he quips.

"Get them, too. She likes them," I say in amusement. "I need to figure out how to get her to adapt."

"If you want her to adapt, you need to pull your head out of your ass and start thinking like a Human, Ryder. You might be the all-powerful Horde King, but she is Syn; she is part Human no matter how much she shouldn't be. If you want her to stay, if you want her to adjust to this life, and you want her to be a part of yours...*woo* her."

"What the fuck is *wooing*?" I snap.

"Do nice things for her; get her gifts. Find out what she likes, and woo her with them. Show her our world; make her want to be with you."

"I'm the fucking Horde King, I don't woo."

"Woo her," Ristan continues.

"I don't woo."

"Woo," he repeats.

"I'm not the kind of man to woo anyone. I can make her scream my name to the rafters, isn't that enough wooing?"

"Woo," Ristan smirks, which only serve to irritate me more.

"Woo," I grind out on an exhale.

"Yes, woo," he says, already turning to walk away. I watch his shoulders quake with laughter.

"Woo," I growl.

"Woo!" he calls over his shaking shoulder.

"Fuck me," I shake my head.

"No thanks, not my type...now go woo your princess."

Chapter
TWELVE

I awoke to Darynda pushing on my cheek. I gave a sound of protest, which she continued to ignore as she tormented and pestered me until my eyes popped open to level a killing glare on her. I slapped at her hand irritably as she smiled enthusiastically. I hated morning people; always had. I'd never been able to climb out of bed and welcome the day. I was more of a glare at the world, and snarl until I'd had enough coffee to appear Human.

"Time to wake up, sleeping beauty!" she chimed happily.

"Go away," I growled low, trying to focus.

"Not a chance. I brought you this crap they said you like; I even tried some of it! It tastes like fairy poop, but it does have magic in it! I feel like I can do a million things at once!" Darynda said, bobbing her head happily as she tried to pass me the cup without spilling.

"How much did you drink?" I asked, wondering if the coffee had something to do with her mouth working overtime.

"Nine cups! It's addictive. Eliran said one cup was enough for you, but he said nothing about me, and well, I just kept putting those little cups in and pushing the button, and it continued to give me more. So of course I drank it."

"Oh." Shit. I was corrupting the Fairy pool. Coffee today, nail polish tomorrow. I smiled as she handed me a cup. "I'm still in the room next to his…?"

"Yes, you are! Claire is still beside herself. She even went so far as to ask him to move you out of this room! He was quick to put her in her place. She deserves it, though; talking crap about you and telling us all how horrible you were. None of it is true, though. You don't look like you could even use a sword! I mean really, you had a job. And the stuff you went through…we are lucky you are even sane!"

"Darynda, breathe," I said, taking a sip and spitting out the straight espresso. No wonder she was on caffeine overload. "You drank it plain!?" I asked in shock. Don't get me wrong, I loved espresso. But in order for it to be good, it had to have some added flavor.

"Well, that was how it was presented to me by the machine!" she said, offended that I spit the espresso out everywhere.

"The machine only brews the coffee, you have to add the rest," I offered in explanation.

"What would you add to it?" she asked, tilting her head to examine me with a curious look in her eyes.

"Where's Ryder?" I asked through the disgusting espresso flavor sitting on my tongue.

"He's holding court, of course. He is the King, and is under pressure to right the wrongs of the Horde

Realm."

"Call for the Demon," I said.

She did, and within moments Ristan was strolling leisurely into the room. He flashed his silver and black swirling eyes and took in the espresso that now decorated the silk covers. "You summoned?" he asked, and lifted those beautiful eyes to mine.

"Need cream and sugar," I explained. Darynda deserved to taste a latté; one made right.

"You summoned me for sugar and milk?" Ristan asked lifting one brow further than the other.

"Sure did. I also need clothes, and shoes," I explained.

"Going somewhere, Flower?" he asked cautiously.

"No, but I'm not sitting around in pajamas all day, Demon."

"Good to know. Let me run down and milk a cow for you," he replied with a smirk lifting his lips.

"Ha-ha," I replied and kicked the blankets fully off.

"Good to see you are back to your old self and not fainting."

"I do not faint, Demon," I replied.

"Do too," he said with a wide grin.

"Do not."

"Do too!" he argued.

"Do not! Now please cream and sugar me,

Demon."

"I think Ryder might get a little pissed if I creamed and sugared you, Flower," he said with a wicked look in his eyes.

"Demon!" I shouted. This creature and his sexual innuendos were dangerous. Get him started, and he could go for hours.

"As you wish," he said, and instantly a delicate porcelain sugar bowl and creamer set appeared on the table next to the espresso maker. An ice blue silk sundress with matching sandals appeared at the foot of the bed, away from where the brown specs of the espresso mishap rested. He wiggled his fingers at us as he sifted out.

It took me twenty minutes of showing Darynda the joyful taste of an actual latté, which she liked a lot better than pure espresso. She helped me to dress and worked wonders with my hair, which was now braided and styled as if I'd spent hours at the salon. Even though she'd assured me she wasn't good with hair, it was so much better than anything I could have managed on my own.

"This is an honor to be placed in the room adjoining his!" Darynda mused after a few moments of silence had passed.

"Really, it's not," I said. I was ready to face him now, and I had a feeling Darynda wouldn't be so accommodating about taking me to see him as she had been about everything else so far. "I need to talk to Ryder. Can you take me to the throne room?"

"He's holding court right now. I'm not sure he will see you."

"Take me to him, please," I said, already heading

to the main door.

"No way! You are a concubine. You are not allowed to roam freely. You would need guards, and permission!"

"Look, Darynda, we need to get a few things straight. I'm not his. I didn't get a choice in this, and while you may think this is great, I don't. He hasn't asked me for any of this, he just demands I be here. I'm not his chew toy, or his pet."

She blinked, but said nothing for a moment. "Concubines are normally given little choice in the matter. The King chooses them, and some are given to him as gifts."

"Gifts? Do you have any idea how fucked up that sounds out loud?" I asked and threw open the door.

Sinjinn smiled and bowed with a courtly flourish. "Princess Sorcha," he greeted.

"Sinjinn," I said, happy to see a friendly face. "Take me to your leader."

"You are to rest," he said as he straightened back up. His eyes scanned my face briefly before he smiled once more.

"I'm done resting; take me to Ryder, now."

"I can't. You need to rest and take it easy. I was ordered to make sure you were not stressed out."

"Okay, well if you don't take me to Ryder, I'm going to scream my fucking head off. It's going to stress me out, and I'm sure he wouldn't want that, now would he? He ordered you to keep me calm, so take me to Ryder!"

He looked to be struggling with what he should do, so I tapped my foot impatiently. I felt bad placing him in the middle of it, but I was not staying in his future wife's bedroom, and that's what this was. I'd read enough books to know that what the girls spoke about yesterday was true—in a castle, the connecting room was the one the wife stayed in.

"He's going to kick my ass, Synthia."

"It's either that, or I scream my head off. You can pick."

He rolled his eyes and started walking. I smiled and threw a triumphant look over my shoulder to Darynda who had been silent through the argument. Her eyes were wide, as if she feared Sinjinn would have been angry at me for arguing with him. She totally needed to get out more.

"How did you do that?" she hissed quietly when she caught up to me.

I looked at her and grinned. "Easy; this isn't my first rodeo ride with the King and his band of merry men."

"Rodeo?" she questioned.

I rolled my eyes again. "I've been around Ryder for over two months now, and he wasn't the Horde King yet. Obviously; because if I'd known, I wouldn't be expecting his child…"

We retraced our journey from yesterday to the throne room. The castle was huge, and had been built of white stone. It was old, but it had been updated so that it didn't look like something out of the middle ages…or older.

Chandeliers dotted the high ceilings of the

walkways, and get this! Candles, yes, actual candles, and flaming torches in the wall sconces lit the way. I had to almost run to keep up with Sinjinn's long strides, but then Darynda did, too. It made it hard to take anything in while running behind him.

The room that was ahead of us was filled with creatures of the Horde. The one currently speaking… err…screaming was a Shape Shifter, if his inability to hold Human form while screaming was anything to go off of.

"They are inside of Faery. What is it you plan to do about it, *King*?" he sneered.

"I plan to find them and bleed them out…slowly. I have scouts out scouring our borders. If you have an issue with this, Silan, say it," Ryder growled as his wings grew wide behind him, even though he was seated on his wicked throne.

Ryder looked good upon the throne. He looked like he belonged on it. The Shifter continued to argue, and Ryder seemed to grow bored with his rant. It wasn't until another man who looked close in looks to the other Shifter stood up and interrupted, that it ended.

"My King, Silan is only worried because his mate is heavy with child. He does not wish to throw down a challenge," the male said.

I took him in. His vivid blue eyes and shoulder length blonde hair made him look almost Human. He was Fae, but instead of being beautiful, he was rugged and handsome, like Ryder in his regular Fae form. I swung my eyes back to Ryder to find him staring at me. I exhaled a shaky breath as the fight and the reason I'd been angry evaporated with the wicked little smirk he gave me.

"I, too, understand the fear of having the Mages inside Faery during this time. Synthia, please, come to me," Ryder said standing, his attention now on me.

I narrowed my eyes, but did as he asked. I was taking the stairs up to the throne when a silver throne with a comfortable looking white square pillow in the center appeared from thin air to the left of his badass throne. I let the electric hum of his presence flow through me as I accepted his hand. It wasn't until I felt his magic flow over my skin that I realized I was now dressed in a red ball gown, with a huge balloon skirt. I raised an irritated brow at Ryder. "Seriously?"

"I like you in red," was his answer to me. To the Shifter he said, "This is Synthia, she is the Blood Princess. She's also pregnant with my first child. So yes, I understand the need to eradicate the threat to our people more than most. Unlike my father," his eyes never left mine, "I do not plan on breeding an army of sons. She will likely be the only woman to carry my child."

"Right," I ground out, sarcastically.

"Do not argue with me in front of the Horde. In my bedroom, in my room, or sitting on my cock you can argue. Not here. Here, I am the Horde King. Here, I have to kill people for less." His voice traveled across my mind, startling me. I knew he did this all the time with his men, but this was a first for me. I gave him a saucy smirk.

"Then leave me out of it, King."

"Never." His eyes sparkled with mischief. *"Will you have dinner with me tonight?"*

"Change this damn dress to something that doesn't look like Cinderella took acid and met Alice in

*Wonderland for a trip, and even though I don't want
to be your damn dinner, I will* have *dinner with you."*

His laugh fluttered through my mind before he
tilted his head slightly to the side. *"I wasn't asking to
eat you. Tempting as it is, I was asking if you would
have dinner with me tonight, Pet."*

"Dinner?" I raised a brow as I threw the answer
at him. He was joking, right? He was holding court,
and we were neck deep in a private conversation, and
he was asking me out on a date? Since I was pregnant,
you would think we would have been past the dating
stage.

I felt another rush of magic, and smiled as I felt
jeans hug my ass and a long sleeve black blouse with
a turquoise scarf that was perfectly fitted around my
neck took the place of the dress. Soft slipper boots
with fur trim that matched the scarf covered my feet.

"Anything else, Princess?" He asked, but this time
he was no longer in my head.

I gave him a crooked smile and shook my head.

"Sit. You shouldn't be out of bed yet, Synthia," he
said as he sat back in his wicked skull throne.

"I'm not a weak female, Ryder. I can handle
walking," I mumbled and sat on the feather-soft
pillow on the silver throne. It wasn't apparent to me
that sitting there was any big deal until the crowd
hushed and looked at me as if they'd just witnessed
something huge.

What the hell had I just done? Oh yeah, I'd sat
in the Horde Queen's seat…with the Horde King's
permission…Fuck a duck. I started to stand up, but
Ryder grabbed my hand and held it in his. His eyes
scanned my face and then he turned back to the crowd,

as if nothing had happened. I glanced briefly and nervously at Zahruk and Ristan behind him. Zahruk looked like he was going to have heart failure, and the Demon looked entertained; like he wanted to pull up a chair and have popcorn for the show.

"Princess," the Shifter said, bowing low at the waist. When his head rose, I noticed his blue eyes were sharp and glowing. Yup, Fae. "I am happy to see you have been found alive. My King has chosen a brave lassie to start his dynasty with. Your story of courage and survival inside the Human world has traveled fast."

"Peachy," I groaned, and the Shifter grinned to reveal a beautiful smile.

"As I was saying, my King, Silan has no wish to challenge your wisdom of the choice to scout for the Mages. Our thought was to offer our trackers. As the alpha of the wolf pack, I am more than willing to use the pack to assist you in any way you need us," he said and bowed his head to Ryder.

"Silas, your father served my father. I understand the need to get the King's attention. Make no mistake; I am not my father. Your father was much like my own, and I have no plans of accepting the favors of those who think to gain it through the ways of our fathers."

"I took my father's head soon after you did the same to your own," Silas said and looked briefly at me. "You took the Blood Princess as a Gift, did you not?"

"I did, but only because my Seer had a vision of our child healing this world. Had it not been seen, I wouldn't have asked for her. I have not asked for a female since the day I made the contract with the

Blood King."

"This child, the one she carries, it will mend our world?"

"I was told this by Ristan, who was given the information by Danu. She gave him the vision and so it shall be," Ryder said, narrowing his eyes as he dared the Shifter to challenge it.

"Then so shall it be." His ice blue eyes swung to me and then lowered to my stomach. I lifted a brow at him, because there was nothing to see.

When his head slanted and an amused grin lifted his lips, I got an uneasy feeling that he was doing more than just looking at the flatness of my stomach. I watched as those beautiful eyes slowly rose to my face and his head righted. "Your pregnancy is definitely blessed by the Goddess, Princess."

I sat beside Ryder in silence, with Darynda smiling like an idiot nearby. Several more cases were heard by the King before he finally stood and announced that he was done for the day. We had to wait until every last creature left the room and there were a lot of them before we could leave. I couldn't, however, get the look of the Shifter's eyes, and what he had said, out of my head.

"We need to talk," I said, barely above a whisper.

"We can talk at dinner," he said, turning as he leaned his head against the back of the throne.

"Who the hell said I was having dinner with you?" I glared at him to get my point across.

"You did," he said smugly, and grabbed for my hand with a smile plastered on his lips. "Sinjinn, next time, tie her to the bed and gag her. She wasn't supposed to be up yet. She's carrying the heir, which makes her health your number one concern."

"Syn is very persuasive," Sinjinn replied, smiling.

"That she is. Come." Ryder held his hand out for me to accept. I stared at it for several seconds before I lifted my head.

"Remove this collar," I demanded.

"No," he replied easily without even considering it.

"Afraid I will leave you?"

"No, Synthia, I should just mark you. It would allow me to be able to find you anywhere you go; you already know how that works. The collar is necessary for now, and it is there for your safety. I told you, I won't allow you to run from me again."

"I didn't run from you, Ryder. *You* handed me over the Dark King with a freaking bow on my head."

"Which won't happen again, nor will you be lost to me. With my mark on your skin, I'd be able to find you if anyone decided to pop in and steal you. I'd rather be safe than sorry where you are concerned. You are a trouble magnet."

"You afraid you can't protect me?" I taunted him. Unwise? Yes. Did I care? No. I'd worn his mark before. It was tempting, but at the same time, I wanted him to trust me.

"You carry my child inside of you," his hand moved to touch my stomach. "There is no fucking chance of anything happening to either of you. Even if it means that I have to protect you from yourself."

Chapter
THIRTEEN

I was dressed via Ristan, who had stopped by to assure me that I *needed* to go to dinner. I, on the other hand, was not impressed. He'd dressed me in a white baby doll dress that barely covered my ass, and black stockings that had the heads of cats on the front of them just above my knees, and tails that went up my legs, and stopped at the lace bottom of the dress. He was chuckling "here kitty-kitty" and prompting me to throw things at him as he winked in and out, sifting as he avoided the missiles.

Darynda thought it was cute and convinced me to keep the outfit on, and then brought in Faelyn and they'd whipped my hair up in a magical updo and by magical, I mean they'd used magic and it was done and once again, my face was done with a light touch of make-up.

"I really don't think I should be going to dinner with Ryder. Not when I want to neuter him and watch him writhe in pain," I mumbled unhappily.

Darynda snorted and scrunched up her face. "You need heels," she mused and glamoured a pair of white heels with black trim. She leaned down and helped me into them.

When she was done, she stood back and smiled. "Looking like that, you guys won't even notice the food!" she clapped happily, proud with her efforts.

I shook my head. "This is stupid," I complained.

"Syn, he asked for this. Just give him a shot. He's trying." Ristan grinned with a mischievous look in his eyes.

"Give him a shot? I'm more likely to *get* shot around him! I'm pregnant; he's done what he needed to do with me. His job as King is finished where I am concerned, so what is the point of this?"

"You should know better than that, Flower. Ryder isn't done with you, nor is he likely to ever be done with you. *He* didn't plan on this pregnancy, and if you need to be pissed at someone about what you have been through, it's me. I'm the one who told him what I saw in the vision."

"That wasn't done with malicious intent, Demon. Ryder played me for a fool, and he will do it again. Can you tell me he won't marry Abiageal? Can you tell me that he will be mine, and only mine?" I saw him flinch, so I didn't need his answer. "I didn't think so. I deserve better than that; I *need* better than that. I won't become just another woman in his growing collection. He's already got more than anyone should ever have. He won't give them up, and I won't change what I was raised to believe. I want more, and my child deserves more." I lowered my eyes and exhaled a shaky breath.

"You need to let go of some of the social mores you learned in the Human world, Flower. They will do you no good here. Sooner or later, you will see that. Now, come, your King awaits his woman."

I took Ristan's hand and was sifted out of the castle to a pool that had hundreds of white roses and lilies floating over the crystalline surface. Thousands of small white lights lit up the sky, and two full moons hung high in the sky. I looked around and found Ryder in a tux, with a cocky smile on his face. Great, I wanted to wipe the smugness off his face. I also wanted to rip the tux off him and do naughty things.

"Princess," he smiled wider.

"Fairy," I groaned.

Why did he have to look so freaking sexy all decked out? It would be so much easier if he were a three-headed monster with a pitchfork. And his smile…he knew just how to disarm me, and exactly how to make my center turn to pudding.

"Witch," he amended.

"Asshat," I growled and narrowed my eyes.

"Okay!" Ristan clapped loud enough that we both turned our glares on him. "Now that we got the foreplay out of the way, we can get right onto the main course."

Ryder snorted, and I crossed my arms.

"Ryder," Ristan said patiently, and I could tell they were doing the mind to mind thing again from the look passing over their faces.

"I'm trying. She's the one who started it!" He growled out loud at Ristan, who shook his head as if he were annoyed with Ryder and sifted out.

I moved toward a hammock that looked comfortable, and sat on the edge. My eyes strayed toward the pool, and I sighed. It looked inviting and utterly beautiful with the flowers floating over the surface.

On the other side of the spread was a small table and pillows set out to sit on. No chair, but the table itself was low to the ground. There were people standing at the entrance with platters of food, which smelled divine.

Ryder walked over to me and extended his hand. I swallowed past the fear of touching him, and accepted it. His warmth flooded through me, and I did my best to stifle the sliver of desire his touch always sent through me. Once I was standing, he walked us across the small distance, and around the pool where he seated me on a pillow.

He probably had enough pillows to give one to every Human back home.

"Serve us," he said loud enough for those by the door to hear. They rushed into motion before the first word was ordered.

Some kind of fruit was placed before us, which almost looked like strawberries, only they were twice the size of normal ones.

"Hybrids," Ryder said after a moment passed in which I stared at the berries.

"Hybrid strawberries?"

"We brought fruit back after our first trip to Washington. We purchased seeds, and brought them back to plant. Faery soil is unpolluted like yours. They came up like this, and the juice and taste are far superior to the fruit I tasted there."

I winced when he had said which state I was from. I missed home already. I chewed my bottom lip and glanced up to catch him staring at me. This had been a stupid idea. I should have just gone to bed and stayed there.

"Here," he said and held one up. I moved my hand to take it from him, but he held it away.

"What the hell?"

"Let me feed you," he grumbled.

"I'm pregnant, not disabled, Fairy!" I sputtered.

"I know that!"

"Then why the hell can't I feed myself!?" I shouted.

"Because, I'm trying to be romantic!" he growled and scowled.

"Oh," I whispered, shocked as I backed up an inch. "Why?"

"Does it matter why?" he grouched.

"No, I guess not."

What.

The.

Hell!?

I opened my mouth and he held the berry up carefully. He allowed me to move my mouth to take it, but he refused to let me feed myself throughout the entire meal. When we were done eating, he smiled like a naughty child and stood, up pulling me with him.

"Come with me," he said and walked me to the

edge of the pool.

"I don't have a swimsuit," I said, eyeing him warily. It was official, Ryder was on drugs.

Before I could voice another complaint, he had me dressed in an ice blue bikini and had dragged me into and under the water with him. Music blared to life from somewhere unseen as my head popped back above the watery surface.

The Fray's *Never Say Never* was playing softly, but loud enough that we could hear it above the small waterfall feeding the pool. I looked around in wonder as small flames leapt from the flowers all around us. We had enough space between us and them that our hair was safe.

I gasped as Ryder grabbed my waist beneath the water and pulled me to him. I placed my hands on his naked shoulders. He'd changed at the same time he'd changed my clothes. Ryder in a suit was disarming. Ryder half naked and wet was devastating.

"What do you think?" he asked, his eyes guarded.

"It's beautiful," I whispered breathlessly. It was. It was beyond anything anyone had ever done for me, or probably would ever do for me again.

"Good, can I undress you now?" he asked with a smirk lighting his eyes.

I shook my head and splashed him and turned to move away from him. As if. He didn't let me get more than a foot from him before he took me beneath the water with him. I fought, but his arms calmed me and before I could even grasp what he was doing, my entire body jerked with desire as his lips landed on mine and he fed me air as he kissed me softly.

When we both came up and broke the surface of the water, he laughed. "Shit, this is actually fun."

"What is?" I asked, narrowing my eyes on him as I shook the water and removed the hair that was plastered to my face.

"Playing with you," he whispered.

"Is that what we are doing, Ryder; playing?" I asked, feeling tears burn in my throat.

"I'd rather we were fucking," he replied in a huskiness that sent heat shooting to places it shouldn't be.

"What exactly are we doing? You've done what you needed to; you got me pregnant. I don't understand what else you want from me," I whispered as my eyes searched his.

"You are mine, Synthia. I've always told you that never have I danced around what it is I want from you. I've kept many secrets for good reason until it was the right time to reveal them. I won't make any excuses for what I have done, or how I got you here, Pet. I'm glad you are here with me, and I'm happy that you are the Blood Heir. It makes it easy for me to keep you." A small smile played on his mouth.

"Is that all you want? Because if I'm just another—"

He quieted me with his lips, and I was helpless to do anything except wrap my arms around his neck and kiss him back. I was pissed, I was hormonal. I was also growing hungry; food did little to fill the emptiness in my stomach. He, however, could fill the ache, and would.

One minute we were in the pool wrapped around

each other, and the next…I was on my back with him hovering above me, a soft blanket underneath us. His hands braced on either side of my head before he lowered his hot mouth back to claim mine. I moaned as his kiss consumed and erased the troubles of my mind. I knew he was doing it on purpose to stop the fight.

When he pulled away, I was left breathless and panting.

"I didn't bring you here to fight or argue," he ground out as he shook his wet head, which made me squeal.

"You are as bad as a wet dog!"

"Speaking of wet dogs, yours is here. He's found a pack of Shifters that has accepted him since his own was killed."

"Gabe is here?" I smiled.

"I missed this," he whispered, going down on his elbows as his finger skimmed the tender skin over my smile.

"Is that all you missed?" I inquired in a teasing tone. I was so lost around him. One minute I wanted him and in the next I turned mafia. I wanted him maimed in very bad ways.

His lips turned up in the corners and he shook his head, sending even more water shimmering from the inky tips. "I missed this," he whispered before he dropped his head and kissed my lips gently. "And this," he said when he pulled away and licked the pulse that was currently speeding up at the hollow column of my neck.

I felt his magic whisper through the air as it

magnified his kiss as if he had a thousand mouths and all of them were touching my skin at once. I moaned and lifted my hips toward where his hardness pressed firmly against my need.

"I miss the sounds you make as I take you. I miss the noise you make when I fill you full of my cock. The way your eyes light up when they meet mine, wanting more," he replied as our swimsuits disappeared from his magic. "I miss the feel of your nakedness against mine," he continued, even as I parted my legs for him.

"I miss this, Pet. The way you let me, even though you're unsure of what will happen," he whispered against my ear, as his fingers skimmed over my stomach and stopped between my legs. "I love how wet you get when you know I'm going to fuck you sweet, long, and hard."

"I need you," I whimpered, fighting the urge to flip him over and just take what I needed from him.

"I'm going to tell you how I plan to fuck you. Do you want to know what I plan on doing to you?" he asked as a growl rose from deep in his chest.

I nodded, unable to make words come out.

"I'm going to spread your legs." He did, holding my legs apart until it was almost painful from being stretched as far as they would go. "I'm going to lick you." His head lowered and his tongue lavished my sleek heat until I thought I would go crazy from it. "I'm going to fuck you like this." One finger entered, and then another joined, and another, until it, too, became painful as he stretched me.

I moved my hips, or tried, but his hold on my stomach held me immobile. I moaned and tried to, anyway. He smiled as his eyes locked with mine, and then slowly he lowered his mouth and flicked the sensitive nub there. He continued to do it, holding my eyes locked with his golden heat.

His fingers entered and slid out, only to plunge deeper. He curved them, finding the place inside that made my mind grow dizzy as the impending orgasm tried to find purchase. The minute I got close, he pulled his hand out and waited.

"I'm going to fuck you so hard and so deep that you will still feel me next week, Princess. Your body will tremble, your insides will melt, you will be wild with need, but you won't come, not until I allow it. I want you so fucking wild with lust that you beg me to come. That you will beg me to allow you to find release, and only then will I allow you to come on my tongue."

"Ryder, please," I begged as his fingers penetrated me again.

"I love my name on your lips; the way you beg for me when I drive you wild," he said as his mouth hovered against my pussy, close enough that his hot breath fanned the sensitive skin.

My hands dug into his silky hair, but he easily caught and detangled them, before he held them with one hand against my stomach. He lifted his head and started to slowly climb up my body.

"Do you want me, Synthia?"

"Yes," I whimpered through the heavy panting of my breath that refused to slow and was steadily becoming labored from his ministrations.

"I miss this." He entered me as his hands held my thighs apart. I hadn't been prepared or ready and his fullness pulled a scream from deep in my throat.

"Fuck, so tight and so sweet. I miss my cock being buried inside of you. I miss this." His hips thrust as his ass gyrated and he plundered my wetness.

I moaned, and the moment I closed my eyes, his hands left my leg and came to my jaw. I opened my eyes and was instantly captured in his golden depths. I licked my lips, but he didn't move to kiss me. He kept pumping his hips at the perfect angle, the perfect beat that matched my heart which was increasing with each thrust, as it pushed me closer to the release I was reaching for. Each time I grew close to climax, he'd pull away and wait, only to start his sensual assault again.

"I need you," I moaned as something burned hotly against the left side of my lower back, right above my butt. But my mind was focused on one thing, and one thing alone. Him.

"I know," he smiled, and claimed my lips in a scorching kiss. The only thing keeping me from melting was the gentle breeze that filtered through the bowers thin see-through drapes that did little to hide us, "but I'm not ready for you to come yet," he whispered before he kneeled back on his calves and his hand stroked me where I needed him to fuck me.

"Ryder, fuck me, please."

He grinned wickedly and his free hand skimmed over my lips and his thumb pressed in until I parted my lips to take it into my mouth. "Get on your knees, now."

I followed his command and got to my knees, even though they trembled with need. He lay back as pillows materialized behind him. He lifted his long arms and cupped both sides of my face before he pulled me down, until my mouth was inches away from his pulsing cock.

I lowered my head the rest of the way, not needing a guide to tell me what he wanted. My tongue snaked out to capture the pearl of glistening moisture on the tip of his engorged head. The salt-tang exploded on my tongue with a sweet bitterness as a shiver of desire shuddered up my spine.

The moment I took the head in my mouth, he groaned a long, low, animalistic sound from deep in his chest. I smiled with the warmth of his cock in my mouth, on my tongue and the musky male scent of Ryder's arousal in my nostrils playing havoc on my senses.

"Fuck!" he barked as I took even more of him into the haven that was my mouth. I curled my tongue around him as I tried to fit more. He was too big for me to take very much, so I opened my mouth wider, and dropped my jaw as I tried to cover my teeth with my lips and took even more of him into my hot mouth. I moved my tongue, even though it felt trapped under the heavy weight of his huge cock.

Ryder was no longer holding still for me to see just how much of his heavy cock I could take inside my mouth. He started thrusting, moving his cock deeper and sliding it out again over my wet lips, steering my head to the steady beat of his passion as he took my mouth and held my hair to keep me there for him to take. "That's so good, take more," he ordered and I did.

I relaxed my throat as he pounded his need in, battering the back of my throat until I pulled back and swirled my tongue over the salty tip of his cock as he moaned against me, taking him deeper as my eyes captured, and held his, until his head rolled back and his eyes closed as he filled my mouth until I was forced to swallow him.

I moaned and fed from his passion, from his emotions that the release had given him. I fed until I was bursting, and he allowed it. He'd known I was hungry, and that was why he was on his back and I was licking my lips satisfied, even though I had yet to come tonight.

"My turn," he growled and sifted. One minute I'd been a satisfied cat, and the next I was filled with him, and he was fucking me from behind. His hands gripped my hips as he drove himself in until I was sure I would explode. He didn't allow it. Instead, he flipped me over and his mouth was ravishing my core hungrily.

I exploded into a million pieces. My legs trembled as heat centered at my core and shot through me. Sweat beaded at the base of my neck as he drove the orgasm on, until I felt it start to abate. He was inside of me before it had ended, and the moment he was, I shattered again.

Chapter
FOURTEEN

Dawn broke, and he glamoured another dress on me. The moment I was fully clothed, the bower which we'd had hungry sex in disappeared as if it had never been there. He'd given me so many orgasms that I'd lost count; between kisses, he sweetly assured me that he was still on a strict diet—me. It was a reassurance that gave me comfort and hope.

"What happens now?" I asked, smiling since I'd been unable to remove it from my lips.

"I take you to see my world, so that I can see it through your eyes."

"You want to see your world through my eyes?" I asked, a little confused by his words. He smiled and my breath caught and held in my lungs.

He was beautiful, even as his powers caressed my skin and he changed forms. He did it effortlessly. One minute he'd been a handsome Ryder, almost Human. In the next, he was anything but Human. His huge wings hugged against his skin, and his eyes turned to midnight with the full galaxy of stars stolen from the sky, now locked inside of them.

It still boggled my brain that my Ryder was the Horde King. It was a relief that he wasn't Alazander, and that he'd killed him. Anyone with such hatred and evilness inside of them needed to be put down.

I was entangled, caught, trapped in his obsidian depths. He lifted his hand and held it out for me to accept on my own. A bevy of emotions pooled through me, deep and profound, and turmoil tried to rear its head among them. I didn't want to think; there would be plenty of time for that later. So I didn't think twice as I accepted his hand and drew in my breath as he pulled me against his naked chest.

"I want to show you something, Synthia. It's a special place I enjoy," he whispered.

"Oh really?" I mused with a smile that wouldn't let up, glued to my lips.

"I'd walk you there, Pet, but right now sifting is easier, and safer. I can't take you everywhere I want to yet. The Mages have followed us here, which limits places I will allow you to see. They are trying to find allies with those who oppose the Horde. They've grown impatient and have brought the fight to us."

"We should kill them, like quickly," I said, placing a protective hand over my stomach without even realizing I'd done it until Ryder's hand pressed firmly over mine.

"Our child will be safe, Synthia. I vow it to you. I'd wipe every Mage off this map and that of your homeland before I let them get close to you, or my child."

Shit, that was actually sweet!

"She will be protected," I concurred.

"She? You have decided on our child being a girl?" he asked, but there was no anger in his tone, only mirth.

"Isn't that what you want?" I asked, replaying what my mother had told me before I'd been given to the Horde King.

"You are predicted to give me a son," he whispered against my ear as he turned me in his arms until my back was flush against his chest.

"So says the Demon, but, he's wrong on things," I said flippantly.

He chucked, and said softly in my ear. "The Demon's visions have never been wrong."

Ryder wrapped his arms around and me, and I smiled; at least, I did until his wings whooshed, and we went airborne. I squeaked an undignified sound of fear and he took us back down the entire inch to the ground.

"Face me, and place your arms around my neck, Synthia. I won't let you fall," he replied, and I did as he asked.

I wasn't afraid of heights. But then, I wasn't accustomed to being in the arms of someone who could freaking fly, either. The first time we'd only shot straight up in the air, and then he'd sifted us out of the Blood Kingdom. This time, he was actually flying. I rested my face against his chest, taking in his heady scent as I did so. I allowed his presence to calm me, and when he took off again, I was ready.

He didn't go fast, and eventually I pulled my head from his chest so that I could see where we were heading to. I smiled and squealed again, only this time, with excitement. "Holy shit, Fairy, you can fly!

I thought you said we would sift?"

"And miss you holding onto me this tightly?" he replied warmly.

He laughed deep from within his massive chest and shook his head as he landed on a long deck that couldn't be more than a mile from the pool we'd just left. I waited for my feet to touch the wood deck and for him to loosen his hold, before I moved.

There was a long, slanted staircase covered with moss, which led to an azure pool of water that was fed by a beautiful cascading waterfall. "It's beautiful," I whispered as I took it in. It was a cove with huge cliffs on all sides, except for the one with the winding staircase that led to the welcoming pool of water.

Vivid emerald vines with white flowers that looked like lilies with more petals hung from them. They covered the sheer rock cliffs. I took one step and then another with Ryder close on my heels. When we reached the crystalline pool, he pulled me back against him.

"I used to play here after training with my father. It's heated from the rocks. We call them Core stones, natural rocks that were once dipped into the cauldron of life; they stay heated for millennia or more once they have been removed from here. Kind of like the natural hot springs of your world."

I escaped his hold, and bent to my knees and placed my hand into the cove's water. It was warm, like a hot tub, but there were no bubbles or big tub like the hot springs back home. "Where are the rocks?"

"At the bottom, but you won't find them. This waterfall has been here since before your world was created, and it flows throughout Faery. It is so deep there are those that thought that there wasn't a bottom. All bodies of water are connected in some way. Everything in Faery has a purpose, and normally works together."

I sat on the platform and dipped my toes into the water, sighing with pleasure. It was eerily beautiful here, and yet even as I sat still, I could see the flowers moving closer to where I sat. "Are the flowers moving?"

He laughed as he sat behind my body, and curled his legs around my frame, fitting perfectly. His feet joined mine in the water's welcoming heat. "Everything in Faery is alive. Those are not flowers, they are Dagdens. They keep this place protected, but expect payment from me, for doing so."

I watched as one got scary close to us, and then gasped as Ryder bit into the palm of his hand to draw blood. The white flower approached and without needing to be told, quickly latched onto to Ryder's palm.

I watched in stunned silence as the white flower turned crimson red. It continued to stay latched onto Ryder, but soon began to fade in color, and as I lifted my eyes to the other flowers, I realized why. They were all feeding from the one attached to Ryder. Instead of the hundreds of white flowers that had been there, now hundreds of light pink flowers scaled the cove's cliffs.

I gasped and curled tighter against Ryder's chest. It was a reminder that I was no longer home, and that this place was anything but safe. I'd have never known that those were not flowers, would never have even guessed it. When the flower had taken its fill of Ryder, it crept silently back across the water to slither up against the rock.

Creepy!

I pulled my toes from the water, wondering what else I had missed.

"Synthia, nothing will touch you while you are with me. The water is safe," he said comfortingly.

"I'm tired," I said, and I was. I had been getting over taxed easily, and I didn't like it.

"Come, you sleep with me tonight," he whispered.

He flew us back to the castle, yes the castle. A real-life castle that looked as if had been picked up from Scotland in the 1500s and deposited in Faery at Ryder's will. Instead of taking me inside right away; he flew us to the hill that overlooked his home.

The castle was built into three different levels of the cliff it was embedded into. There were hundreds of stairs, maybe thousands that led from one castle to the next. It was lit up, but not from light bulbs; from torches that were inside the stone walls.

"It looks like something I would read in a romance novel," I said, because I knew he was waiting for me to comment.

"It's older than any of those books," he said with a snort. He took pride in his world, and I wondered what it would look like through his eyes if he was seeing it as a child.

"You should read some of them, Fairy. You might learn a thing or two from them."

"Like how to throw you over my shoulder and carry you home to pillage and plunder your sweet honey?" he teased.

I snorted and rolled my eyes. "That's a Viking. I was thinking more like a Scottish Highlander." I smirked where he couldn't see it.

"So you want me in a kilt? Is that so you can have easy access, or so that I can?" he mused as his lips smiled against my hair.

"Maybe it's both?"

"Does my lass want her mon to speak with a thick brogue?" he asked, and it sounded so natural off his tongue that I shivered with desire.

"Nae she does nae." I smiled, mimicking him which made him throw back his head and laugh.

I grinned and turned in his arms. This was nice; this I could live with. We were happy and together— but it was short lived.

Zahruk sifted in silently. I felt the slight tingle in the air that came when someone sifted and quickly turned around.

"Ryder, we got problems. The Shifters were just attacked. It was very bad; we think it was the Mages, and a message from Cornelius has arrived. He and Abiageal will be here soon to start preparing for your wedding. I think this is his way of forcing the issue now that you have ascended," Zahruk said, but I'd noticed he wouldn't look at me. He kept his eyes fixed on Ryder's as if I didn't exist.

"This couldn't wait?" Ryder asked in an angry tone.

"No, the Mages are getting bolder. This attack wasn't on the colony of Shifters; it was on the pack that just left this castle."

I shivered and stepped away from Ryder.

"We are not done, Synthia," Ryder growled, noting I'd stepped away and dropped my arms to my sides. I'd let myself forget that he was marrying someone else.

"Go be the King, Ryder. I'm tired," I whispered past the tears constricting and burning in my throat.

Chapter
FIFTEEN

Ryder slipped in and out during the night, and I slept right through it. I had been a mess after the outing, and sleep had been escaping me until Darynda had brought in some soothing tea that had knocked me down for the rest of the night.

Time was running out to make Ryder love me, and finding a way out of that contract so he didn't have to marry someone else was weighing on my mind heavily.

It sounded easy, but things with Ryder never went smooth. I was always expecting his mood to change, and with my own plagued with hormones, it wasn't a simple matter. We were adjusting, but the pressure from those around us was also smothering. It would be nice to go back to the night in his arms before he'd handed me over to Adam.

"He has to marry her. I don't see what the big deal is. They have been betrothed for close to thirty years now. Alazander made the betrothal contract, but neither side was in a hurry to consummate it as they were each getting what they wanted without making it official. The Horde needs the alliance that they share to stay as it is. No offense, but I don't see him getting that from your family."

"And what, may I ask, is that?"

"Thirty thousand fighting warriors and ten thousand iron warriors who can wield iron with magic."

"Oh, is that all?" I snorted and shook my head. Okay, so Ryder was getting a lot from his soon-to-be bride.

"I am the Blood Princess, and I have the cure to Faery growing inside of me. Can she say the same?" I shot back, because a twinge of jealousy roared within me. Shit. "I'm sorry, I just don't understand why being the Blood Princess doesn't seem to count for anything," I amended, because I didn't want to offend Darynda who had grown up in this world.

"It's okay. Being the Blood Princess is a very high station, higher than Abiageal's. It's just that her contract was negotiated first and the Horde got exactly what it wanted with both contracts," she said thoughtfully, and then switched topics so fast it made me dizzy. "Did you know that The King has called the Dark Prince into attendance? He's supposed to be super-hot."

"Wait, Ryder called Adam here?"

"Cadeyrn," she said, narrowing her eyes in disapproval.

"Um, no. It is Adam now, and he wants to be called Adam. It is the same as I was Sorcha, but going by a different name for so many years has a way of making the new name stick."

"You really should call him Cadeyrn. It's what his mother named him. Anyway, he should be here later today. All the women in the castle are humming with excitement, because it's known he is openly looking for the Light Heir now that you turned out to be Blood."

"Adam is looking for the missing Light Heir?" I felt my heart clench in a vise. Not because I wanted him to be mine, but because the thought of him being with someone other than Larissa felt wrong.

"Yes, Ryder is helping of course. If all four heirs and the relics come into place, Faery could be healed. People would stop worrying about pregnancies, and dying infants."

I felt a chill snake down my spine.

"I'm so sorry!" Darynda cried, placing her hand over her mouth with wide eyes.

"It is fine." It wasn't fine. I was having a child in a land where they didn't survive. Nothing was okay in this situation. I'd been so wrapped up in my own head, that I had forgotten the mortality rate of the children here.

"How many infants have died in the Horde this year?" I asked hesitantly and very afraid of the answer.

"One in twenty; that's the odds of them making it through Transition," she said watching my face.

"That's not so bad," I said, feeling a weight start to lift off my chest.

"One in twenty will live," she replied, dashing it and placing the weight right back on it.

I bolted to the bathroom and threw up. I was still kneeling, calves to ass, when Ryder picked me up. "Eliran has medicine for this," he growled.

"Does he have something to ensure our child lives?" I asked on a giant sob that rocked my entire body.

"It's going to be okay, Pet. Ristan has seen the child, which means he will live to his birth."

"Has he seen him grow up? Has he seen him anywhere besides in Adam's arms?" I was starting to freak out. I hadn't wanted to be pregnant, but now that I was, I needed to not lose this baby.

"We are working on it. I promise."

~~*

I was being given nausea medicine when Ristan sifted in. He was sitting beside me now, and his hand was rubbing my shoulder. "I haven't seen the baby beyond the vision in Adam's arms. Unfortunately, I can't just make the visions come, Flower."

"So he could die?"

"Yes," Ristan replied, as Ryder growled, and Eliran shook his head.

"Ristan," Ryder warned.

"Would you rather I lied to her? She needs to know the truth, no matter how bad it might be!" Ristan shouted over the glowering looks Ryder and Eliran were throwing at him.

"I need the truth. I want the truth. I can handle the truth. What I can't handle is allowing anything to happen to this child. Do you understand?" I asked, looking up at Ryder and Eliran, and then over at Ristan.

"Syn, just because—"

I grabbed the Demon by his shirt and pulled him closer until we were nose to nose, the tips touching. "The truth. It's all I want. You saw me hand Adam a son. Was he alive, did he move at all?"

Ristan swallowed slowly, his eyes never leaving mine. "I have to assume he was based on what I saw. I just do not know if he makes it to Transition. I also do not know if that is the child you are carrying now. Based on the severity of how fast our world is dying and what Danu has shown me, I have to assume he is. Those are two big educated assumptions." I slowly released his shirt, letting him sit back a little.

Okay, this was a little better that I had thought at first, but still not good enough. Ryder trusted him, a lot, and Ryder said that Ristan was never wrong. It was just some things had to be interpreted. It was plausible he'd seen me handing my child to Adam, because well, I'd want my best friend to see my son. I'd want him to hold him.

"You're sure it was me, and that it wasn't the real Light Heir who was handing him her son?"

Ristan looked uncomfortable as he answered. "I saw you, Synthia. I'm sure that it was you in the vision with Adam and you were both smiling. From all of the visions I have had, I do know that you, the Blood Princess, will give Ryder a child, and I am sure that child is the start of the cure to this world. That Danu is pushing and pulling your fate where she can is another thing I am sure of, because not even you can deny the odds of you taking the job from the Guild and ending up inside of Faery. You found your way back here, Flower. Through all of this, you were brought back to our world for a reason," he finished with his hands in his lap and a steady look in his eyes.

"Maybe Danu hates me. Ever consider that?" I

asked, feeling the nausea rise again, even though I'd taken the meds. My heart was hammering wildly, and it wasn't helping that I was really starting to wonder why Danu thought I was so freaking important.

"Synthia, you need to rest. You need to allow the medicine to help you," Eliran said, taking in my shaken pallor.

"I can't *lose* this baby," I whispered as my chest burned with fear and unshed tears.

"Syn, no one in hell will touch our child, including the sickness. Not even if we have to take him to your world to save him," Ryder said, scanning my face tenderly.

"Get Alden here, and Adrian and Vlad. Adam is on his way. When they get here, we go Mage hunting," I said, fighting off more nausea.

"You are not going hunting," Ryder argued.

"Who the hell is going to stop me? They're the ones causing this sickness in the children. So I say we catch one and torture the prickless bastard until he tells us how they are doing it. Then we stop it. We make this world safe for *our* child, Ryder."

"I have men out searching for them," he continued to argue.

"Yet, they attacked the Shifters. Which means they are attacking the smaller creatures of the Horde, the ones they stand a chance of fighting. Something drew them here, and there's a reason they are attacking the smaller clans. We just need to catch one of them and figure it out when we do," I snapped.

"You get some rest. I'll send out a notice that we need one of the Mages alive. It's the best I can do for right now, Pet. I need to get the Horde under a bit more control before I can leave for any length of time. I'm under constant challenges right now, and I'm needed here."

"I need you here, with me," I whispered. I needed his warmth and the comfort of his arms right now more than anything. I was handling everything this world was throwing at me, but he was a big part of why I was handling it so well.

He might not say the words I wanted to hear. He may not have broken the contract. But I could tell he was trying and he truly cared about me. And right now, that meant everything.

Chapter
SIXTEEN

Adam was waiting for me in a formal receiving room, wearing jeans and a loose fitting black silk shirt when I saw him. I wasted no time in running to him and throwing my arms around his body in a bear hug. His arms wrapped around mine, and we stood together like that for a while.

"I thought I had lost you," he whispered.

"I thought I was going to have to kill the Horde King!" I pulled back and studied his handsome face. He looked well; he looked really well. I put a little distance between us, and smiled. "Wow, you got buff," I observed. His lime and emerald eyes were brighter now, the black line that surrounded them more defined.

I wrapped my arms around his neck and pulled Adam closer. "I missed you," I whispered.

"You too." He smiled against my neck. His hands warmed against my back through the thin cotton dress I wore. Turns out, hormones can make you easily overheat. I'd noted swelling as well, in my boobs… I'd decided that pregnancy sucked monkey nuts.

"How are things with you?" I asked as I finally let go of his neck.

"I'm on the hunt," Adam said, smiling wickedly.

"For the Mages?"

"For my fiancée," he answered, a small grin lighting up his face.

"Me?" I asked, watching as his grin faltered, and his lips turned up into a semblance of a smile.

"No, Sorcha," he said, and I notice he's enunciating my name on his lips, teasing me.

"Then who?" I asked, because just name me George and put me in a monkey suit, I was curious to see if Darynda got the gossip right. He had been going to marry me, until I'd been snatched from our handfasting ceremony.

"The Light Heir. I'm still engaged to her. The prophecy still says we are the other half to putting Faery back together. My father thinks it's a good idea we begin looking for her a bit more aggressively. The sickness is getting worse in the Dark Kingdom now, and more land is being affected and more children have been dying over the past few weeks. It's heart-breaking to see it happening."

"Oh," I said quietly. I had already done one freak out, and this was a sore subject right now.

"I hear I'm going to be an uncle?" He smiled until it met his eyes.

I rolled my eyes. "How the hell did you find out, anyway?"

"Ryder sent word to my father," he explained.

"You mean Ryder boasted about his virility?"

"Pretty much," he confirmed and shook his head. "Having the Horde King's love child? I never thought I'd see the day that Synthia Raine McKenna had a love child…with a Fairy." He ducked quickly as I threw a punch at his shoulder, but missed.

"Are you upset?" I asked carefully.

"That we didn't make a baby? No. Syn, I came to an understanding when you were taken. I don't love you that way. I mean, don't get me wrong, I totally thought I did," his eyes scanned my face, "but it wasn't my love for you that I felt. It was what you were feeling for him. You love him."

I swallowed and considered the nearest exit to escape and hide in. I wasn't a coward, and I knew that had been why Adam had been acting the way he had. We had a bond, and it fed him my emotions as surely as I could feel his. "How's your dad?"

"Syn, this is me. You can't lie any more than I can. You can tell me anything, and you know that. I can feel the hurt, the love, and most of all, I can feel the fear you are feeling for your child."

"Guilty, but that doesn't mean I plan on saying it out loud. Now, how did you get here?"

"Ryder said you needed to see some friendly faces, and I am hoping that Ristan might get a solid lead on the Light Heir."

"That's good, but are you ready?" I asked, thinking it was a little too soon for him to be doing this. Larissa had just moved on, and he'd loved her.

"Faery won't wait for me to figure it out, Synthia," he said lightly. "I don't need to love her to make a child; I just need to fuck—"

"Got it," I cut in quickly, not wanting him to paint a vivid picture for me. "You should at least want more than just a quick fuck, Adam." I rolled my eyes when he awarded me with a smile.

His eyes looked harder. We'd aged. Not in years, though; mentally. We'd been through hell together, and yet we'd both hung on and made it out on the other side alive. He at least remembered his childhood in Faery now, so he was far more accepting of their ways than I was. It still felt weird that he had such an acceptance of his role in this world. I hoped he could find his way back to being the sweet man I grew up with and could always count on. I smiled at him. "Wanna grab something to eat?" I asked.

"Synthia, are you asking me to put the moves on the Horde King's girl?" He shot me a mock look of horror.

"I'm not his girl," I barked, shaking my head at him.

"Oh you are. You just won't admit it."

"I am not!"

Yes, I was arguing for no good reason, but it was Adam.

"He marked you. He couldn't have said you were his any better way than that." He smiled, knowingly.

"He didn't, not this time."

"He did."

"No, he didn't. Last time it was…awkward. I'd have known if he had, Adam."

"Syn, I have Fae senses, and they are telling me to back the fuck off. Very violently."

"I'd know if he had marked me," I argued.

"Would you?" he countered with a small frown creasing his forehead.

"I'd have seen it." I wasn't sure who I was trying to convince, myself or him?

"You are marked," he shook his head, and smiled again. "Let's go grab some food, and we can talk some more. You need to feed my nephew."

~~*

I left Adam at the door to his room, which was only three doors down from mine. He'd been told to ready himself for dinner and that he would escort me himself tonight.

I was so happy the Fae actually ate food, and some of it was incredible. The fruit that Ryder had fed me was amazing, but then, it could have been because he was feeding it to me and my senses had gone all haywire. I was standing with Darynda in the room when Ryder stuck his head in.

"There is a dinner tonight for the Dark *Princeling*... Syn needs to be dressed in something red to symbolize the Blood Caste." He was gone as soon as the last word was said.

I was fighting the nausea again, but the meds were helping. It sucked that being Fae didn't cancel out the bad parts of pregnancy. I had asked Darynda for an actual bath, and was pleased when she had conjured water into the huge tub.

She'd also brought bath oils and towels, which was

nice since I couldn't for the life of me glamour fabric onto my ass. I was starting to think it had something to do with the necklace Ryder refused to remove.

Dinner had been casual, and I had been informed that there would be a huge feast and celebration very soon for the crowning of the Horde King, since he had skipped the formalities in his haste to get to me.

I enjoyed seeing Ryder and Adam interacting with each other now that Adam and I were in on the secrets. When Kier had taken Adam away from the presentation, evidently Ryder had given him permission in those parting words to let Adam in on everything. The first thing Adam had wanted to do after finding out the truth was kick his ass for scaring the crap out of everyone. The second thing he wanted to do was kick his father's ass for tricking him into thinking Ryder was his brother.

It was a relief knowing that Adam was here, and that I could go to him when I needed to. I was sure that had been why Ryder had brought him here, and for whatever reason he had done it, I was happy he did.

It was refreshing to have Adam close by. It was also a subtle reminder of how many people I had left in the world. Ristan was slowly making his way to my heart. He was a hard one not to like. Ryder had been a little distant, but then he had a lot on his plate right now.

He had ascended, and with it, came everything he had put off to find me and help the Dark King retrieve his missing heir. He was running a kingdom now, and we were both trying to figure it out as we went through it.

I was grateful for the time it gave me to think, but

also afraid that if I thought too much, I would want to run. I had nowhere to go now. My house was gone. The apartment wasn't an option; not after what had occurred there. Adam was now with his father, and it was where he belonged.

I just needed time to figure out where I belonged, and time to wear Ryder down, and make him see that I was worth fighting for. There would be no running from this; not now that I was pregnant. I couldn't leave a world to die either; not when the child I carried could be the cure.

No, I just needed to find my place and make sure it was beside Ryder. Even after everything I'd gone through with him, I was willing to fight to keep him. I just needed to give myself some time to adjust to the different culture, and the new world I'd found myself living in.

It was both thrilling and terrifying. Change always was, though. The part that scared me most was having no control over my own life. If I stayed, I'd be giving most of the control to Ryder, but wouldn't loving him and being with him also give him full control?

Ristan's advice helped me, and I was appreciative for it. The idea of being placed in the pavilion and left there bothered me the most. I wasn't sure if he would do that, but it was still there in the back of my mind that he could do it, and easily.

I was inside my room before I thought to look for Ryder's mark, and I found it on my lower back, right above my left cheek. I could have thrown a fit over it, but it looked sexy, and Ryder would be expecting a fight. I could easily give it to him, but I wanted to be unexpected. I wanted to make him wait for it, and he would. He loved it when I gave him attitude, but the truth was, if I was ever taken—I wanted him to find me.

For now, I'd let him think he'd won.

Make him wonder why I was so accepting this time.

He needed to feel as if he had control over me, and I understood that he wanted to keep the unborn babe safe as well. Strangely, this gave me a level of warmth and pleasure knowing he'd go out of his way to protect us both.

Ryder would be a fierce father and protector of our child. This was the safest place to have our child, and I wasn't an idiot. I needed to be here where they could help save my child if anything went wrong. I was right where I needed to be. For now, anyways.

Chapter
SEVENTEEN

A few days went by at somewhat of an easy pace while I spent my time passing the endless hours in the bedroom with Adam. Darynda had been great through it all—including the one fit I'd thrown when Ryder had left to go scouting with his men.

I was going stir crazy and had never been one to be idle. Ryder seemed to think that I would be meek and timid now that he had become the Horde King and I was pregnant with his heir. Yeah, right…so not going to happen!

Today I had asked Darynda to find a swimsuit, and since she didn't seem to understand what I was looking for, she was currently out trying to find someone who could do just that. It wasn't until Zahruk came to the door that I groaned.

"I was informed you were in need of swim wear?" He asked, scanning the room before he pushed through the threshold and smiled.

I crossed my arms over my chest and leveled him with a narrow eyed gaze. "I am, I'm tired of sitting in a room and watching the clock tick by until Ryder allows me out to play."

"Allows you out to play? You have free reign of the pavilion. No one can get in or out of it without us knowing. You were kept here because Ryder was worried about your comfort."

"Just dress me up and let me out."

"As you wish." Zahruk bowed his dark blonde head and flashed me with his electric blue eyes. I felt his magic cut through the air as a simple blue bikini replaced my skirt and top. He nodded, but before he turned to walk away, a simple white cover of sheer silk was wrapped around my form.

"Thanks," I mumbled and watched his wide back as he walked away.

"Ready?" Darynda chimed in with a brilliant smile as she returned.

In the pavilion there were women sitting around doing different activities together—or there were, until we walked in. Every eye in the place turned in our direction as we entered, followed closely by Sinjinn and Aodhan.

I smiled and ignored the dirty looks the group gathered around Claire tossed at me. She'd been nice when we'd first met, but I was willing to bet it was because she hadn't planned on me sticking around long.

"Flower," Ristan said as he sifted in beside me.

"Demon," I tossed over my shoulder as I continued to the pool.

"I take it this isn't for relaxation?"

"I need to stay in shape, and sitting in a bedroom won't do that," I replied as we entered the back of the pavilion where a more private pool was. They had three pools. One for the children, which, I'd only seen a few of them so far. Another was in the main room and was full of women splashing and playing around in the nude—no wonder Darynda was having a tough time with the idea of the swimsuit.

I was still a bit miffed that the first time I had seen the pavilion, I had no idea I was in the Horde Realm.

I'd chosen this one because it was currently empty, so I could swim paces and work at keeping my physical form in shape. Baby or no baby, I was a warrior and that wasn't changing due to a mommy status being stamped on my forehead.

"Sooo, I take it you are a bit restless?" he ventured.

"Brilliant deduction, Sherlock," I gritted out. He smiled annoyingly at me.

"I'll see what we can do about providing some adequate entertainment for you."

"Like spin the Fairy? Pin the tail on the Demon?" I snapped.

"Oh, ouch! Touché, Princess. I'll keep in mind to manifest a few bottles, and a donkey for you. Wouldn't want to end up with a tail pinned to my ass, now would I?" He slid his hands to his butt protectively for a moment. "I was actually thinking of the libraries, and getting you acclimated with our history, seeing that sparring and weaponry are off your schedule for right now," he went on mischievously. I looked at him gratefully.

"I would prefer the sparring, and sticking a certain Fairy with a dagger has a nice appeal to it. Okay, the libraries would be a nice change. Please?" I gave him the pleading puppy eyes, and he laughed. At least that would go a long way to relieving some of the boredom.

I shook out of the silk cover and let it slide to the floor effortlessly. Ristan and the men quietly left the poolside room, leaving Darynda and myself alone. I sat down and let my feet slip into the cool water. Obviously, this wasn't one of the heated pools.

I let the stress run off of me as I let the water calm the racing of my heart. It hadn't slowed down any since Transition, and everything was moving entirely too fast. I'd been devastated at the thought of losing Ryder when they'd said I was the missing Light Heir.

Now that I had him, and knew what and who he was, I wasn't sure where that left us. I wasn't about to become his just because he could keep me here by sheer force. The night he'd taken me beside the pool had been amazing, but he'd only come to feed once since then.

He was busy being the Horde King, and I knew that wasn't going to get easier for a while. He'd spoken of being challenged by his own people and the other Castes of Fae; ones that his own father had tormented.

"You keep glaring like that, and the water might turn to ice," Darynda said, sitting beside me.

"Sorry, just thinking about things," I mumbled and pushed off the side of the pool. The water was shockingly cold and a gasp left my lips unexpectedly. "Shit, that is cold!"

Darynda laughed but made no move to jump in. She'd glamoured on a swimsuit as well, now that she knew what one was. "Mind if I leave for a few minutes? There's someone I'd like to go see really fast."

I shook my head. "Go ahead. I'm going to get used to the water and just do a few laps." I wondered if it was to see someone or some male—hey, I knew enough about how things worked around here, and I understood that my girls had to feed, too.

As soon as she was gone, I started to run in place, letting my body get accustomed to the chill of the pool. I turned my head and stared at the closed door, wondering if my guards were just outside, or if they had moved onto somewhere else.

I felt a ripple tear through the air around the pool, and before I could do more than turn around, Liam appeared.

"Sister," he said with coolness to his tone.

"What are you doing here?" I asked, moving closer to the side of the pool he stood on.

"I've come up with a plan to get you out of here," he said, kneeling down as he shook his blonde hair from his face. His blue and purple gaze looked a little too cocky.

"Um, what?" I asked, not sure if I wanted his answer, but curious enough to ask all the same.

"News has traveled to the Blood Realm that the Horde King has a child on the way," he answered as his eyes scanned the door and came back to rest on mine.

"So I've heard," I whispered, wondering where the hell he was going with *that* line.

"I plan to kidnap her and ransom her for your own release. If he even thinks this child could be his Heir, he'd void out the contract father made."

"By kidnapping the concubine that is pregnant?" I asked for clarification.

"Yes, I need you to help me, though. I need you to sneak me inside the pavilion, and point out which one is pregnant."

Oh the irony!

"You know that the pavilion is full of guards... right?"

"Synthia, I don't have much time. This is the only way I can get you out of here. I can't just take you from here; you are bound by the contract. She, however, isn't. Not if I take her with me."

"So, let me get this straight," I said, watching him scan the room and the door. "You steal the Horde King's concubine, and you exchange her for me. Then what? You think he wouldn't come after the Blood Fae over this?"

"He is a new King, sister. He will be bombarded by challenges, and trying to rein in the Horde for months," he said, holding out his hand to help me up from the pool.

I accepted it and exited the pool silently.

"You will need to cause a scene, something that will make the guards go after you. Can you do that?"

I blinked and shook my head. I knew how much it had taken him to come back here. He'd been tortured here, his hands cut from his body. He'd endured more than any one person should ever live through. And he'd come back to this place, for me.

"Liam, we can't do this. I'm sorry," I whispered.

"We can, and we will. Right now the Horde King is out checking the borders. He won't be back for a while," Liam said, standing up to his full height.

"Liam, I am the pregnant concubine," I whispered, meeting his eyes that were so much like my own.

I watched as he shook his head and did the math inside his head. "Look, if you want to be his whore, you can just say it!" He growled, his eyes flashing with anger.

"Ryder is the Horde King. He's the same one who brought me back inside Faery; the one who accidently undid the protection spell on my skin. He was playing a part, and since the Dark King was his uncle, and had adopted him—he played that part well. I had no idea that he was the Horde King, or that it was him when I was being gifted to him. But this plan? It won't work, because I'm pregnant with his child," I said, watching as his features fell from the news.

"Fuck!" he whispered vehemently.

"I'm okay here," I assured him, but his eyes were now wild and when I reached out to touch him, he recoiled from my touch.

"I have to go. I'll find a way to save you sister. I will," he said, and sifted out.

Chapter
EIGHTEEN

I finished my exercises in the pool, disturbed by the desperation that had been stamped on Liam's face. There was also the sudden absence of the guards, and Darynda. And, well, there was the fact that five minutes after Liam had sifted out, they'd all returned together.

They'd known. I kept the fact that I knew that they knew to myself. I waited until I was back inside my bedroom to excuse myself from Darynda, and entered Ryder's room—to find him leaning against a wall, bathed in shadows.

"Nice try," I said, stopping just inside the threshold. I crossed my arms over my chest, feeling a slight chill from the window he had opened.

"Hmm?" he made the noise from between his full lips.

"Liam was here, but then you knew that already," I accused. He'd set me up!

"I always know when someone sifts inside my stronghold. He was allowed inside. He was also allowed to leave. I am aware of everything that goes on inside these walls, Pet."

"Why? Why allow him in; to see how faithful I was?" I was done being nice, he'd actually set me up to test me. I'd passed, but he had no idea how much in love with him I was.

"I needed him to see that you were unharmed so that he could return and report it to your family. I wanted him to see that he couldn't take my concubine without breaking the contract. Liam is a warrior, and he needed to see with his own eyes and hear with his own ears that you are mine. I respect him. The entire time he was a *guest* here, he never begged for mercy, and he never complained."

"A *guest*? You cut his hands off and sent them to my parents! If that's how you treat your guests, then I'm afraid to see what you do to your enemies." I rolled my eyes at his flippant comment concerning my brother.

"Liam was in my father's custody for years. He'd already been caged and tortured when I found him rotting in the dungeon. I took his hands, yes, but only because your parents refused my offer. Synthia, I did what I had to do in order to get you. I don't regret what I did, nor do I regret the fact that I have you here now."

"As your concubine," I growled.

"I'll take you however I can get you," he answered with a grin that I could see even through the shadows that bathed his face.

"I thought you were out patrolling the borders?"

"I was, earlier. I got word that the Mages had moved their encampment; they'd been tipped off by someone. They have someone inside the walls of this kingdom, or close to it, helping them. Most likely it is Dresden. He's not happy that he is no longer in the favor of the Horde King. My father was of the same ilk, not me. His challenge has been issued, as well as many others. Your brother told you as much. Did he not?" He finished and stepped from the shadows. "How are you feeling?"

I narrowed my eyes on him coldly. "Like I should throw up on your shoes." I was tired of the games. "Next time, Ryder, if you want them to see me, just invite them in. Stop with the fucking Fae games, or just keep me out of them."

"We found another relic; one we can get to," he said, smoothly changing the subject. "I leave in the morning to get it."

"I'm going with you," I said, meeting his golden stare.

"No, you are staying put."

"I'm pregnant, Ryder. I'm not made of glass. I am going with you. If it gets dangerous, I'll leave. I won't let anything happen to our child."

His eyes lowered to my flat stomach. "Our child," he tested the words on his tongue.

"I'm going," I repeated.

"I'd rather you stay here where it is safe for you both."

"I'd rather be with you," I protested, making sure to stand my ground.

"Fine, but you need to be cleared by Eliran before you can go," he growled and pinned me with an angry look.

"Fine," I chirped triumphantly.

"Fine," he said on an exasperated sigh. He held his hand out, and I quickly accepted it. He sifted us into the medical ward, which was where Eliran could normally be found. We'd been there less than twenty seconds before Ryder started bellowing orders. "Eliran, now!"

"You don't have to shout," I muttered.

"Synthia! The medicine not working?" Eliran rounded the corner with his hair sticking up as if he'd been resting, or worse, feeding before we'd so rudely interrupted.

"They are working wonders," I smiled and thanked him. In a matter of moments, I ended up on a table next to one of the 3D ultrasound machines. From the looks of it, Eliran had been busy back in the Human world.

"This is going to be cold," he said before squeezing a container that looked like something ketchup would come out of over my stomach. I rested my head on my arm as I got comfortable.

He placed the globe looking wand over my stomach and pressed in gently. I watched the monitor silently as he moved it up and down until he stopped and flipped on a switch. The noise coming through it sounded like static.

"That's the heartbeat," he replied to my silent question.

Heat flushed through me and my eyes swung to Ryder's with a grin from ear to ear covering my face. My baby had a heartbeat!

"Oh, crap," Eliran said.

"What's wrong?" Ryder and I both asked at the same time.

"There's a head," Eliran said, pointing it out on the screen, "and there's another one."

I felt my stomach drop. "Oh my God, my baby has two heads!?" I cried, feeling as if the table had fallen out from beneath me and my entire world was crumbling.

Ryder looked at me, and the look in his eyes was of sheer pain, and unmasked horror. Our baby had two freaking heads!? "Can he live like that?" Ryder asked.

Can he live like that!?

Eliran shook his head and I felt my heart shattering. He swept the wand over my tummy slightly.

"You misunderstand. Your babies each have a head of their own," he said with a bright smile on his face. Two heartbeats could be heard like they were beating through a tunnel.

"Say what?" I asked, unsure I'd heard him correctly.

"Twins, you are having twins. There is no mistake. See?" He pointed to one of the heads and followed the lines with his fingers. "There are two arms, two legs, and a head and torso. And this," he did the same again with the second one, "has the same. It explains Synthia's acute case of morning sickness."

I wasn't listening anymore. I was shaking as the ringing in my ears echoed through my head. "Fucking, Fairy!" I growled, turning my eyes to Ryder's face. I lost every single ounce of the desire to throttle him as fast as it had formed. He was staring at the screen with wonder in his eyes.

"How many other cases of twins have there been in Faery, Eliran?" Ryder asked, ignoring me.

"None I know of personally."

"One," he corrected him and lowered his smiling golden eyes to meet mine. "Shit," his eyes lifted back to Eliran. "How safe is it for her to have twins?"

"I have no idea, but I will ask around and see if anyone has heard of twins being delivered by a Fae mother. I do know that there was a case over millennia ago, but it didn't work out for the mother. The children, however, were born safely. We have Human technology, though, and I can look through the information I brought back to learn everything I can about delivering twins."

"You do that," Ryder whispered.

"Genders?" I asked, trying to ignore what they were talking about. I had lived through Fae ripping my family apart, a serial killer, and had faced the Horde King. No way in hell would I die giving birth!

"Too soon to tell, but they look healthy. Heartbeats are very strong, considering they are only two months along by Human standards. They look good, and so do you, Synthia."

Ryder's hand lowered with a tissue and he wiped the gel from my stomach without waiting for Eliran to remove the wand. "Is she well enough to mission travel across Faery, possibly for several weeks?"

"She is, but only if she is feeling up to it," Eliran said, turning his head and winking at me over his shoulder.

"I'm ready to go," I said, smiling up at Ryder, who was even now holding out his hand to help me up. I dismissed it and sat up.

"Synthia, I'll do everything I can to ensure you are okay. Twins are a good thing; it will give the people hope."

"Of what? That the Horde King can shoot an egg and fill it twice?" I asked, raising a brow. "Or that he's virile as a flipping rabbit?" I glowered when Ryder snorted and grinned devilishly at me.

"Let's go, Pet. I have a meeting with the Guard to go to, so we can plan this out. We will have to make a few adjustments if you are going with us."

Chapter
NINETEEN

Less than an hour later, we met up with his Guard in a warded meeting room. A sense of excitement stole over me as I moved toward the table…that was round. The sight of it made me smile. "A round table?" I asked, tossing a curious look toward Ryder, which he caught. I watched his lips turn up in the corners before he sat down.

I moved my eyes to look around the room, taking in the wards that lined the walls. I'd been in a room like this in the mansion, one that had knocked Larissa to her knees. It had been the first indication that I was Fae, and I'd done my best to ignore it.

My eyes slipped back to Ryder, who was watching me closely. I rolled my eyes as his grin grew into a blinding smile as if he was thinking the same thing. I sat down in a chair. At least this time I didn't feel like I was the hired help.

Ristan stormed in through the door and stopped cold looking down at me. His eyes lowering to my stomach, and filling with a look of absolute wonder as Ryder's had done. He took the seat beside me and Ryder swung into leader mode effortlessly.

"Okay, so we know that the relics in Tèrra have all been relocated," he said and glanced at me. "Tèrra is what we call your world, Synthia. Zahruk and a few others have confirmed they are being moved once a day, easily obtainable in transit. Alden, with the help of one of the Guild's librarians has discovered a scroll written in our language. It's believed that it was obtained some time ago, but we are unsure of how it ended up in the hands of the Guild," Ryder said smoothly.

"Alden is still at the Guild?" I asked, feeling my stomach sink with the knowledge. It was too dangerous for him to be at the Guild when we now knew the Mages were running it. Leaving him inside was asking for trouble.

"Alden is fully aware of what he is doing, and the danger of being inside the Guild. Ristan is keeping in touch with him and if he even thinks Alden is in trouble, he will pull him out and bring him here," Ryder said with his eyes watching me for any sign of objection.

I turned and looked at Ristan, who was still looking at my abdomen. He looked as if he was trying to see inside of it. "Ristan?" I asked, watching as he lifted his eyes to mine.

"Twins," he said softly, "how the fuck did that happen?"

"Well, do you want the short version or the long one, Demon?" I asked, grinning from ear to ear. I was scared shitless of having twins, but I wasn't passing up an opportunity to mess with the Demon.

He gave me a blank stare before he lowered his eyes again. "She didn't let me see twins, Flower."

"I would hope not, Demon, because had you seen them, and not told me, I'd be kicking your ass."

His eyes lifted to mine, the silver inside of them shining. "Only you would have twins, just to fuck with me."

"I blame Ryder," I said, and smiled as snorts and grunts of agreement filled the room.

Ryder was smiling, as were his men. He shot me a smoldering look before he got the meeting back on track. "Like I was saying, the scroll that was found indicates there are more relics than we'd originally thought. We have one out of four that were hidden inside Tèrra, but this document shows that there are more pieces to the puzzle. Each relic has two pieces. These counterparts that were hidden inside of Faery are the activation pieces for lack of a better word." He paused and looked around the room before continuing. "I couldn't make the scepter work beyond coming to life, but at least now we know why it wouldn't work correctly. Based on the scroll, Ristan was able to locate one of the secondary pieces. The problem is, it was hidden by the Fae. We hid it, and it won't be as easily obtained as those inside the Human world will be. Ristan, the room is yours."

"I think the secondary piece was hidden to protect the power of the relics from being used by the Humans, or in this case, the Mages. We had always thought that the relics would only work in the right Fae hands. However, the Mages have proven themselves to be resourceful and they have been systematically finding ways around many of our magic's. I think the ancients knew what might happen, and put safeguards in place for the relics. Those who have gone into slumber are even now being awakened. They would be able to tell us what they know, and exactly why they were hidden. Unfortunately, we don't have the luxury of waiting for them to become fully awake. The Mages have followed us here, and we know they are not stupid." Ristan nodded to Zahruk, who then took over the room.

"Okay, so it's the same as last time. It's going to be heavily-guarded magic, but we have no idea of what kind, or if there are creatures set in place to thwart us from entering. What we do know is it won't be as easy as the last one," Zahruk said, winking at me.

Shit, if that was easy...what the hell were we in for this time?

"This is what we think is going to be there." Zahruk flipped on a monitor and worked the flat screen from where he sat beside Ryder. On the screen were drawings and diagrams for what looked to be a huge cave. "This was set up by the previous Dark King; it's the labyrinth." Several strings of violent curses erupted from around me before Zahruk turned his eyes on me. "For those of you who don't know what that is, I'll be explaining it," he said slowly, as if I was lame in the brain department.

"It's where the Dark King used to send his warriors as a final test. If they made it through the course, and most didn't, he would place them in his secret guard. Only very few of those who went inside made it out alive. Which is why Kier shut it down when he took the throne," I said, trying to pull all the data and information from my brain. Details about this place were sketchy, but I had come across some information about this bad boy before breaking into the Dark Fortress.

"Impressive," Zahruk said with a tilt of his head. "But it's not that simple. Those who make the journey can use no glamour, no magic. Those who journey with us can use simple glamour, but not to assist those who will try to enter the labyrinth."

"Define simple glamour, because nothing with you guys is ever simple," I quipped, eliciting snorts from the men.

"Fair enough," Zahruk mused, with a sexy smirk lifting the corners of his mouth. "We can glamour things like food, water, and fire. Basic survival items only, nothing defensive, meaning no weaponry so we will have to glamour what we think we will need ahead of time and bring it with us. This actually applies to as many of our basic needs as possible so we won't be tempted to use magic unnecessarily. No sifting as we use the ability in battle, so this trip will be on horseback. Break the rules governing the labyrinth, and you cannot go inside."

"Shit, so you guys will be roughing it." I laughed, the men did not look happy about this thought.

"Well, anything regarding the labyrinth is called a trial for a reason. It is supposed to test your mind, body, and resolve," Zahruk countered.

"This is going to be good. I can't miss or be tempted by something I hadn't gotten the hang of yet. You guys on the other hand..." I teased them with a small smile. "I studied what information was available on the labyrinth before I took on the Dark Fortress. If Kier shut it down, does he have any idea of what is inside? We can't afford to go in blind. It's a Fae creation, so it's gonna be full of tricks and crazy shit."

"We know a little about it. Kier has given Adam a rough idea of what should be there, but like many things in Faery, it will have changed with time since it was given life from Kier's father. Everything in Faery changes. Unlike your world, Synthia, Faery gives rights to the land. Which means it's a living, breathing world. We are going to have to go in fairly blind, and hope for the best," Zahruk replied.

Every eye in the room turned to Ryder as he made a disgruntled sound. "Kier said whoever we send through it has to be pure of heart, pure of intention, and sane of mind. There's nothing in the Dark Kingdom that shows how to make it through this labyrinth. He sent Adam to help us, since we need someone from the royal line to access the start of the labyrinth."

"Question, the Light Fae had all the relics, so why didn't they know about the other pieces?" I asked, thinking out loud.

"The Light Fae wouldn't use the relics. The Queen wasn't stupid. She was blinded by the love of her child. We think one was hidden by the Dark King, and one by your grandfather, Synthia. Two were hidden by my father, and those we will save for last, since he was a sadistic prick."

"So the ancients might have known about these safeguards, and this scroll had the information on it. I'm surprised that at least the Heirs weren't told about it. Seems a bit short sighted to me," I said.

"Not necessarily." Ryder mused. "I was barely through Transition when they hid the relics, and even though I knew most of what my father was up to, he didn't tell me everything. This would have happened sometime around the eleventh century. Our history is much like yours. Over time, it becomes useless and forgotten. Unlike you, we don't always teach our children of our history in books. The fact that your Guild has our scrolls is telling, because that means the Mages infiltrated one of the Castes. That's the only way to explain how they would have obtained it. Alden is looking for more, but we are out of time. We need to start collecting them before the others figure out what we are up to."

"Okay, so we have the Dark King's son helping now. You also have me to open the Blood…err whatever theirs is called, or where it's hidden. And, we have you to find your father's. So why are we still sitting here?" I asked, tapping my fingers on the table as I watched him.

"Because we need to be fully fed before the trip, and since you are coming with, I'm bringing more people than I had planned to. Eliran will also be coming with us, as well as a few others. This won't be a simple thing, Pet. We can't sift until the trial is complete, nor can we use magic for protection. Riding there will take weeks."

"I don't need to travel with a doctor, Ryder. I'm pregnant, not sick."

"You're pregnant with twins, Synthia, and that is a rarity within the Fae. You also carry *my* twins in your womb, so plan on being at the back of this retinue with armed guards protecting you at all times. You will be guarded and kept safe for the entire time we are out of the kingdom. Do you understand? There are many who will want you dead for the simple fact you carry my child in your precious womb. Say no to any of the safeguards I have put in to place, Pet, and you stay here in fucking bubble wrap."

"*Children*, Caveman; I carry your children inside my womb. I don't mind guards, but if you try to put bubble wrap on me, know this: I'll kick your ass *while* I'm popping the damn bubbles," I smarted off. Fucking bubble wrap me!

"They don't know that. No one outside this room with the exception of Eliran knows you carry twins, Synthia. You may tell Adam, but you will tell him to keep this information to himself. It's important that we keep this quiet for now; I need to keep you protected. You are a target, as you were before, Synthia. But now, you and the infants you carry are all targets for my enemies to use against me. Liam was allowed inside; anyone else who comes will be killed. You will always have one of the thirteen close at your side from now until you give birth. Pick one, and remember he will be with you like fucking glue," Ryder said, narrowing his eyes. He'd ignored my bubble wrap comment, which was probably for the best.

"I pick the Demon."

Ristan grinned.

"Ristan, any arguments?"

"No, Ryder. But I will need time to clear up a few things before I can babysit," Ristan said, with a playful grin on his face.

"That's fine. Okay, we will meet in the main hall in the morning when the others have arrived. Asrian, you will stay here at the castle, and keep things moving along with the Horde petitions and hearings. Get the help of a few of the others as well. I suggest you all feed and rest tonight."

"As you wish," Asrian said, bowing his head slightly. "I will hold down the fort, you take the guards you need, and I will keep a skeleton crew here with enough show of force to let those who think we are weak in your absence think twice."

"Summon Vlad, and get the others back here as soon as possible."

Chapter
TWENTY

We were walking back to his chambers when he finally said something that didn't include his plans to wrap me in a protective bubble. "You sleep with me tonight, Pet."

"In bubble wrap?" I asked, tossing him a serious look. I refused to be wrapped in anything. I may have been pregnant, but I was still a warrior. I was never helpless.

"In my arms," he replied smoothly in a seductive voice. "Bubble wrap is only for when you are away from me."

"Smart ass," I growled through a smile that spread quickly across my face.

"I'll show you my ass if you show me yours, *Fairy*," he said mimicking my nickname for him. I raised an eyebrow at him, surprised, because he was playing with me. It was out of character for him, but it was one of his many surprises of character.

"You got it all wrong, Ryder. You are the Fairy, and I am the Pet. Keep it straight, Ryder. I'm pregnant; I get confused easily in my current state." I teased him, until I turned to catch the heat burning in his golden eyes. I swallowed over the lump forming in my throat. Shit, he was hot!

I could play coy and act like I didn't see the smoldering heat burning in them, but I was weak, and he wouldn't let me go with him unless I'd fed. And let's be honest, the heat in his eyes? I wanted to see it as he drove himself deep inside of me.

"Now you admit it?" He continued to play. I liked this lighter side of him, even if he did want to bubble wrap me and lock me in a panic-room until I gave birth.

"No, I'm not a Fairy. I'm Fae, and even though I suck at being one, I'm here. My old life is gone; you knocked me up. So yes, Ryder, I admit that I'm Fae, and I'll even admit to being Blood Fae, and hell, while I'm at it, I'll admit I like you. Now you, you're still a Fairy," I said, smiling impishly.

"You like *me*," he said, shaking his head. "You *like* me."

"Yes, it could be the hormones, but you are kinda cute…for a Fairy."

"For a *Fairy*?"

"You should really get this hallway checked out, seems to have an echo in it." I smiled even wider.

"I guess I could admit a few things," he replied in a sexy voice that was filled with heat.

"Such as?" Yes, I was curious to know what he felt, since he never said anything apart from wanting me. Shit, we were having twins! And I had no idea where we stood on this.

"You've got a great ass," he said, never taking his eyes from mine as we walked, oblivious to anyone watching us. "Your screams when I fuck you? I like that shit, too. The noises you make when I drive my cock balls deep and you ask for more? Fuck, I seriously like it...a lot."

Okay, maybe I fell right in to that one. "Flattery will get you nowhere," I continued to tease him.

"I love the way that your eyes glaze over with heat, and your bottom lip quivers when you scream my name. I love the way you come on my cock," he continued playing.

I swallowed and shivered involuntarily. Freaking Fairy had game! And he was using it all on me, and I was allowing it. "I like the way you fall over when I kick your ass."

"You've never kicked my ass," he replied easily.

"Never say never, Fairy," I said before I turned and kicked out with one foot, while I planted my hands against his chest and shoved him. I stayed long enough to catch the look of shock on his face, before I turned and ran as fast as my legs would carry me down the long hallway. I squealed with laughter from the look on his face as I ran forward.

I'm not sure what I'd expected, but c'mon, he was Fae. He sifted in front of me, which I hadn't seen coming until it was too late. I ended up colliding full-force with his much larger frame. Hitting Ryder at a full sprint was like hitting a brick wall. I screamed as I started to fall backward, but he caught me easily.

"Shit!" he growled with a hint of laughter in his tone.

I was quickly pulled up and pressed against the

warmth of his wide chest, which I'd just a second ago face planted. "What the hell do they feed you? Cement?" I said as I relaxed against him.

"You knocked me on my ass, Pet."

"I did, didn't I?" I snorted, happily flashing him a haughty smile.

"I should spank that pretty ass for doing so," he whispered heatedly as he stalked me. I was walking backward toward the door I knew to be behind me.

"You wouldn't," I said, already knowing that he would. He was the epitome of a male. He was strong enough to do it, easily. I was almost surprised by the heat that erupted from the mere thought of his hands on my ass.

He took one step for every three I had taken. He caught me the moment we passed through the door to his lavish bedroom. One hand snaked around to the small of my back, and lifted me up against his immense chest, the other finding my ass where he then smacked it softly, almost teasingly. I smiled and bit into my bottom lip. He continued walking toward the bed, as if my weight didn't hinder him at all.

His eyes burned with intensity as he turned us around and lowered himself to the bed with me still pressed against his body. I spread my legs until I was straddled on his lap. I lifted my face until our mouths were close enough for either of us to make the first move to kiss.

Neither of us did so. Instead, we sat like that for minutes, just together. Both of us were afraid to move to dispel the peace, which was so new to us. No snarky comments came easily to mind no brutal alpha male shit, either. Just us. This was the man I'd fallen in love with, even with his sheer dominance and his need to control.

Right now there was none of that between us, and it wasn't needed. I wanted him, and even though we had many issues to work through, right now wasn't the time to discuss it. I had a craving, and only he could give me what I needed the most.

His mouth lifted and brushed against mine, softly. His breath wafted to me, with a subtle hint of rum on his tongue. I inhaled and drank him in, even as his hands tightened on my ass. He rocked his hips slowly, showing me the desire he felt, and I had created.

I moaned and ground my body against his massive erection. He growled hungrily from deep in his chest, the sound sent chills racing down my spine. It created a spike in my temperature, and my nipples hardened with the need for his attention.

"You're so fucking beautiful," he whispered through the thickness of lust.

"I need you inside of me, Ryder."

"I can smell how wet you are already," he growled and sifted us around, until I was beneath his massive frame. I spread my legs to accommodate his length, as he pressed his body against mine. His hands cupped my face, and tilted it to give his mouth full access, to ravish it.

I moaned louder, but his mouth captured it as his tongue delved deeper to find mine. I felt his possession as his mouth warred with mine, and won. His hips gyrated against mine, placing pressure against my wetness. Creating a fire that smoldered, and burned white hot inside of me. He was still kissing me as his magic filled the air, and removed all of my clothes, except the slinky black lace panties.

When he finally pulled away, I cried out from the loss of the heat from his body. He stood back and gave me a devastating smile. I watched his face as his eyes slid down my naked chest, until they rested on the lace that covered my pussy. The heat from those eyes fed my need, and before I knew what I had done, I'd lowered my hands and was rubbing where I needed him to be.

"Fuck," he said with so much heat in his voice that it went directly to my core, sending a new wave of heat rushing over my body. I felt his magic radiate through the room until it was kissing my nipples and caressing my thighs. "You're so fucking hot. Do you have any idea how beautiful you really are?"

I wasn't comfortable with beauty. I had never thought I was pretty, and even though I was Fae now, I still wasn't comfortable with my own looks. Ryder saying it, not once but twice, made me blush and something inside of me felt warm as tears threatened to fall from my eyes with the sincere tone in his voice. This beautiful beast thought *I* was beautiful.

I fought against the thickening in my throat that his words had created, and I blinked back tears as I sat up to go to him. He stopped me with his eyes alone. The possessiveness in their expressive depths was enough to stop me cold. This man was saying he wanted me, without having to move those beautifully skilled lips.

I stayed rooted to the bed, as if I'd become a part of it. I felt melded to it and unable to move from beneath the amber hunger that was burning for me in them. This beautiful creature dominated the space, filled it brimming with his presence. The air grew thick around me, and I knew what was coming before it kissed along my spine and rained tendrils of a thousand kisses over my neck and face.

"The beast needs to feed, Synthia. He wants to feed from you," he said, even as his body began to change, as if he couldn't stop it from happening.

"Ryder," I said as a sliver of ice crept up my spine, which did little to cool the heat that was coiled in my belly. His eyes blinked from gold to obsidian, and brands that had been stationary now slithered over his skin. Skin changed from being bronze to pale as he stood before me. I ran my tongue over my dry lips and stifled a violent tremor that fought to be let loose.

"You've been with him before, Pet. He was there in Transition with us."

I shook with the memories from Transition, as if I'd known it all along but hadn't been able to believe it. My mind went back, as if I was back in the room during my own Transition, and watching it from above. Ryder was there, but he was different; he was larger. His skin had been paler, and he'd been inside of me, the beast had.

He'd spread my legs, and spread me from the inside. His tongue had grown, and it hadn't just been Ryder who was with me, but the beast. He'd ensured I had made it through Transition, and now I knew why Ryder hadn't needed the help to bring me over. He already had help in the form of his beast.

"You allowed him to fuck me without asking me?" I accused.

"He didn't need to ask you, and it's not like he really could at the time, anyway. You challenged him, and he accepted. You allowed him out, you wanted him! You may not have been able to admit it back then, Pet, but you knew. You have seen him in my eyes often, and you chose to ignore it. You took him in small measures during the hunt, on our first night together. You have nothing to fear here. Not from us," he said even as his hair grew longer, darker, and his features became more defined, his skin paling to a soft alabaster.

His eyes smoldered with desire even as his voice dropped a few octaves. His hands rested on his hips, as his body grew larger by about six inches overall; his brands writhed and changed. His wings unfolded until they were spread behind him, wide and beautiful.

"Say yes," Ryder urged. "I'll be right here with you. If you want him to stop, all you have to do is tell me."

"Yes," I whispered, and as he stepped back from the bed, allowing for me to stand, I did.

"Sit," he said after I'd stood in place for only a few seconds.

A small bench with a soft pillow placed a top it appeared, materialized by his magic. A thin metal pole appeared after that, with a chain that hung from a small connected metal that was embedded in the pole itself. I tore my eyes from it and looked at Ryder, who was smiling roguishly.

"Yes, I plan to tie you up and take full control of your passion. It is how I like you; at my mercy, begging me to allow you to come," his voice came out multilayered and husky as hell.

"You always have control," I replied honestly. He was always in control; he didn't need chains to do that. I stepped closer until I was inches from the bench and lowered myself until I sat on it. I lifted my hand without waiting for him to ask and spread my legs until my knees rested on the bench.

He said nothing; his eyes just watched my movements as if he was memorizing each line, every curve of my body. Those eyes shifted, and the stars in them became my focal point. His body shimmered and his brands pulsed with life. He cracked his neck as the pulse in his jaw ticked. He stepped closer and ran his thumb over my face before he released it to grab the chain that hung above my head.

"You will have no control this time. He's going to be hungry and demanding. If you don't want this, Synthia, tell me now."

"I can handle the beast," I replied, finding the thought of finally knowing what was taking me thrilling. I'd always thought that Ryder had something inside of him, and even though I hadn't been aware of it at the time, I'd fed his beast, and in return, it had knocked me up.

Ryder had been as surprised as I was that his beast had intentionally impregnated me. Ristan had told me how he'd found out moments before I'd been taken from my own wedding to Adam, and now his gentle caress of my stomach in my dream made complete sense.

The metal clicked into place, restraining my hands above my head, and I watched as Ryder lowered himself until he was eye level with me. His mouth pressed against mine, and the kiss was consuming. This was what the songs wrote about; with one kiss, I was helpless to pull away. With one kiss, I was a boneless mess, and with one kiss, I was his.

He pulled away, but in his place now stood his beast. The Horde King knelt before me, his silken eyes taking in everything. The room grew thick with his power. The electricity he created, slithered over my skin. "Are you afraid of me?" he asked, his voice layered and hypnotic.

"Yes," I replied, and my lips quivered as I did so. I wasn't terrified, but to say that I wasn't afraid at all would be a lie. I could now see the difference of Ryder being in control of this form and his beast.

His hand came up and tested the weight of one breast, and then the other. He smiled, and I sucked in my breath. He was terrifying, but he was also the most beautiful creature that I'd ever seen in my entire life. I leaned my head back against the pole and watched him as he caressed my skin, until a moan stole from between my lips. His eyes watched every reaction that I gave to his touch.

"I smell your wetness," he said, his fingers sliding over my skin until they rubbed my clit through the silk panties that Ryder had left me in. I hissed with pleasure as his skillful hands pressed against me, right where I needed them to be. He removed his hands and placed them on the delicate skin behind my knees, and lifted them until my legs were bent and spread for his wide girth.

His mouth lowered until he was raining soft kisses along my inner thighs. His hands rested on my knees, holding them apart for him to devour my flesh. And he did, with his lips and his tongue. His mouth was the match to the kindling of which he started the fire with. My entire body came alive for him, the panties soaked from the desire he was creating inside of me.

Knowing he was a part of Ryder made this okay. Seeing the gold flecks in his eyes made it okay for me to do this. This was the being that wanted me, and he was a part of the man I loved. I felt his head lower until he pressed his mouth against my panties. His wings expanded until they blocked out the light from the candles of the room.

Stars erupted behind my eyelids as his breath fanned against the wet sleek heat of my need. He licked around my panties, his hands sliding beneath my ass and lifting it easily. I opened my eyes and was met with the galaxy of stars in his inky depths. I'd been wrong before; it wasn't a constellation of stars locked in his endless depths. It was the gold from Ryder's own eyes, as he watched me from inside the beast.

His mouth lingered against my thigh a moment before his teeth nibbled against my tender flesh. His teeth pressed against me as his tongue slid over the wetness, scorching my flesh. I watched him nibble and tease me with his fangs as he tasted my blood from the small pin-pricks his fangs had left. I found pleasure from his bite; no pain was forthcoming. My eyes found his again, and I gasped with pleasure as he sucked on my clit through the panties.

I felt the panties rip, and looked down to find them gone. I shivered at the thought of his strength, but that thought was fleeting as his mouth replaced the silk, and everything inside my head turned to one focus. That the beast was using that tongue, and fuck was it good!

It pushed against my opening and entered until I could take no more. He was pushing, and pulling, and his nose was pressed against the sensitive nub, which was a crescendo of sensations all at once. He growled against my skin, and I moaned louder as I pushed against the pole, trying to give him more range to torture me with.

And then it was gone, and he was kissing me.

Hard and passionate; curling my toes until I thought they would cramp. This beast was made for fucking, and I was his target. He changed what he was doing so quickly, that my mind would register one thing, and he'd have moved on to another thing.

His finger entered my wet sheath, and then another and another until I cried out from the pain and pleasure that assaulted me. I was crying out, pleasure sending waves of heat rushing through my entire body. I felt the chains lower, which meant he'd undone them with magic, and I took full advantage of it, pulling his head closer. Magic kissed my flesh, and then I was on my back on the bed. He didn't fuck around. He was in full control, and I was at his mercy, his will was my own.

"Fuck, your body is so tight; it fits me like it was made for me, alone!" he growled as he parted my legs and looked over my head. I did so, too, following his eyes. The length of chain laid forgotten, and the need for it gone. He wasn't done with them yet, though.

He smiled, and as I turned back to look at him, I saw the fangs. Full sparkling white fangs, which I hadn't noticed before. I blinked, and when I looked again—they were still there. I shivered as he brought his tongue out to lick one, and then the other.

"I am the spirit and power of every breed of the Horde. I am their leader and in being the King, I can take any shape; any form at any time."

"So, you are a Vampire, too?" It was a lame ass question, but hey, I was currently fully exposed, and getting scared now wasn't an option. He nodded and flicked his wrist, much like Ryder did. The thin chain that had held my arms to the pole had now been secured to the thick wood of the headboard.

"I am whatever I choose to be, or whatever Ryder

needs me to be. I have been with Ryder since his Transition. Once Danu decided he was a strong enough host, she unlocked the rest of my power and allowed us to merge as one. It is the difference between a Fae, and the Horde King."

"Uh, do you have a name? I mean, Ryder called you his beast, but is that your name?" I asked uncomfortably.

"I have no name, little one. I am part of Ryder and he is part of me. I can truly be the beast he calls me. However, I will not hurt you," he said and sat back on his haunches. "I am always with Ryder, and even though I am death, I could never hurt you, Synthia. Even before Ryder knew he wanted you, I was there, telling him to go after you. He fought against it, not understanding the need I had for you. You were mine the moment I first laid eyes on you. I cared not how I got you; only that I did. I could have killed you, killed this little obsession that I felt, but the first time he took you, I was lost. When you took us into your body, you knew he was not alone, and yet you asked for more. I could have easily killed you while taking what I wanted, had you denied me. You are my match," he said thickly, his voice echoing off the walls. "That is what Alazander did not have."

"A match? What do you mean by that?"

"Alazander, as a host, did not have a match. He was not as strong of a host as Danu needed him to be. Over time, his beast took complete control while seeking his match. He became frustrated, endlessly seeking, never finding her. Alazander was weaker than Ryder, and thought the beast made him invincible. Ryder will not make the same choices of his father. He's a good host for me."

"So, is Ryder like the brain and you are the

brawn?" I ventured sheepishly. He threw back his head and laughed.

"I have my own brain; he is the mental strength and conscience to my power. If we are not balanced in his manner…it is very bad. Faery will be feeling the effects of what happened to Alazander for a long time."

"Can he hear you when you have control?" I asked, finally allowing the cat inside of me to get curious.

"Only if I allow it. Right now, all he can see is you talking." He smiled, and it was dark and deadly.

"Why did you get me pregnant?"

"Because I wanted it, and our child will be unlike anything Faery has ever encountered before," he said with a roguish grin. "He would have let you go to save this world, even though he wants you with everything he is. I wouldn't. He has one purpose, and that is to save Faery. I wouldn't allow it to happen. You belong to us, forever now."

"Children," I said.

"I promise we will make many babes together," he said as his fingers slid over my flesh.

"We're having twins," I said, wondering how much Ryder had allowed him to know. They might be one, but they had a way of blocking one another that they used. How many kids did this thing want from me?

"Twins," he said with a huge self-assured smile on his lips. He climbed over my body, and kissed my lips. "This pleases me, and now I will please you."

I shivered with his words, and as the air grew thick

around us with magic, I moaned. It was everywhere, touching, kissing, and then his mouth was on my center, and his fingers parted my flesh. His tongue slowly licked up and down over and over until I lifted my hips.

"You taste of heaven," he growled.

I now knew why Ryder growled so much; it wasn't always him doing it. He shared his body with this creature, and it stood to reason that when he disapproved, he let Ryder know with the deep inner growl.

His tongue entered me hard and fast. My hips bucked from the bed even as he lifted them until he had me at his mercy. He continued to move inside of me, until I was wet and slippery on his face, a mixture of juices and a boneless mess.

"Are you ready to scream for us, Pet?"

At the name Pet, I opened my eyes and nodded.

"I can't hear you," he said, as he let my hips fall to the bed, and his knees parted my legs easily. "Are you ready to scream for us?" he growled hoarsely.

"Yes," I growled back at him, and spread my legs until they could go no further apart.

Magic filled my body, heating it from the inside. Magical kisses rained down over my face, and nipples, and then I felt him nudge against my entrance. His hands landed on either side of my head, and his eyes locked with mine from where they sat right above me. His brands slithered over his torso, but his wings were now hidden behind his back.

He pushed into my opening, and nudged his way inside. It wasn't until he rocked his hips that I knew

I was in trouble. He was much larger now than he normally was. I felt fear flicker up my spine, but I'd taken him before, and he wouldn't hurt me. Ryder wouldn't let him hurt me.

"Stop thinking, and just feel me," he whispered against my ear. I swallowed and tried to relax, but it was easier said than done. He pulled out and shot forward, impaling me on his cock. I cried out as shock radiated through me. Pain erupted as a whimper exploded from my lips.

It wasn't until he started moving that the pain lessened, and friction took over. He growled his approval and captured my lips with his. "This is why I wanted you. I knew from the moment I saw you, that Danu made you for me. They can't take what I can give. You can," he grounded out as he plunged his cock deeper inside of me.

I moaned and moved my hips, needing him to move to stop the pain. It was a unique blend of pleasure and pain, and the orgasm was cresting in the middle of it all. I was fucking the beast, and I liked it. I liked knowing that Ryder was watching me, that this was another part of him that wanted me. I was a freak, but damn if this wasn't worth being one.

He pulled out and flipped me over until I rested on my stomach, and then he was pushing back into my wet heat. The gentleness was gone, and I screamed as he filled me to the limit. He grabbed my hair, and pushed with his hand on the small of my back, all while driving his cock inside of me.

I exploded without warning, and the room disappeared. I was floating. I felt lost, and even as the darkness stole over my mind, I could feel Ryder's presence, urging me back from the unknown for which I teetered on. He was here, with me and his beast.

Not controlling, but guiding and urging. I shivered as something pulled and pushed against me. Hands touched my face, pulling me back until something hot consumed my mouth. It demanded I open, and allow it control.

I was being kissed and fucked, and it was pure blissfulness. He'd grown inside of me, his body long enough to claim my mouth as he fucked me. I exploded again and again, until I finally felt myself feeding from him. I pulled on him, and before I knew I had done it, I'd flipped the beast over and had straddled him.

I moved, my hands finding my breasts and fondling them as he watched. Shock had registered on his beautiful face briefly, but it was gone just as quickly as it had come. His eyes slanted with heat and grew languid, his mouth slack as I rode him. He moaned and I smiled. There's something fucking hot about a man moaning, because he can't stop it from coming out. He couldn't either, and even though I couldn't grow as he could, I leaned over and grabbed a fist full of his hair, and brought his mouth to mine.

I chased his tongue hungrily with mine until he fought back, and then I was in trouble. One minute I'd been riding him, and the next he was between my thighs, fucking me. He nuzzled my neck and bit me as he rocked his hips. I detonated with a scream, sending him over the edge as he pounded into me, both of us in a frenzy of feeding.

I'm not sure how much time elapsed while we fought to get our ragged breathing under control. He had braced his arms on either side of me, keeping his massive frame from resting on my body. He gently lapped at his bite on my neck. My hands came up, and wiped the wet hair from his face, and then I claimed his lips gently.

He smiled against the kiss, and whispered into my mouth. "Beauty and the beast," he said with a chuckle. "Sorry, but I don't own a library." His beast was playing with me? I smiled. I could play, too.

"Bitches love big libraries. The Demon said there are several just lying around. Work on getting me one?"

He threw back his head and laughed. I smiled and shook my head. "I wasn't joking, I love books. Big books, momma porn, romance, adventure, I love it all. You are going to need a lot of books to entertain me."

"Who says I plan on letting you out of bed long enough for you to read?" he asked, but even as he did, Ryder was once again taking control of the shared form.

I smiled and shook my head as golden eyes stared back at me. "What makes you think you can keep me in bed, Fairy?"

"I can think of a few things to do that would make you beg me to stay in bed, Pet."

"Oh really? You think you are that good, hmm?"

"Are you saying I'm not?" he asked, as he climbed over me, and spread my legs with his knees.

I smiled, already lost to the passion and heat smoldering in his eyes. "Prove it, Fairy. But I still want my library."

Chapter TWENTY-ONE

The next morning I awoke to Darynda tapping on my forehead. She was smiling like an idiot, but she was also holding coffee. I instantly forgave the fact that she was tapping on my noggin, and sat up to take the delicious-scented coffee.

I smiled, but managed to hide it behind the rim of the mug. After a few deep sips, I looked up to find Darynda still smiling excitedly. "What's the smile for?" I asked, straight to the point and not bothering to beat the bushes.

"I get to go with you! The King said you would need someone to tend to your needs should you have any. I told him you were not like the other royalty and that you could handle it, but he said I should travel with you!"

"Um, thanks, I think," I replied, not sure if she'd actually given me a compliment, or not.

"So, we need to bathe you soon. The men are already gathering in the great hall. He even summoned those he had in the Human world back because of the Mages being so close to the borders. Have you ever been on a trial? Because I've never been and since we have to actually travel and cannot sift for it, it's going to take us about a couple of weeks," she blabbered on, as I emptied the coffee cup and held it out for another absently.

"One cup; you are carrying the King's heir," she said with a smile.

Gloves off, I wanted the second cup.

"Two cups won't hurt us, I promise."

She sighed and wagged her finger at me. In the end, she filled the cup and started the bath. I sighed as I crawled out from the opulent bed and stretched, before finishing off the second cup with a happy sigh. I was sore, but not sore enough to ask Ryder for help fixing it. The bath would help, anyway.

I slid into it, not caring that I was naked in front of Darynda. I'd grown up in the Guild, and privacy wasn't something we got a lot of. I'd lived with the other girls, and we'd all shared one shower. The water was hot, but not so hot that it burned my skin; rather, it cured the aches from the previous night.

When I was bathed and finished getting dressed, I smiled at my reflection. I had on tight leather pants, which fit like a glove, with soft suede boots that slid on like heaven and came up to my knees. The top was a pink long sleeve shirt, and Darynda handed me a hooded faux fur lined winter jacket that was white, long, and beautiful.

"A coat?" I asked.

"The weather can change on the Goddess's whim in Faery," she explained. "It's best to be prepared for anything she can throw at us. I have packed for all weather, and you won't have any problems with wardrobe. We will not be allowed to use magic once we leave the protection of the castle walls, so if there is anything you can't live without, I need to know now so that I can obtain it for you before we leave."

I blinked, trying to imagine a world where weather could change that fast. I hadn't spent very much time in Faery, and I was putting my trust in her as to what I would need. She smiled as she picked up a large pack, opened the bedroom door and shouted an order to a male servant, who scurried to take the pack from her.

"Okay, Princess! We are ready. We can meet the King and all of his warriors in the great hall," she announced, already turning to leave the room.

"All the King's horses and all the Kings' men…" I mumbled under my breath.

"Yes?"

"Nothing," I huffed with a grin lighting my lips.

"They will be present," she continued.

"And Humpty, will he be there?" Oh hell, I was going for it.

"I do not know a Humpty," she confessed with a frown.

"He's an egg," I started to explain, but felt eyes on me from behind. I turned, even as Darynda rambled on.

"He's an egg? You name eggs in your land?" she asked.

Claire was behind us with a haughty look in her eyes. She was trying to catch up with us, which I couldn't have cared less if she had. She managed it with her long legs and dug her hand into my shoulder.

"Why is she allowed out of the pavilion?" Claire demanded of Darynda.

"The King wishes it so, and so it is," Darynda said, tilting her head toward Claire, who stood a few inches taller than us. "It's his choice."

"We will see about that. The room she is in belongs to my sister!" Claire screeched, as if she was trying to cause a scene, and achieving it.

"Then why don't you take it up with Ryder? If you are so fucking outraged on your sister's behalf, talk to the man who placed me there and not Darynda, who can change nothing!" I growled, feeling my brands start to move, which had happened only twice so far since I'd turned into a freaking fairy.

I turned and headed off down the hall without waiting to see if Darynda had followed. I wasn't dealing with Claire's shit right now, or ever for that matter. She was inconsequential, and I was glad to be leaving her behind for however long it took to get the relic.

We made it to the great hall when I got my first look at everything that was being prepared to go with us, including the men.

All of the thirteen were here in full armor, as was the Shifter from the throne room where Ryder had given him an audience to hear his complaints. There were men running back and forth, as women came in carrying packs. I noticed some of them preparing to go with us—including Claire. I swallowed the rage at the idea of her journeying with us, after I'd thought I was getting away from her.

She noticed my glare and turned on me. "What's the matter, Witch? Oh, you thought I wouldn't be summoned to journey with the King?" She batted her brown eyes and lifted her hair from her face with her fingers.

"I was hoping that, yes," I said, already dismissing her.

"You think he would forget me so easily after all we have shared together?" she continued.

"Pretty much!" I threw over my shoulder as I wound my way through the large crowd, trying to spot the *King*. She continued talking, but I ignored her bitchy comments easily. Darynda was close on my heels, and was doing a fine job keeping close to me as I sped through the crowd.

"She isn't going to stop, Synthia. Not until you make her," she said from behind me.

"I'm not playing her game. She isn't worth my time," I replied crisply.

"She's Fae, and that means if she needs to, she will prove she is worthy of his bed to reclaim his eyes."

"What is that supposed to mean?" I snapped as I spun around on her, narrowing my eyes.

"It means she will turn to trickery or any other means to hurt you, Synthia. Strike first, fast and hard."

"No," I said as I shook my head. "I may be Fae, but I'm not into proving who is the better bed mate. Ryder wants her? He can fucking have her, but he won't touch me ever again." Having a chat with Ryder's beast gave me a measure of confidence that I hadn't felt before. Ryder may think that he had to fulfill that contract with her sister, and Claire could try and crawl into his bed, but I had a feeling the beast would have his own thoughts on the matter.

I turned and caught a glimpse of Ryder, who was dressed pretty much as he was during the Wild Hunt. He wore the heavy obsidian cloak again, and I shivered with the memory that outfit brought with it. The heavy fabric was absorbing the light from the many windows above Ryder, catching it and giving it a colored façade. Under it, he wore the same form fitting black armor the others had on, but the cloak itself was once again tied together with the black studded onyx jewels that held it together. A single red dragon was embedded in the middle of the silver disc that hung from his neck.

Sinjinn walked over to me when he noticed my presence, and held out a matching cloak. His chocolate brown eyes, with the sea green centers smiled as he approached. "Hey, little momma. It is cold outside, so I get to wrap you," he said in greeting as he held out the matching cloak.

I took the cloak and unfurled it, and almost sighed at how soft the fabric was. I'd felt it before as I'd leaned against Ryder after he'd claimed me in the hunt. I swept the fabric out and over my long coat. Sinjinn was quick to manifest the matching dragon clasp that would secure it in place. His fingers worked deftly as he locked the clasp and stood back with a smile.

"Thanks," I said, tossing him a small smile as I took in Ryder. The man was impossibly sexy. He radiated sex off of him in turbulent waves, which washed over my skin.

"Anytime," Sinjinn said as he stepped out of the way and glamoured on his own cloak over his armor.

My eyes swept the hall. One of the men turned and I realized he wasn't one of the thirteen, but he wore the armor of the Elite Guard. He had long bright blond hair, and as his eyes met mine, I jumped as I realized they were gray and aqua. It was the guard who had tied me up on my first night here. He winked and wiggled his fingers at me before returning a comment to Savlian. I tapped Sinjinn on the shoulder.

"Who is he? I never saw him with you guys back home," I said, lifting my chin to direct him.

Sinjinn looked over and chuckled. "He is one of us. That's Lachlan; he was the one holding down the Horde while the future Horde King was out wearing lipstick and prancing around in tights." His lips twitched with his words. "He and Asrian are trading duties for now." He grinned at me as the realization dawned. "Yes, we assigned him to be your guard at your presentation. We figured he was the only one of us you wouldn't recognize right off the mark." I shook my head at him. I should have known; Ryder always was one step ahead.

"Lift the hood, Pet. I'd have you covered before we enter the bailey," Ryder said, offering his hand in my direction. I took it, and I quickly put the hood over my head and followed Ryder as he led us out of the bustling hall and into the bailey of the castle.

Remembering my brief stint outside with Ryder; I placed our current position at the upper most castle; the biggest of the three tiers. The Horde Kingdom looked as enchanting as any Scottish castle from the fourteenth century from the outside, and inside it was breathtakingly beautiful. It was a bit of a mind bender for me as I always thought that the Horde was scary and that they must live in an awful nasty place. Then I remembered the flowers of the cove and realized that the Horde had a dangerous beauty about it. As if they wanted those coming in, to be lulled into a false sense of security. Ristan once told me that they came from one of the most dangerous places imaginable, so that had to be the case. Put in that perspective, it made sense. It was just another way for them to show their strength to those opposing them.

"You will be riding with me," Ryder said thickly.

The men looked like we were gearing up for war, and I was ready for it. Even in my condition, I wanted to be busy. I wanted to be out and about, instead of locked away and bubble-wrapped. "Riding?" I said after his words registered in my brain.

"Yes," Ryder said with an impish grin lifting his lips.

The words had barely left his mouth when I heard the clip-clop of hooved feet over the cobblestones. The horses were being led into the huge courtyard. Ryder's warhorse was the same one that had been with him during the hunt. He was huge with blood red eyes that were sharp and alert. I stepped back instantly, colliding with something hard. I turned to find Aodhan with his blue and black hair looking down at me with a cheeky grin on his lips.

"By all means, Princess," he said, and pulled me against his body. His ice blue and electric blue eyes searched my face as I looked up at him from where I was pressed against his hard body. "I don't mind at all."

"Aodhan, if you want to keep your hands, I suggest you get them off of her," Ryder growled as he reached for me and pulled me against his body.

"Just seeing if she's into me, my King," he said.

"She's not," Ristan said as he pushed his way through to where the Elite Guard had gathered. Darynda was standing beside Z and Adam, who would be joining us for the trial according to Ryder. He wore black armor as well, but on his was a coat of arms that marked him as a royal from the Dark Kingdom.

Darynda waved to me, but she was eyeing Zahruk with something akin to hunger in her eyes. I shook my head as Ryder headed to the horse and easily mounted him. He turned back to me and held out his hand. I accepted it, and was assisted by Ristan, who had snuck up behind me.

"Allow me, Flower," he said smoothly, as he hefted me up to Ryder, who placed me astride the horse, in front of him.

I was wrapped in one of Ryder's big arms as he turned to address the crowd gathering in the huge courtyard. "We ride for the Horde!" he growled over the crowd, and it erupted in cheers that sent my skin tingling with the sheer volume of it. "Those who stay are to protect the kingdom, and those who ride protect the princess and the future heir!"

I rolled my eyes. The big guy was a little too happy that his little warriors got the job done.

It was a once-in-a-lifetime thing to see the Horde warriors and the elite guard ride out of the castle. They moved like a well-oiled machine, the entire assembly was three horses wide, and as far as the eye could see when I tried to look back.

"Am I riding the entire time?" I asked as I noticed a few wagons toward the back.

"You ride with me. I can make sure you are safe this way. The Mages are in the area, and the Shifter is here to sniff them out if they get too close. I'm not taking any chances with you. We won't be able to use glamour, or cast magic when we leave these walls. It is part of what I was telling you last night;

to be mentally ready, we must walk as mortals. The elders thought it gave the warriors time to reflect on their past as they prepared for their future as a chosen warrior," he replied against my ear.

"You plan on squishing me with your arm for the entire ride?" I countered as I turned my face and looked up into his beautiful amber eyes.

He laughed and loosened his hold on me as I shifted to rest against his chest. "How long of a ride is this?"

"A few days journey to reach the trail to the labyrinth. After that it should be two weeks or so, to reach the labyrinth itself. The men and Adam will stay with you when I enter the trial."

"Ryder, Vlad and his men have arrived," Ristan said as he rode up beside us.

"Good, find the Shape Shifter and see if he has caught any scent of the Mages."

When it got quiet again, I closed my eyes and rested against the protection of Ryder's body. His soothing scent wafted in, and even though it was morning, I fell asleep in his arms. In the last month I'd been falling asleep with an ease I wasn't used to. I was willing to bet it had something to do with being pregnant.

Chapter
TWENTY-TWO

I awoke to Ryder whispering in my ear, and opened my eyes to see everyone around us dismounting. I yawned and turned my face to his. "Are we there yet?" I asked, knowing we weren't.

"No; we need to water the horses and rest them for a little while. You slept for a couple of hours straight," he informed me with a twinkle of amusement in his eyes.

"That's what happens when you keep me up all night," I shot back, barely concealing a smile and slight blush. He dismounted and held his arms out for me, so I slid from the horse and was instantly pressed between his body and that of his huge war horse.

"I enjoyed last night. Didn't you?" he asked, and my heart melted right into my feet. I had. I'd enjoyed being with him and his beast. It had felt right, as if this was where I was supposed to be, and I was his. Right about the time I was going to reply, Claire came strolling up to where we stood.

"Darynda is looking for you, Synthia," she said sweetly, as she batted her almond shaped eyes at Ryder. "Is there anything you desire from me, Sire?"

"Not at the moment, Claire," Ryder replied, and I felt my claws extend. I pulled away from Ryder and took off without asking where Darynda was. Only when a hand landed on my arm did I notice that I'd started walking without asking where she was.

"Princess," Silas said, as he stopped me from entering the wooded area. "It's not safe to wander around unprotected."

"Who says I'm unprotected?" I asked, lifting a brow at him. I may have wandered off, but I was never unprotected.

"I wouldn't wander too far, Princess, you might get eaten by the big bad wolf," he continued.

"Is that so? I have an army behind me, and I assure you that I am never defenseless," I dropped my voice a few octaves to make sure he understood what I was saying.

"You're pregnant," he replied, as if that alone meant I was a defenseless female.

"I am, but I'm also a trained assassin of the Guild. I enforced the laws inside the Human world, and I was damn good at it. I may be pregnant, but I can still kick ass."

He smiled, his eyes lighting up with something akin to pride. "You will be a worthy queen to our King." He bowed his head, causing his shoulder length blonde hair to brush against his shoulders. "I'll escort you back all the same. I'd feel much better knowing you were safe within camp."

I didn't argue with him, since I hadn't meant to come in this direction, anyway. I didn't stand around to see if he followed as I headed back in the direction I had come from. I made it five feet before I was surrounded by Ryder's posse and Ryder himself. He and the Shifter stared at one another for a moment with tension so thick you could cut it with a knife.

"Don't get all pissy with him, Ryder. He only told me to turn my ass around and come back to where it was safe." I wasn't sure why I stuck up for the guy, other than the fact that I knew he hadn't done anything wrong and didn't deserve to be throttled by the crew currently standing around us with their hands on their weapons.

"Silas?" Ryder growled his name, as though it was a vile thing on his tongue.

"I caught the scent of the Mage, who has been trailing us for the last mile. I didn't think it wise that she go toward it in her current condition," he explained.

"Z, Sinjinn, Aodhan, go scout. Synthia, come to me, now."

"You guys do know that pregnancy isn't a condition, right?" I mumbled, even though I had stopped worrying about it. I was more worried that Mages were on our trail. The fact that they were in Faery meant they had followed us, but why? I knew they wanted to ruin Faery, but this shit was getting personal really quick.

"Why the hell did you wander off?" Ryder demanded as soon as the men all hurried off in different directions. "I told you to stay close!"

"Oh, I'm sorry. I figured you would want me to make myself scarce so you could service Claire!" I'd spun around on him with my hands fisted at my sides. Great way to hide the fact that I was jealous of that tramp! Ninny!

"You sound jealous," he purred.

"Suck it, Fairy!"

"I don't plan to suck anything. I plan to lick it until it flows down my face. Now answer the question; are you jealous?" he continued.

I wanted to scream no, but being that I was now Fae, I couldn't lie. This sucked! I narrowed my eyes while watching his smile break across his lips. "And if I was?"

"Are you?"

"If I was?"

"Are you?"

"Are we, what?" Ristan asked just as the entire camp shook from an explosion. Ryder grabbed me quickly, and pushed me behind his back.

"To me!" he shouted with enough force to bring every guard in the camp to us. They created a shield around me and the other women that were pushed inside the protective barrier of the men. "Vlad!" he ordered, and I watched through his arms as Vlad, Adrian, Zade, and more men that Vlad had brought with him moved protectively to the front of us.

"On it," Vlad said, and began shouting out orders rapidly. Smoke rose from the trees where the men had gone to look for traces of the Mage. I looked in the air, and saw some of the tree tops on fire, but rain pelted them now, as if someone had placed a cloud above the fire.

I turned and watched as Darynda moved her fingers in a circular pattern as she made her way to me. She made it rain! I grinned to myself, and kept that it was her to myself as well. The rules of the trial did say we could manifest water. When she reached me, it was to shiver violently before she clasped my hand.

"Are you well?" she asked, and I nodded at her question.

I felt something touch my shoulder through the cloak, and turned to find the Shifter watching me closely, with his hand pressed to my shoulder. He removed it and nodded to me, before he turned and melted into the crowd.

"Are you sure?" Darynda pried.

"Me and bombs are on a first name basis," was my reply, which caused her to look at me as if I was insane. "We are close, like this," I crossed my finger and wiggled my eyebrow, trying to reassure her I was fine.

I could smell blood before Aodhan came into sight with it oozing down his face. I felt my fangs pulse in my mouth and brought my hand up to hide them. I smelled the iron that was thick in the air as well, and knew he'd be harmed with the deadly metal. I felt the pull to heal, and pushed at Ryder, who turned and looked at me.

"He's hurt," I said.

"Stay there, Synthia. They didn't come here for Aodhan; they came for you and the child you carry," Ryder growled.

I didn't push, though. Instead, I nodded. "Then bring him to me. I need to heal him," I said quietly, for his ears alone.

"Synthia," he warned.

"Don't you *Synthia* me, Fairy. I *have* to help him."

I felt the urge pulling inside of me. It wasn't a choice; I needed to help him. If I didn't, I'd be violently ill. It was like something else was inside of me, trying to come out. My hand trembled with the need to touch him, to run over his skin and pull the iron out. As more men came through the wooded area, the need to help them become all consuming.

"Synthia," Ryder said, his hands framing my face as everything inside of me was set on fire. "Fucking hell! Bring them here, now!"

They were brought one by one and laid at my feet. I dropped to my knees, even as Eliran dropped with me. I closed my eyes, and allowed whatever was inside of me to cure the tainted blood from their system. When I was done, my eyes grew heavy, and Ryder watched me with worry set deep in his eyes.

"Get the horses, there's a copse a few miles from here. We can secure the area in case the Mages follow us. She needs rest," Ryder ordered, and everyone ran to obey him. Of course they did, he was the freaking Horde King.

It was an hour on horseback before I was pulled off and handed off into waiting arms. Ristan, who was now my official bodyguard, and Adam both took turns holding me as camp was set up and secured. They set up enough tents to house half of Spokane easily. I'd wondered why they hadn't glamoured anything, but then I remembered Zahruk telling me how the trial required that outside of the basics of food and water, no magic could be used. They might as well be mortal.

I was in Adam's arms, with my head nuzzled against his shoulder when I felt well enough to stand. I told him, and he placed me back down on my feet.

"Thank you," I said, and watched him smile.

"No problem. Don't mind holding you, Syn."

"I know, but I feel better." And I did.

"They are as mortal as we were when we first met them," I said with a wide grin. Ryder was efficient, as if this wasn't his first Trial, but some of the men were scratching their heads, and cussing at the tents as if they'd been built by the devil himself.

I wanted to laugh, but I hurt and I wasn't sure why. I looked to where Ryder stood talking to his men, and caught the eyes of the Shifter on me. For some reason him staring at me was disturbing, and yet I felt no violent feelings from him. Something was off about him, but I couldn't put my finger on it.

Ryder turned and motioned me closer, and I smiled at Adam and kissed his cheek before moving over to Ryder.

"Our tent is set up and ready for you. Follow," he ordered, and I did because I wanted to lie down. I felt as if I'd run in a marathon today. Inside the tent was basic, with a crude makeshift bed, and covers that looked thick and welcoming.

"Synthia," Ryder said, stopping me before I made it to the bed. I turned and looked at him carefully. "You can't do shit like that now. You need to think about the babes," he said carefully.

"I couldn't stop myself, Ryder. I don't know what the hell it is, but something happens to me when they are poisoned with iron. It's like a drug to my system, and the need to help them is more than I can bear," I replied honestly, with tears forming thick in my throat.

"Shit," he said, raking his fingers through his hair.

"We were afraid of that. Ristan has seen you healing people en masse. We need to figure out if you are collecting the iron in your system, or where it goes when you are done."

"I have no clue," I said, eyeing the bed longingly.

"Get some sleep, Pet. We leave at dawn," he replied, and kissed my forehead, before running his fingers across my flat abdomen.

Chapter
TWENTY-THREE

Dawn came fast. The air was chilling, and there was somberness to the group that hadn't been there yesterday. The excitement of going on the trial was tarnished by the Mages' attack and their attempt to escape the men when they'd gone looking for them. The injured had been all healed—by me. I was still drained, but I wasn't about to ask Ryder to feed me here.

I'd wait until the next camp, and ask him to put up a thicker tent. I might be Fae, but I'd been raised by Humans and being in the middle of an open camp surrounded by others wasn't where I wanted to feed. I wasn't shy about nudity, but screaming with pleasure was another subject. I'd be damned if I screamed his name where everyone could hear it.

"Coffee?" Ristan's voice caught me off guard, but the mouthwatering aroma was welcome. I turned to find him holding out a cup of coffee.

"How did you manage to get this?" I asked, as I took it and brought it up to my nose for inspection. It smelled like heaven, and I'd figured there would be no coffee available during the trip.

"I lived as a Human for a while, Flower. I have many moves," he held his arms out wide, "and moves you haven't seen yet. Stick around; I am also a master on the grill."

Leave it to the Demon to be a coffee expert over a campfire. I could see water being tossed on several as I sipped the coffee, wondering where he had gotten the cream and sugar. But then again, I probably didn't want to know.

I finished the cup and handed it back to the Demon, who held his hand out expectantly. He didn't move from where we stood. "You pissed that I chose you for guard duty?" I asked, lifting an irritated brow.

"Nah, I eat hearts and fuck shit up. I specialize in the shit, so obviously I'm the right man for the job when it comes to protecting my delicate little Flower. Besides, I got to watch your little handmaiden blush when I tried to tell her you and I went way back. She didn't buy it, can you believe that shit?"

"Delicate?" I flipped him the finger even as he started to laugh. I'd noticed that out of all of Ryder's men, I let the Demon get away with more than any of the others. He gave me a lot of shit, but he was also the one who was helping me adjust more than the others were.

I was still trying to come to grips with the idea, that it was his visions that had set off the chain of events that had brought me to this point; he himself did not deliberately do this to me. I found I just couldn't blame him for something he had no control over; he was only telling it how he had seen it. The guy was cursed.

It had to be hell to be given glimpses of the future, and then told to figure it out. I'd walked in one of those visions with him, and the pain I had from it still lingered in my mind. How many of those visions did he get on a daily basis? How was he still sane? Well, somewhat sane.

"When do we leave?" I asked, since he had yet to break the silence from me flipping him off.

"Soon; Ryder and a few of the men went to check the perimeter of the camp. When they come back, we should be ready to go. Most of the tents are coming down now," he said as he watched the movements around camp.

"Thanks for the coffee, Demon."

"Hey, I like you better with coffee in you. If you need to use the bushes…I will escort you there," he offered.

"I do," I replied.

When I'd finished and was walking back to the camp with Ristan, the men were riding back in. Ryder was atop his black warhorse, proud and beautiful as always. His men flanked his sides as they rode in a V formation through the remains of what had been the camp.

When he reached us, he dismounted and patted his horse lovingly. He wasted no time as he walked to me briskly. "Feeling better?" he asked, and I smiled.

He'd held me through the night as if I was his most prized possession. "I am. I was just drained from healing the men."

"Good. We need to move out," he said, nodding his head to his men who left to help get rest of camp moving.

"Trouble?" Ristan asked.

"No, but that in itself is trouble. Silas couldn't pick up their scent. I'm not sure it's worth finding this fucking relic, when your safety is my main concern now, Pet."

"I'm fine, Ryder. Besides, this relic is one of the keys to the survival of this world. This world *has* to accept our unborn children. Too much depends on us getting them."

"It's not worth it if it threatens you," he argued as fire lit behind his golden eyes.

"It threatens our children if we don't finish this, Ryder. We finish it, period. This isn't up for discussion. I want this place fixed, like yesterday, for our children. Their lives hang in the balance, and depend on the Goddess and this world to accept them, so don't tell me we're going home! What we're doing is finishing this trip, and getting the damn relic. If we find any of the Mages, we'll kill them. Shit, Ristan can gorge on their hearts!"

"Now that's a woman," Sinjinn said as he winked at me when I turned to where he stood.

"Sinjinn," Ryder warned with his tone threatening.

"Hey, he's just saying what the rest of us are thinking," Sevrin said with a roguish wink in my direction.

Twenty minutes later, we were riding again. Once again, I rode in Ryder's arms, pressed against his massive chest. "You know, you may yet cause a mutiny with my men," he rumbled in my ear.

"They're loyal to their King. But, I have tits, and you don't. So I guess it's possible," I replied, resting my head against him and enjoying the feeling of being safe in his arms.

He laughed and shook his head. "You do have really nice tits," he agreed.

"Good enough to cause a mutiny over?" I asked as a smirk covered my face.

"Good enough to cause a war," he replied, causing me to laugh.

"Good to know. Next time you argue with me, I'll just start playing with them," I replied impishly.

"You do that, and I'll let you win," he replied silkily.

"After I'm done playing with them, I'll make sure to award you with a gentle nibble…" I continued to tease him, enjoying the subtle peace that sat between us out here in the open.

"Nibble on me, Pet, and I'll fuck you until the bed breaks."

"Really? I don't see any beds out here…but I'm willing to try," I said, turning to look into the fire that was now lit in his eyes. I loved his eyes, but I loved them more when that fire started to kindle and burn for me.

"I wouldn't offer that right now. I may be tempted to stop this horse and make a bed just to fuck you on it," he said smoothly, his voice already growing hoarse as he pressed his massive erection against my back.

"You wouldn't," I said, trying to sit up. He wouldn't allow it, though. Instead, he pulled my body closer to his, and his hand lowered until it was pressed hard against my sex.

"You wouldn't," I repeated, even as I pressed his hand closer with my own, moving it to where I needed it. The others around us seemed oblivious to our antics, but Ryder covered me with the cloak, covering his hand in the process.

"I would. Now lean back; and no sounds, Pet, I mean it."

The authority in his whispered command had me leaning back quickly. I smothered a gasp as his hand lifted the skirt I wore and parted the panties out of his way. The movement from his horse, and his hand worked against me. I wanted to moan. Hell, I wanted to beg him to make a bed, just so we could break it.

"Good girl. You want me to fuck you, don't you?" he crooned.

"Ryder," I whispered as his fingers played gently with the soft flesh between my legs.

"God you smell so fucking good; so ripe and ready to be fucked," he ground out through clenched teeth. "I want you, right here, right now, beneath the sky. I want to take you until you beg me to stop," he continued, his voice growing thick with lust.

"Please," I begged, even though I wasn't even sure what I was begging for. I just wanted him, and right now I felt as if it didn't matter that eyes were watching us, or that we were mounted on a horse. It only mattered that he do as he was threatening to do now.

His hand moved away and my brain began to function. Ristan was riding up beside us with a smirk on his face.

"Ryder, the Shifter would like permission to approach you," he said.

"Not now," Ryder growled.

"I think you should hear what he has to tell you."

I remained silent through their exchange. My body was still fighting to gain control after Ryder's magic fingers had set it to blaze. I swallowed as heat lit my cheeks. Ristan knew. I could see the quirk of his lips, and the knowing look he gave me. Sex was a necessity to the Fae, but I'd been raised differently.

"Fine," Ryder replied.

The moment Ristan turned his mount around and nodded, the Shifter came forward. Silas eyed me, before turning his attention to Ryder.

"We're being followed. I've caught his scent five times in the last hour. This one is on his own, and not a Mage, Ryder," Silas said, pinning me with those stunning eyes.

"How many?" Ryder asked, as his arm came down protectively over my waist.

"Only one following us, and he is strong. I can catch his scent, but every time I think I have pinned his location, he moves."

"Which Caste is he from?" Ryder asked calmly.

"No idea, but he is moving with a purpose. He's been on each side of us. I think he is throwing his scent, trying to keep his presence masked," Silas said with a sharp twist to his lips. His eyes once again landed on me, and that uneasy feeling came broiling back to life.

"Zahruk," he shouted over his shoulder, "take two guards and scout ahead, but stay within shouting distance. No magic unless a life is dependent on it. I would rather repeat the trial than lose one of my men to the Mages."

Chapter
TWENTY-FOUR

It was several hours before Zahruk and his scouting party came back to the group. We'd been traveling for what felt like forever when Ryder called a halt next to a bubbling stream. I was still looking lovingly at the natural springs that seemed to bubble up from nowhere.

"We will camp here," Ryder announced.

"We are moving about as fast as snails," I griped. My ass was sore, and my legs hurt from the endless gait that his horse had trotted here with.

"We are making good time," Ryder replied. "You are in need of respite. We will leave at dawn, and push on further into the Gnarled Forest. Tonight, we need rest, and those who have never been in the forest need to know the dangers of entering it."

"Like what?" I asked, feeling my curiosity spike.

He slid from the horse, and looked back up at me expectantly. When I made no move to get down, Ryder smiled devilishly and easily plucked me from the horse. "Like don't tempt the beast, because he likes a good game of cat and mouse."

I swatted at his shoulder. "I'm serious."

"So am I," he said as he leaned over and kissed my forehead. "Come; I'll bathe with you in the springs."

I eyed the spring, and then eyed the beast in front of me. "I'm not getting naked in front of an army of men."

"You think I would allow anyone to see what is mine?" Ryder asked, as he turned back to look at me, hiking his brow up until it wrinkled.

"Who says I'm yours?" I taunted him.

"I do," he said to me. To Sevrin, who stood closest to us, he issued orders and the poor guy jumped to do it. I watched from where I stood, as they erected a cover around one of the springs that was surrounded by large oval rocks.

"They are heated, so it should help to heal the soreness of traveling," Ryder said when he caught my curious look as the bubbles floated up disturbing the watery surface.

"Oh!" I said, surprised.

"You think the Humans have the only natural hot springs?"

"No, but I honestly didn't expect to find one here." But I was thrilled that he had. The little cove with the blood-sucking flowers was interesting, but this place looked safer.

"Darynda," Ryder called to the group of girls walking by. When Darynda came up to us, he told her what I would need, and where to put up the tent. When she ran off to secure the items from the many packs that were laden on the wagons, he turned and grinned at me mischievously.

"I've seen that look before, Fairy," I replied, while trying to keep the grin from spreading across my lips. "It always ends up with us and a bed."

"Does it?" he asked as he pulled me closer to him. "It also ends up with you screaming my name as I make you come for me."

I shivered deliciously. He had a point there. "We're surrounded by people," I pointed out.

"So we are. I fail to see what that has to do with what I intend to do with you," he replied with an intensity that made me squirm.

"If you make me scream, everyone will hear us," I hissed, as his lips tipped higher in the corners. "I'm serious, Fairy! You may not care if everyone hears you getting off, but I do!"

"So you don't want them to hear me scream your name with passion?" he asked with a twinkle of mischief in his eyes.

"No, I don't want them to hear us doing it!" I replied hastily as Ristan walked up to us.

"Doing what?" the Demon asked with a devilish grin on his lips.

"Nothing!" I almost screamed, but caught it, and it came out more as a strangled growl.

"Oookay! Someone is a little hormonal today," Ristan said with a wide smile. "Ryder, your oasis awaits you." He executed a slight bow before he took off again.

"It's this way." Ryder laughed as he pulled me

toward where black curtains had been set up.

When I entered the area, I gasped.

Partially because I knew they had done it all without magic. Cherry blossom petals floated above the welcoming water. A few candles had been set on the smooth surfaces of the rocks. I shook my head with wonder, before turning to catch Ryder smiling.

"We won't be disturbed here," Ryder assured me.

"Wow, I'm impressed," I said, taking in everything. We even had a small basket that held something that smelled divine. "So I guess you expect to get some for this?" I lifted my eyes in time to watch him remove his shirt.

My eyes drifted over the thick cords of muscle and the magnificently molded abs, to the brands that pulsed on his bronzed skin. His pants hung low on his hips, revealing the thin dark patch of hair that led below the waistline.

He continued, working the button and then the zipper of his pants easily, efficiently. I pulled my eyes away as he let them drop and stepped into the inviting water. I heard a splash and turned to see if he had slipped, and found him standing waist-deep in water. He whipped his hair back, which had been doused in water, sending tendrils of water over my skin.

I slowly walked to the water's edge and sat on one of the many rocks. I silently removed my cloak, boots, and the silk socks from my feet. When I had finished, I placed them in the water and sighed happily. "This is heaven," I whispered as I lifted my face to the sky. The skies in Faery were beautiful.

It was late afternoon and the most beautiful sunset was already spreading across the skies. Faery had two suns and two moons, as if a mirror had been placed against them. Like everything in Faery, beautiful yet deadly and still perfectly balanced. The greens of this world were bright, as if everywhere had water running beneath it. I'd yet to see a place in Faery that wasn't beautiful.

"What are you thinking of, Synthia?" Ryder asked, as he pushed through the water until he was between my legs.

"I was thinking of how beautiful this place is," I replied, enjoying the heat that his touch brought to my skin. He smiled and shook his head.

"This spot was picked out by Ristan," he said, as if he wished he had picked it out.

"I was talking about this world," I whispered as he got closer.

"I'm glad you approve," he said. "You are a little over dressed, though." He smiled mischievously.

"Don't even think about it!" I screeched, but it was too late. He pulled me easily from the rock and into his arms.

I was soaking wet, but in his arms still. He took us down, until only our heads were above the water's lusciously warm depths.

"I thought about it," he said as he smiled against my cheek.

"Now my skirt is wet, and everything else," I complained with a smile, unable to stop it from spreading across my lips.

"That's not the only thing that is going to be wet," he growled as his mouth found mine, and kissed me deeply, until I threw away my inhibitions and wrapped my body around his. I felt his hands skimming my back, caressing my flesh as he ravished my mouth.

When he pulled away, I groaned from the loss of his heat. He helped me pull off my sweater and skirt and threw them with wet splats on the rocks, and then moved with me in his arms until I felt the smooth surface of the rock behind my back and his sleek muscles against my chest. He pushed one leg down, and then the other.

I watched in wonder as he slid slowly down my body, until his head was submerged in water. I felt his hands pulling against my undies, and sliding them from me. I tried to control my breathing as he followed the path of my underwear. His hand slid down, with his fingers caressing my skin like silk until he lifted one foot, and then the other.

He didn't come up for air, and right when I started to get worried, I felt his mouth press against my naked sex. Kissing and nipping at the swollen flesh, and then slowly moving up, kissing me until he popped out of the water. His eyes were now glowing like two hungry orbs of fire. My breath hitched in my lungs as I felt my body approve, and my brands as they moved in rhythm with his.

"Ryder," I said, worried that something was wrong. I'd never felt my brands with so much life on my skin before. Well, there was the one time when I was wrapped in his wings during my presentation, but I thought that was him doing it.

"It's Faery, Synthia. She's giving us permission. She approves of our union," he whispered as he pulled me against himself, and cupped my ass from where it no longer was hidden beneath the silk panties.

"That's good," I replied.

That's good!?

"Yes, that's good," Ryder replied as his hands wrapped around me. His mouth crushed against mine, as he entered me in a skilled move. He captured the moan that exploded from my lungs, holding it within his mouth to keep it from being heard.

When he pulled away, he smiled and moved his hips. I bit my lip to keep from making any loud noises, but it was futile. He drove himself in, and pulled out until the water was sloshing over the rocks. I let my head roll back on my shoulders, even as his mouth lowered and found my throat, licking across the vein silkily.

"This is heaven, Synthia. Inside of you is my heaven," he whispered, so softly that I wasn't even sure he had said it.

I rocked myself as he pumped and pushed inside of me, until the world faded away and with it, my self-consciousness. I wanted him to know how he made me feel, I wanted him to hear it in every noise I made, and every breathless moan that escaped. I exploded around him, milking him as I shattered into a million pieces.

His mouth found mine and captured it hungrily. His hips began moving in a fevered pitch, as he rode my body. I clung to him and held on as the water continued to rush from the pool as he fucked me. When he exploded, the air around us grew heavy, and rain loosened from the sky to pelt us relentlessly. He fed us deeply, until I felt as if I would explode from the fullness he'd created inside of me.

We stood in the water, motionless as the rain

continued to fall. We labored to catch our breath, as the world came rushing back to us. He pulled out slowly, and set me back on the rock he had plucked me from.

"Grab my cloak, and cover yourself, Pet. We have company."

Chapter
TWENTY~FIVE

We had company, but it came in the form of wolves from the Shifter's pack. Silas had sent out a call to those he commanded for help. Help to track the ones who were hunting us. They didn't ride with the group. Instead, they tracked the woods around the caravan. They had heightened senses that came from being one with the animal within them. It came in handy when hunting an invisible foe.

I had been wondering about Ryder and his pissy attitude toward Silas, and when I asked about it, all he would say is that he didn't trust them because of some things that had happened in the past, but they were a necessary evil right now.

It took us seven days after leaving the Gnarled Forest to reach the base of the Willow Mountains. Everything in Faery had a name, and you knew the moment you left one place and entered the next. The air would grow dense and the surroundings changed without further warning.

By the time we stopped, I was exhausted from riding on the horse. My bones jarred with each sure-footed step the warhorse took. I hated to admit it, but I needed rest, and a bed sounded like heaven right now.

It left a foul taste in my mouth, but I caved and asked Ryder to make camp on the last day. We would sleep like the dead tonight, bone-weary and exhausted. I didn't wait for Ryder to finish his check of the surrounding areas before I sat on an old log.

I was still sitting there when Ristan came over and sat beside me. He held out a flask and winked at me. "It's water. Drink some. You look like you could use it."

"How much longer before we reach the beginning of the labyrinth?" I asked, and Ristan shook his head.

"Not quite sure, Flower. It can move as all lands inside of Faery do. Kier gave Adam general instructions on how to locate it, but part of the trial is the actual search."

"Great, so we could be chasing our tails?"

"Didn't know you had a tail, but I'm game to examine it," he replied with a serious look on his ageless face.

"Buddy, the only tail you are going to see is your own, when I kick your ass."

"That's my girl. Your tent is ready. Let me walk you to it. You need to rest and be ready for whatever tomorrow brings.

I stood and accepted his help up. He took me to Darynda, who smiled as she welcomed me, even though she looked as tired as I was. "I'm to wait with you until the King returns."

"Fine, but I won't be good company. I'm so tired I could face plant a rock and sleep for a week."

"Me too, so you will find no issue there," she said

even as she yawned.

I fell asleep before my head hit the pillow.

The next morning, the camp was alive with activity, and even as Darynda tugged on my shoulder, I blinked my eyes open.

"The Demon is making you coffee. Get up; we leave within the hour. The Mages are close behind us."

"Great," I said, standing up to dress myself as she tossed me a pair of jeans and a long sleeve shirt, that had a skull in the front of it. I slipped the boots over my feet and stood up to button my pants. They were tight, and I ran a shaky hand over my stomach.

It wasn't a huge bulge, or something anyone else would notice. But I could feel the change in my body from Ryder's offspring that had invaded my body. "Darynda, can you get me something else to wear?" I asked, embarrassed that I had to.

"Those don't fit?" she asked, unaware of the angry tears I was trying to hold back.

I was changing, my body was changing, and it sucked!

"No, I'm too fat!" I growled.

"You are pregnant; but don't worry, I planned for it," she said, handing me a pair of black yoga pants that had Booty written across the butt, in pink.

"Wow," I replied.

"I'd have gotten something better, but this trip wasn't really planned in advance. I noticed the small bump the last time we stopped to change, so I asked

Matilda to borrow these for you."

"They're fine," I said, shoving one leg and then the other into the pants and pulling them up.

"Wow," Ristan said as he came in, barely containing his laughter.

"If you laugh at me, I swear I will gut you, Demon," I growled, turning to look at him.

He smiled and handed me the coffee he had been bringing, and left as soon as he did. His lips continued to shake as his eyes kept watch of my reaction. I hated that my body was changing, and I couldn't stop it from happening. "Give me the cloak, please."

"Synthia, you're pregnant, and it's a good thing," Darynda said as Ryder walked in to hear the tail end of her words.

"What's the matter?" he asked carefully.

"I'm fat," I mumbled, shooting him a look of mixed feelings. Mostly fears. If I was fat, he was bound to set me aside in favor of someone with more to offer him. I'd watched Witches of the Guild being sequestered because of their misshapen bodies when they got too big.

"You're not fat, Pet. You are carrying my twins."

I was overreacting, and it sucked! I couldn't make my brain stop thinking it. My eyes were leaking tears now. "I'm going to be huge," I replied, flashing him angry eyes. "You just had to knock me up!"

He smiled, walked over to me and wrapped me in his arms. "You're the most beautiful thing I have ever seen, Synthia. Pregnancy will not change that. The fact that you are carrying my babes only makes it more so."

"Whatever; let's get this shit over with before I only fit in sheets," I gritted out.

"I prefer you in nothing more than sheets," he murmured huskily in my ear.

My cheeks heated with a blush as he kissed me.

"We need to move. Grab the cloak and finish the coffee. Ristan assured me you would be more Human with it in you. I prefer you Fae, personally."

"Fairy!" I glared.

"I'm going. Drink the coffee, it will help. Be ready in ten minutes, though, the Mages are close."

"Ryder, if they get too close—"

"If they get within a hundred feet of you, this ends. I will sift you home where I know you are safe, and then I will come back and finish them off."

"Deal," I said, not because I wanted to hide, but because I had more than just myself to think about now. I had to worry about protecting our babies from those insane assholes. I wouldn't allow what had happened to Larissa, to happen to me.

I waited with Darynda and Ristan until the shrill whistle cut through the chilly morning air. Within five minutes, we were loaded up and heading through the mountain.

It took us three days of riding and another day of coming through a mass of willow trees before we reached the next camp. The men had to cut through the willow trees at the base, because they'd grown too thick to trek through.

The next place was unlike anything I'd ever seen before. The Darkness was what the Fae had called it in hushed whispers. The entire land looked desolate, and was encased in a thin layer of ice, as if it had been frozen, and left that way. Tall, thick trees towered sporadically in either side of the thin patch of walkway. Fortunately, we only spent two days freezing our butts off there and the moment we stepped over the thin veil, everything changed again.

The trees were lush and green. Vivid colors made an ocular feast for our eyes. An expanse of vivid blue skies stretched above us as sun shined across the valley. A waterfall gurgled in the distance, and what looked like a thin walkway was actually a brilliant bubbling spring that led deeper into another stretch of forest.

"It's beautiful," I said, watching as a small bird flew by us.

"It is, but it's also what Kier described as the beginning of the labyrinth. We should reach it within the hour," Ryder whispered against my ear.

"Great." That was just what we needed. We'd been on this journey for just a little over two weeks, and we had yet to make it to the location we needed to be at.

"Zahruk, send the scouts out to set a perimeter," Ryder ordered.

I watched from the safety of his arms as a circle closed around us, and those who Zahruk shouted at spread wide led by Lachlan. The Shifters were just catching up with the group, as they had been around us but not with the caravan of people.

"No scent of the Mages for the last two days. We either lost them, or they gave up trying to figure out the terrain. The lone Fae male is still out there, though. That's all we know for sure."

Ryder tilted his head behind me, in acknowledgement of the Shifter's words, but he said nothing. I was beginning to think there was more to this story than Ryder had mentioned to me, like these two had some sort of twisted history from the stiffening of spines of the men. They went on high alert every time Silas got too close to Ryder.

"Clear," Ristan said, as a series of whistles pierced the wind.

We dismounted, and the men from the wagons began to set up camp once more. I walked beside Ryder and Ristan and the rest of the men as we headed toward the small spring to water the horses. That was where everything changed.

The men continued to talk to each other, seemingly unaware of what was happening. Silas was close behind us with his own horse, and the men had fallen in behind as they always did. Our backs were never left exposed, or unguarded.

"The horse, it needs water," Ryder said, and his eyes flashed sideways to me.

"That's why we're walking them to the water," I replied. Maybe being on the horses so long had rattled his brain.

"Water, yes," he replied.

I glanced at the others, who were carrying on varying conversations with each other. None of them made a lick of sense. It wasn't until Ristan said something that made me go on alert.

"This isn't right," he muttered as his skin turned

from ivory, to crimson red. I caught a glimpse of fangs, peeking from under his upper lip. "Something is off," he continued, his eyes flashing as he took in each male.

I smiled at Ryder, who was smiling gently at me. Everything seemed to move in slow motion.

Sevrin was smiling at Savlian, and when I looked over my shoulder, I blinked in confusion. Something was very off here, and my stomach was sinking with apprehension with every step I took.

I turned to look at Ryder, who was walking beside me, and caught his eyes flashing with a yellow tint that Ryder didn't normally have. His eyes were gold, amber, or black. Never yellow. Ristan met my eyes and shook his head.

"Flower," he whispered, barely audible.

"Demon," I replied back.

"Duck!" he shouted as he pulled his swords, and swiftly took the head from Ryder's shoulders. I felt my knees buckle, as everything inside of me went numb with disbelief. Ristan had just decapitated Ryder.

Chapter TWENTY-SIX

I ducked as Ristan swung his sword in the direction of the next man standing closest to me. The moment his blade pierced Vlad's heart, I screamed. I cried out as I tried to pull magic around me to take out the Demon. He'd stabbed Vlad! He'd killed my fucking Fairy! Why was it my magic had to leave me now? Screw the trial and not using magic, I was going to kill him. The Demon had fucking lost it!

I felt bile rise in my throat as everything inside of me shook with rage. I was unarmed and my brands either failed to notice I was in danger, or were inactive within the strange barrier. Tears burned in my eyes as I tried to summon the strength to stop the Demon before he could kill anyone else.

I couldn't move, even though I wanted to take him out. I needed to get away from him, and yet I couldn't make myself stop screaming. I needed to protect my unborn children from the Demon from hell. Yet, I couldn't stop crying and screaming with rage so deep and foreign that I'd thought I would sink to the depths of despair from it.

I screamed until I thought my own ears would bleed, and it wasn't until I caught sight of Ryder over

Ristan's shoulder about a hundred yards away that I stopped. Ryder stood with the rest, separated from us by what looked like an invisible barrier. His hands were pressed against it, with a look of horror on his beautiful face—his beautiful alive face.

I turned and looked at Ristan, who was preparing to go after the others on our side of the barrier with those wicked looking blades he was wielding. They were over three and a half feet long and double bladed. I had never even dreamed of such a thing. He'd known it wasn't Ryder; not the real one, anyway. My heart still raced as my mind focused on those golden eyes.

I moved closer to Ristan, but made sure to stay out of swinging distance. He swung his blade at the fake Savlian and continued killing until only Sevrin was left. He pulled his blade back high in the air, and sent it sailing like a missile toward his target—but it disappeared in mid-air. He pulled his hand back and looked to where he had aimed the sword, and his bare hand. The blades were both gone now, as were the bodies that had littered the ground.

I moved quickly to stand beside him, feeling the air grow thick with the electrical fuzz that came with power. I watched in disbelief as Sevrin changed from a huge brunette male, into a petite raven haired beauty with piercing, ice blue eyes. The woman was dressed in a white silk top that showed off her midriff and matching pants that hung low on her small hips.

The look on Ristan's face was warring between lust, anger, and reverence all at once. He had his eyes locked on the woman before us. His skin faded from crimson to its normal color once again.

"Do you see her, Syn?" Ristan asked softly.

"Yes," I replied, not sure what I should do. Ristan

was looking like he was about to go beast mode and jump her—hungrily. I was pretty sure we'd left Kansas on a tornado, and this was one of the Witches we should be trying to avoid. He, on the other hand was not necessarily thinking as I was.

"Do not look so surprised, Ristan," the woman said in a low seductive voice.

"Danu," he whispered.

"I told you that I would come when needed, oh ye of little faith," she smiled, and I found myself wanting to touch her.

"I have faith, Danu, but I'm not sure it's always well placed."

Oh hell no. I shook my head to dispel the urge.

"Where have you brought us?" he asked.

"To the maze of warriors," she replied easily. "Or, as the Dark Fae of old called it, the labyrinth."

"We came for the relic," Ristan pointed out.

"You think I wouldn't know that? I'm the one who brought you here. Ryder has proven himself with his deeds. He has proven, over and over again, how far he will go to heal Faery. He passed his last test when he gave her away to another Fae, just because he thought she was the Light Heir and that he was fulfilling the prophecy. You, my Demon, have yet to show me how far you will go, but that's not why I brought you here. She chose you as her bodyguard; I brought *you* because you know me. You will see her through this and ensure that she wins," she said as she sifted close to Ristan, and ran a thin hand over his cheek.

"Let Synthia go back to the others. She's pregnant.

She has nothing to do with this," Ristan said, finally finding his inner Demon again.

"She has everything to do with this. The lives of her children depend on it," she said simply.

"This isn't her damn fight!"

"Then all is lost. She is only part of the cure for Faery. The other players have yet to be put into the game. Sorcha needs to find her place, and make her heart belong to Faery. She has yet to accept what she is, and still fights me. She feels the power I have bestowed upon her, and she refuses to open up and allow it to come out. She is a born leader, and a warrior queen. I'm in the fiber of her being, as surely as I am a part of Faery. I set the events in motion that made her who she is, and now it is up to her to accept me so she can find what she needs to be."

"Will my children live?" I asked, not messing around with words.

"I can't tell you that yet. If I did, you'd stop fighting. I need you to fight, Sorcha. I need you to play your part in saving my world. I can do a lot of things, but I can't directly interfere with saving this world. That has to be a choice that my creations fight for. I chose you before you were even born. I make destinies, but you are right about one thing, Sorcha; you choose what you can handle and what you can't. You choose which path you take to get to the end. But in the end, you are where destiny wanted you to be," she said and winked. "And you got all that without having to eat funky brownies or wear a badass headdress. Although, personally I think I'd look pretty wicked in one."

"I need to know if they live," I stated, tired of word games.

"I know you do," she said and stepped back away from us. She materialized Ristan's swords and tossed them at his feet. "You have five hours to find the exit of the maze. For every wrong turn, a challenge will be issued. You will receive one grace, and then for each challenge you fail, someone from your group awaiting you outside the labyrinth, will die. Should you fail, you die," she blew a kiss to Ristan, and with that, she sifted out.

"Wait! When will we get to the actual relic?" I screamed, but only the sound of my voice echoing off the trees in the forest was heard.

"She is always so fucking beautiful," Ristan said absently. "Those blonde curls," he whispered.

Blonde curls? "You mean black?"

"She has blonde hair, with the greenest eyes I've ever beheld," he said, narrowing his eyes on me.

"Uh, black hair and blue eyes," I said and narrowed my eyes.

"That's what you saw?" he asked.

"Yep."

"She is beautiful."

"She's deadly, very deadly," I said, ignoring that she had appeared to him in a different form.

"That's one thing we can agree on, Flower. She was pushing a tremendous amount of power at us," he said, and turned to look at Ryder. I watched his face before I turned to look at Ryder too. He was staring at Ristan, and I realized with clarity that they were discussing what had just gone down.

"What is he saying?" I asked, watching as those golden eyes slid from Ristan to me. There was a look of helplessness in them that I wanted to wipe away.

"That if I allow anything to hurt you, I will be singing soprano," he sighed, and looked me in the eyes, "and *then* he will kill me."

"Oh." I snorted and looked at Ryder with a small smile lifting my lips. "*I'll be okay*," I sent to him, hoping he could hear it through the mental link.

"Be safe, Pet. Stick close to the Demon," he sent back. *"Come back to me,"* he finished, as I gave him a small smile, and blew him a kiss.

I'd thought I'd lost him for a minute. It had been the worst minute of my entire life. I'd lost a lot that I'd lived through, but it wasn't until I thought I'd lost him that I'd known some of the most unimaginable pain in my life, and it had cut deep and quick.

"I thought you killed him," I whispered through tears that still clung to my throat.

"I knew it wasn't him. They were the guardians of the labyrinth and the first test. I didn't have time to warn you; not with the odds being in their favor," he said as he pulled me close and turned me toward the cave, the start of the labyrinth. "We need to get moving. If Danu has been playing with the old Dark King's maze, we could kill half the people outside that barrier by the time we figure it out."

"I thought you knew her?" I asked.

"She's a sadistic bitch who loves to fuck with me. She gets off on trying to find new and inventive ways to screw with me," he said tightly.

"Nice. Does she scramble the brain cells as well?"

I asked sarcastically.

"And then some," he replied.

We continued walking toward the cave in front of us. I turned one last time and looked at Ryder, who watched us as we slipped out of sight, into the labyrinth.

Chapter
TWENTY~SEVEN

We walked slowly into the cave, and before we got very far into whatever hell Danu had planned for us, Ristan stopped me with a hand on my shoulder.

"Here," he said, handing me one of several short swords from beneath his cloak. "Now just because I'm letting you touch my sword and play with it, Flower, doesn't mean we're dating and shit. Don't go getting the wrong impression here. I like my balls. Ryder would be having them for dinner if he thought there was something going on between us. Now, I know the lure of a Demon is strong, but this shit between us? It's platonic. I like you, and even though the allure of swapping spit between us is appealing, fight it."

"Seriously, Demon, you're so full of it," I said, shaking my head as he grinned from ear to ear.

"C'mon, admit it. You like me," he said as he also handed me a dagger, and we started walking further into the maze.

"Oh I like you, but I like you better from a safe distance," I replied with a wide grin.

"Come on, admit it, you want me."

"Dream on, Demon," I said. "So what's between you and the Goddess?"

He growled, which caused me to give him a sideways glance. "It's complicated."

"You don't say." I smiled and looked around the colorful, glittery cave that surrounded us. It looked like something from a movie.

"She wants me to submit to her, and I don't want to. I can't say no, either. She has too much power, and if I say no, I could jeopardize everything Ryder has worked for. Everything we have worked for. You have no idea how much power she has, and how much shit she could cause for us. She fucks with me just because she can. About a century, or so ago, she took over the body of a female I was feeding on, and she has been doing it randomly ever since. One minute, I am in control of the feeding, and the next she is. Some people have to check their food to make sure it is fresh; I have to make sure mine hasn't been hijacked. I have to have control. It is very important to me, because if I'm not in control, my partners can die. Trust me, it is tempting to submit. The sex is amazing. But those who submit to her that way; well, let's just say it never ends well for them."

"That's harsh," I said as we walked carefully between massive stalactites and stalagmites that almost touched each other. As we passed through the giant formations, the cave led out to green pillars of shrubbery on both sides that veered sharply to the left, indicating we were now in the maze. "So she wants you as a boy toy then?"

"You could say that. She doesn't allow me to form attachments to women either. The moment it turns to anything more than just feeding, they die. I can't prove it's her, but why else would a fully Transitioned

Fae woman just die without any signs of sickness?"

"And you are sure you haven't drained their souls?" I asked. I had heard Demons fed from souls, and if they fully fed and gorged on one, there would be no coming back from it. There would also be no rebirth, either.

"I'm careful when I feed, Flower. I learned that lesson long ago. The hard way. I also wasn't feeding when these women died. Danu has been forcing the issue a lot more lately. I'm not sure why, or how to handle it. Not sure why I am telling you this either," he said, glancing at me sideways.

"Because we're friends, Demon. It's what friends do; they listen to problems and help find a solution," I chimed in and threw him a cheeky smile.

"Hmm...Most people don't like or trust Demons," he replied easily.

"I haven't met any other Demons to form an opinion, and you have to admit that Demons don't exactly have a good reputation. But you, you've grown on me like a fungus." I smiled when he snorted emphatically. "Most feed to kill. You don't. You're different, and while I planned on hating you, I decided I should pick my battles wisely. I've been wrong about a lot of things. Like Ryder...I never planned to be here with his children planted in my body...making me fat. And yet, here I am, walking through a maze in Faery, pregnant with his twins, fighting for a world I would have gladly helped destroy only a few months ago."

"Life is funny like that, I guess. One minute you know what needs to be done, and the next you are fighting against things you never saw coming," Ristan said, and I had a feeling he was referring to the visions he was given.

"Do you think she gives you the vision as a gift, or as a curse?"

"A curse. Definitely a curse, because half the time she feeds me visions that piss off the guard, and even though they are accurate, I am sure those are just to fuck with me. The other ones, however—I think those are honestly ones she gives me to save Faery. She can't help or interfere directly, so she helps in other ways," he replied. "Mostly by setting events in to motion and letting freewill take over. The vision she sent me of you handing Adam one of your children, set in motion Ryder sacrificing you for Faery—yes, I noticed she mentioned that Ryder had done that, so it was part of her scheme to show how much he was willing to sacrifice his own wants for the needs of Faery. Let's see, what else? You being taken into the Blood Realm to be returned to your parents to discover that you were the Blood Princess, and then handed off to the Horde King. Do you know Ryder almost killed me when I shared that vision? But that is pretty typical of how she gets her way, fucks with my head and still abides by the rules," he grumbled.

"I couldn't imagine seeing what you do, and remaining sane."

"Who says I'm sane?" he quipped with a wicked smile.

"Okay, mostly sane," I amended.

"Shit," Ristan said, coming to a dead stop at the first directional divide. The path was a three way divide, and there was a thin piece of vellum on the lush green grass that had a few words scrawled on it. He picked it up gingerly. "Riddles, I hate fucking riddles," Ristan growled and shook his dark head. "Why couldn't she have sent a minotaur, or maybe David Bowie and a bunch of Muppets to mess with us?"

"Probably because that's what you would be expecting?" I ventured as he nodded absently.

"The left is but a vision of pleasure. The right is just a vision of horror. The third is the easiest of the three. Choose wisely, for only one will take you in the direction of which you seek to go," he read from the vellum.

"It's written on spell paper?" I asked as my fingers itched to touch the vellum.

"Yes, it's written on spell paper because even now your fingers twitch to touch it." He pointed at my hands, and sure enough, they were itching to grab the magical paper.

"Sneaky bastard," I griped.

"Sneaky Goddess is more like it," he replied as he placed the paper back on the ground. "So, pleasure, horror, or the easy way?" he asked.

"Horror," I replied after a moment of hesitation.

"Sounds lovely," he said.

"Pleasure is a given. If we took it, it would probably be hell. The easiest way is what you would think to take, but since were dealing with Danu I'm going to take a gander and say we'd kill someone for taking it. Horror is the one most people wouldn't take, so we go with it."

"Blades out, and stay behind me. But stay close, Flower. I like my balls just the way they are."

"Deal," I said, and giggled at my own inner thought process.

"What's so funny?" he asked after a moment had passed.

"I was thinking that I don't have to run fast if we get in trouble. I just have to run faster than you."

"Funny girl." He smiled, but didn't take his eyes off the path of the maze row we had taken.

It all changed as we got further into the maze. It was worse than a fun house. Grey clouds rolled in above us as thunder clapped so loudly in the sky, it rattled our teeth. The tall maze shrubbery changed into wicked looking thorn bushes, which twisted and tangled around us.

Ristan hissed and cut through thick tendrils of thorns that threatened the path. "Horror may have been the wrong choice," he said after a few more branches pushed in front of us, blocking our way.

"It was the only one that didn't sound tempting. I've learned never to take the easy way out of anything; it always ends up with people dying. Pleasure, don't get me wrong, I like it, but I'm not taking any path that leads to pleasure with you or the Goddess."

"Good point," he said with a short laugh before he started whacking at another vine.

We followed the path for what felt like hours before we finally came to another fork, and another piece of vellum. We stayed there for a little bit, and I was pretty sure it was Ristan's way of making sure I rested. He took his time before he read the slip of vellum.

"To find the goal, you must concentrate, for within these walls there is one at stake. Which path would you prefer to take? Death, or life, the choice is yours, but keep in mind, even immortals can make mistakes."

"I say we cut a path right down the fucking middle and kill anything that moves," I growled.

Ristan raised a brow and whistled. "Damn, Flower. That almost made me hard. Shock me with that blood thirsty little inner vixen." He smiled and helped me to my feet.

"You choose, Demon. There is no right path on this one." I sighed. Life or death? I chose life, but I had a feeling it was a wrong choice.

"Life," Ristan said. "We choose life, Synthia. Some things are worth fighting our way through."

The moment we stepped foot on the path to Life, everything turned dead. Shit. I felt sick, and instantly bent over and started retching my guts out onto the path. Ristan grabbed me quickly and stepped back into the fork for the paths.

"You're okay, I got you."

I felt Ristan's hands touching me, but Ryder's comfort filling me as I emptied my stomach until nothing was left. "Death," I said and sat back against the Demon, who had sat behind me to comfort me as I spewed my guts up.

"Death," he agreed. "Let me know when you are ready."

"I'm ready, Demon. Let's show this bitch who is boss."

"That's my girl," he said, and helped get me back to my feet once more.

Death was lit from within, and beautiful. Roses had grown on the vines, and the sun had taken place of the clouded skies. "From death comes new life,"

I whispered as I watched birds fly together, and butterflies as big as my head fluttered around us.

"No more easy ways. From here on out, you choose."

"We choose together," I said, and palmed the blades at my sides.

"Together," he agreed.

"Ryder is trying to help us," I said after we'd been walking for a while.

"No, he's helping you. He's freaking out and can feel your unease. He is connected to you, and he feels everything you do right now. Trust me, he's only cussing me out and threatening to geld my boys every time you feel afraid, or pain."

"Good to know," I muttered as something shot past my head.

"Fuck!" Ristan shouted, and took me to the ground.

Chapter
TWENTY~EIGHT

"Don't move," Ristan muttered as his immense body held me against the ground. "Someone just tried to blow your head off," he growled from deep in his chest.

"No shit, Sherlock," I mouthed, and felt pain throbbing in my shoulder. I kept it to myself, but had a feeling Ryder would be cussing up a storm soon. Sure enough, within a second, Ristan stiffened up.

"Dammit, Synthia! You're hit," he snarled as he rolled off me, and looked at my shoulder.

"I'm fine; it's a flesh wound." I turned and glared at him. "Tell that fucking Fairy to shut it. It hurts and burns like the fires of Hades, but I'll live."

"Let me see," he said and moved to sit up.

"Stay down! Someone is still shooting at us," I whispered vehemently.

"Good point," he said, and lifted his head over my chest to look across the twisted vines of blood red roses. "Stay put, Flower. I'm going hunting."

"You're leaving me here?" I complained.

"Well yes. You are shot, and I have a very angry Horde King in my head telling me to gut the mother fucker who did it."

"Fine. I'll be here, in the bushes, on the ground. Just laying here, waiting for you to come back with your big manly self."

He snorted and shook his thick mane of hair. "Promises, promises." He kissed my cheek and left me on the ground. "Stay put, Princess, while I go slay the beast."

"Now who is making promises?" I teased to take off the edge of being planted on the ground with a painful shoulder. The bullet had only grazed me, though, and I was more worried about being left on the ground than I was anything else.

I brought my hand up and ran it over the area which had been grazed and applied pressure. Whoever shot at me had crappy aim. I heard a scuffle, and then Ristan was back and ripping part of his cloak to make a field dressing.

"He's dead, but I think he was dead for a while before I got to him. Danu brought those who got lost in this place back to life to fuck with us."

"Peachy." I ground my teeth together tightly, as he pressed the black coarse material to my arm and then tied it there. "Wait, if she is bringing those that got lost and died in the maze back to life, where they hell did they get the gun? I mean, if this place was shut down when Kier took his throne, that was centuries ago; way before firearms would have been around."

"Fuck if I know. Bermuda Triangle, perhaps? The one I killed—again—looked like a Spanish privateer. Can you walk?"

"He grazed my shoulder, Demon, not my ass."

He laughed and the light caught his eyes and twinkled with humor. "Oh the things I could say to that," he whispered as he helped me to my feet.

I was barely upright when the next attack came. There were several men who looked just like Ristan had said my shooter looked. Their clothing was from the 1600s; cutlasses, old flintlock pistols, and decomposing faces. "Ristan," I warned, as I looked at those coming closer to where we stood. "Are those Zombie pirates?" I asked, trying not to sound crazy.

"What the hell?" Ristan asked as he reached for me, only to stop as a loud explosion sounded.

We both ducked as what looked like a ghost cannon sent a round black ball sailing over our heads. "They're firing cannons at us?" I asked in shock as guns were drawn from the sickly looking men who were growling and making strange gurgling sounds.

"Shit," Ristan said, half laughing, half shock. "Syn, there's too many of them. Get behind me."

I didn't have time to reply as one of the Spanish pirates rushed at us. On instinct, I dropped and brought my foot out to trip him. When he was on the ground, Ristan brought out his wicked looking sword and severed his head.

Another rushed in, this one with his gun pointing at my head. I dodged it easily, maneuvering around its sluggish gait. "They're slow," I blurted as I used the dagger to pierce its heart. "Ristan, they're slow."

"No shit, but so are you!" he shouted as the cannon's booming noise sounded again.

"I'm not slow!" I growled as I took a second to

level him with a killing glare.

"Synthia!" he shouted as a zombie sifted in beside me. I turned quickly; avoiding the rusty sword it aimed at me, and made quick work of it. "You're pregnant, which makes you slow. Get behind me," Ristan continued as he took out another zombie.

I swung the short sword Ristan had given me at the beginning of the maze and decapitated another zombie. "Just because I'm pregnant, doesn't make me slow, Demon!"

He took out another zombie and turned to give me a disgruntled look of irritation. "I like my head on my shoulders. If you so much as get a scratch on your delicate flesh, Ryder will remove it!"

I rounded on him and glared. I didn't have time to argue, and the look on Ristan's face confirmed it as I turned back around and swung the sword, taking two heads off with one swing. I was relieved that the zombies did not get back up once they had been dispatched. "Ryder knows I can take care of myself. You really think I'd let him remove your head?"

"You really think he'd wait for your opinion if you were hurt? He's unstable when it comes to you."

"Unstable?" I asked as I swung the blade again, severing yet another head. I looked at the blade, and then at Ristan. "These blades are wicked," I mumbled as I watched him take out three zombies as easily as I had taken out the one. I looked around the dark green grass, to where the zombies were now all littered upon the ground.

"Well, that was educational," Ristan said, as he wiped his blade on one of the pirate's jerkin. "Goddesses, Pirates, and Zombies, oh my!" he joked with a smile twisting his lips.

"The Zombies were the pirates." I smirked and took his lead in wiping off my own blade. The blood from the pirates was black, and just not natural. "These beings don't belong to Faery. Look at this," I said, reaching down to grab the pouch one of the zombies had tied to his belt. The pouch contained Spanish gold. "These are actual pirates," I said in confusion.

"Come," Ristan replied, pulling me up to my feet from where I'd kneeled beside the pirate.

"You having to help me up is really getting old, really fast," I complained.

"I don't mind," he replied, and we both stopped cold as another fork presented itself. The bushes parted to open up into a three way junction once again. "More riddles."

"Let's hope there are fewer bullets on this one."

"Agreed," he said as he bent low to retrieve the message. "Take the path for which you seek, but keep in mind, not all will take you to what you need. Illusions abound, tempt and deceive, and while men covet that which holds great beauty, humility is often the key to the King's needs."

"Well that's about a cluster hump of dumb luck," I replied, smiling. "But seriously, that's crap. I hate illusions," I complained out loud.

We walked through the maze for at least another hour that was slow and go, due to the pathway being lined with landmines for at least a quarter of a mile. I guess if the ancient Chinese could rig these nasty toys, so could the Fae.

The maze finally ended in a square area that had

many different items placed on pillars made from the same shrubbery that formed the maze. Most of them shimmered, while others seemed more corporeal. We'd arrived at the illusions for which the vellum spoke of.

They were all cauldrons. Ryder and his men didn't know which relic it was—the scroll just spoke to one of the legendary Fae treasures being hidden here, and as I scanned the cauldrons, I realized it was the fabled Dagda's Cauldron. The stories said it was bottomless and no man was ever unsatisfied. The irony wasn't lost on me that the maze only allowed someone who was once a witch and her bodyguard to go for a cauldron. Brilliant.

"We have to choose?"

"Very carefully," Danu said, as she appeared in front of us from nowhere. "Choose wisely, for you only get once chance. If you choose poorly, the maze will start over and someone who awaits you outside will pay the price with their life."

I stared at her, seriously wanting to kick her ass, or have Ristan do it. Those choices sucked about as much as Indiana Jones uber fast-aging, head-exploding poor choices.

I scanned the selection and looked back to Ristan, who was once again staring at Danu with a mixture of love and resentment. I ignored them both and searched through the relics, for the one true one.

Most were made out of gold; one had even been made out of wood. There was one in which my eye kept going back to, but it was made from platinum and iron. They were all round in shape, and looked like bowls or basins.

"Which will you choose, child?" Danu asked, as she walked over to me. "The gold is beautiful, is it not?"

"It is, but the Fae have never really put a lot of stock in metals. The platinum would be the smarter choice, but again, it's made of metal. No, the Fae of old kept their relics hidden in ancient settings. They were arrogant as a people, and sparkly, shiny things didn't really sway them; they were typically into natural things. The staff was made from oak, and it wasn't until Ryder held it that anything happened and it transformed into its true shape and it was beautiful." I looked around and found the wooden bowl, which was battered, but still intricate in the carvings that spanned the base. It was made of oak like the staff, and the Fae loved oak.

It had too much fine detail, but beside it a few feet away was a rough, hand carved stone basin. The side was cracked, but it was natural, and even though it was plain in looks, it was still beautiful. "This one," I said.

"It's broken, Synthia," Ristan hissed beside me.

"It is, but so is this world and it's still beautiful. Like this bowl, it's cracked and needs to be fixed. In the right hands, it'll become beautiful and whole again."

"You choose wisely," Danu said as she picked up the bowl, and it changed into a beautifully chiseled work of art. She handed it to Ristan carefully and turned to me. "You were the right choice for the Queen of Faery, Synthia. You see beyond the beauty of something, and into its heart. Keep to the path I have set, accept me, and you will be able to save your unborn babes. Stray and everything will be lost," she said as her ice blue eyes slid down to my belly.

"Let yourself be free here, Synthia. Find something worth fighting for, and those powers will come forth once you have embraced me and all that Faery has to offer. You have to trust what you are, and what you want the most, to find who you truly are."

And with that she disappeared, and I felt a weightlessness come over me. I screamed as the feeling of falling took hold of my body and mind, and then I crashed against something hard and warm. I inhaled and looked into perfect golden eyes.

Danu was wrong. I knew what I wanted, and I was already willing to fight for him.

"Synthia," Ryder growled from low in his chest and pulled me against him tightly. He pushed me away a second later and was undoing the Demon's field dressing, and checking the graze.

"It's only a flesh wound."

"So I heard," he replied and crushed his lips against mine.

Yes, I had found something worth fighting for. I was going to fight to keep the elusive Horde King as my own. Every beauty needed a beast, and he was mine.

Chapter
TWENTY~NINE

She smiles, unaware of how close she and Ristan had come to death. I sifted the entire party of warriors back to the Horde Kingdom within seconds of her landing in front of me. Taking no chances that the enemies who had been trying to creep into camp, could lay eyes on my beautiful woman.

She's a weakness within me that I can't explain. Her body grows ripe with my babes planted firmly within her. Never has a woman been more beautiful to me. The subtle change is there for the world to see, for Adrian to see.

Her breasts ripen as her once slim abdomen grows round. It's there, even though she's only a little way into the pregnancy. Twins. Only my warrior queen could gift the Horde with the blessing of twin heirs. I should have known nothing with Synthia would be done in half measure.

"You should get some rest," I tell her, and watch as those beautiful eyes swing around to smile at me. She hates that I demand it, and I'm learning with her. "Lay with me, Pet. I'm in need of you."

She smiles, and that wicked little twinkle enters her vivid eyes. I reach out, and pull her against me. She moans. My dick jumps at the noise; such musical sounds she makes when I'm fucking her deep and hard with my cock.

"I thought I lost you," she whispers, and I tremble at the force her words have on me. She watched Ristan fight an image of me.

"Never," I assure her. "I'll never leave you."

Never will I concede to death when she's in my grasp. This beautiful creature is my match. She's burrowed her way into my heart, and into my soul. Finding out she was mine, and was the one I'd been searching for in the Human world, was intoxicating. Watching her at my feet as she was given to me was the most exquisite feeling in the world.

I run my hand over her swollen abdomen slowly. Knowing my children are safe within her is exhilarating, and yet scares me. I could lose them all, if the fates are cruel. Ristan has seen her with our son, but he hasn't seen the other child. Nothing yet, anyway, and it bothers me to even comprehend what it could mean. The possibilities scare me, and nothing scares me but the idea of losing her. It fucking knocks the wind from my lungs.

"How do you feel?" I ask, as I eye her bandage from where the bullet grazed her flesh. I place my hand over the strip and send a shot of power through her wound, helping her flesh to speed her healing time. I'd never been so fucking out of my mind as I was when she'd been inside that maze. Unable to see what was happening, what she was seeing. It was beyond torture leaving her in the hands of another, to depend on them for her survival.

"Good, and hungry," she whispers, so quietly that I pull her closer and run my hard, throbbing erection over her ass.

"That word has never sounded so good, as it does from your lips."

"Is that so?" she asks, and my cock jumps for her. She grins as her face turns toward me. I fucking love this, having her in my bed. She's finally in my world, without secrets between us. She stretches like a cat, pushing her perfect ass against my cock.

"You keep pushing that at me, and I'll fuck it," I growl heatedly into her ear. When she grins wider, I growl louder. She doesn't know how fucking tempted I am to fuck her, hard and deep.

"You wouldn't dare." She cries as I thrust the growing erection harder against her pert ass. I've had her every way possible, but it was in Transition, and she wasn't aware of what was happening.

"I would," I warn her, the beast purring like a kitten with what he knows is coming. "I would take anything you give me, and more."

"Is that so?" She hikes a blonde brow high on her forehead, and I turn her over until I'm leaning against her gentle curves with both arms pinning her body between me and the mattress. I smile down at her, and lean in to steal her lips.

She moans against my mouth, and I curse—fuck, she undoes me. Those sweet little noises when I fuck her, the way she takes me without a care that I am part beast, part man. She took the beast between her thighs, and fucked him as if he were me. Without question, she allowed him inside her body and made him come like some untried youth.

I pull back and lick my lips, enjoying the exquisite taste that is hers. Peace is a fleeting thing between us, and I intend to enjoy it while it lasts. I remove our clothes with a single thought and take in her sweet womanly curves.

Pregnancy suits her; her body is glowing with radiance from within. Her pink nipples have darkened to rose-tipped twin peaks. I lower my mouth and suckle one greedily. I suck harder, flicking it with my tongue as my lips clasp against it. I enjoy the hiss of air that escapes her lips.

She spreads her legs, but I'm not giving in to the seductive temptation to take her hard and fast. Slow and steady this time. I plan to fuck her until she's sore from it. I bring my hands out and spread her wide. At the same time, I draw my magic around us and kiss her with a million soft, well-placed targeted lips. It's good to be King right now, good to have the ability to become more than one man.

I attack the other breast with the same assault, licking and flicking her tight budded nipple as it hardens between my lips. I inhale the smell of her pussy at it grows moist with need. *Not yet*, I tell myself. I pull away and catch her hands as she brings them up to grab my erection. If she starts to touch, I will lose control.

I'd bend her over and fuck her as hard as I could, but she needs gentle right now, so I move slowly against her, waiting for her to be ready for me. She needs to know I need her in my world. I was raised to hide feelings, and she makes me feel too much. It's hard to control the urge to spill it out, like some besotted fool.

I pin her hands on the gentle curve of her blossoming belly. She glares, but it is short lived as I send my magic to her sweet petals that even now grow moist with need. I use my free hand to part her flesh, and impale her with a single digit. "You're so wet," I say, and watch as she moves her slim hips to push my finger in further. "What do you want?" I want to hear it from her lips the thought of her begging for me to fuck her is wild.

"You, Ryder, I need you," she cries as heat flushes her supple body and her pussy sucks against my finger.

"Not yet," I say. I send my magic slithering across her naked flesh, kissing, licking it until her pussy tightens against my finger, milking it. I lower my head until her pink flesh is slick against my mouth, and then I feed on her sweet pussy like a starving man at a banquet who can't get enough.

She cries out, and I lick her harder while adding another finger and then another. I send more magic into her body. Her nipples harden as I watch the magic take over where my mouth has just been. Her legs fall apart, opening to allow me more room to make this sweet flesh purr with pleasure.

I growl my approval as she moves her sweet hips, thrusting me further inside her sweet treasure. I remove my mouth and replace it with magic. I get to my knees between her thighs and watch as she is fucked by a single thought from my mind. "Good girl," I growl as I grab my cock and stroke it hard.

She rocks my fucking world with those sweet fucking noises she gives and the seductive look in her expressive eyes as she relinquishes her control, to my full domination. I relish that she allows me to take full control of her mind and body. I can smell her orgasm hanging just out of reach, and I keep it there. I pull the magic away every time she gets close. Every time I feel her going over, I pull it back and watch as her eyes glow with hunger and heat with pent up lust. I remove my fingers and let my magic cock fill her sweet pussy until it can take no more.

She has no idea how much she turns me on when I watch her take my magic. The beast is prowling, watching with approval as he adds to the magic—and I allow it. "Fuck, you look so seductive right now. You're so fucking exposed, Pet."

She moans, wild with her pending orgasm and unable to make coherent words come out. Just the way I like her. Even though I love her sassy fucking mouth, I enjoy her screams and cries of passion more. I lower my mouth and continue to lick her sweet, juicy flesh as it flows like a river from what I am doing to her.

Another cry escapes her lips, and I smile with triumphant pleasure. She's mine, all mine. She's my little freak in bed. My submissive to my inner control freak. She comes out of that perfect little shell and becomes my everything. My world. Out of bed she's the perfect queen to my people, but here, between the sheets all bets are off. Here, we agree on one thing, and it's her complete submission that I am in full control of.

I push against her pert ass with my finger and she stiffens. I pull back, and meet her eyes as she leans up, but then I attack her with magic until she's helpless, and boneless. I enter her ass, slowly, but fast enough that her mind won't comprehend what I've done. Her entire body trembles with a mixture of shock and awe.

I fill it until it tightens right along with her tight pussy. I remove the finger, and replace it with magic. She screams as she's filled from behind with it, but then I'm there, entering her sweet flesh with my cock; swiftly, but careful of the magic taking her from behind.

"Fuck, you're so perfect. You're my fucking world." I let the words slip and instantly want to take them back. I can afford to show no weakness, not to anyone. I've worked too hard to get here, to save my world.

I switch my train of thought, and ask her what she wants. She moans, and cries out as her legs slip further apart and her ass moves against the magic. Fuck! So tight, so fucking perfect. So wet and ready to come for me. "Good girl, that's it, let me in. Let me fill you until you can't take anymore." I growl as I add more inches of my cock into her tight sweetness. She's so fucking wet that I try to add more, until I've filled her so full of me that she cries from the mixture of pleasure and pain.

"Tell me what you want," I demand, and wonder if she caught my slip, but she delivers it and I am humbled by her words.

"Bend me over, pull my hair, whisper more dirty things that will make me tremble with need, Ryder, and then fuck me like you mean it. Fuck me like I am the air you need to live. I don't want to be your world; I just want to be your favorite part of it."

I tremble with pride as my cock goes in and out of her tight sheath. I pull out all at once and watch as her body shivers with need. I flip her over carefully, and roughly shove her head down into the pillows as I use my other hand to lift her ass and part her legs. Her ass is glistening with sweat, her pussy soaked from her own juices.

"You like it rough," I growl and watch her as she tries to lift herself with her hands. I smile, and release her head to bring her arms behind her back. I secure them with a hand tight against her ass as I release the hold of my magic. I allow it to enter her ass, even as I nudge my cock back into her sweet core.

She cries out and I lunge, filling her sweet pussy full of my engorged cock. "That's it. Take it, good girl," I encourage her. I'm feeling everything. Her ass, her sweet pussy, and her pending orgasm as it threaten to explode. I grab a handful of hair, and pull it until her head is lifted to my own. "You like me in control?"

She moans, but the yes is ripped from her lungs.

I claim her mouth in a hungry kiss, a demanding one, and she allows it.

"You like me buried deep inside your sweet flesh?"

Another yes is screamed from her lips.

"Then come for me. Show me how much you like it. Come fast and hard, so I can fuck your sweet flesh harder." I release her hands and hair, and watch as she crumbles to the bed. Fuck, she's a goddess! She lifts her ass and pushes against me, meeting every thrust I give. She bucks with need until I feel it. She explodes, shaking and trembling with the force over her release. Her pussy grows slick from it, and before I can stop myself, I explode inside of her, feeding her my own release.

Chapter
THIRTY

~ Synthia *~*

I awoke with a smile from ear to ear, and blushed to my roots. Ryder had taken me until I'd crawled away from him, fully sated. He, however, was insatiable. He'd grown hard within seconds of the first explosion of orgasms, and I'd taken him in my mouth and had used the Blood Fae ability to make his cock come for me.

We'd gone at it like teenagers in a fight to determine who was in control, and the answer was simple. He was master in the bedroom, and I was his sex slave. I'd never been taken that roughly, but I was ready for him to do it again.

"You're blushing," he whispered as he stretched beside me.

"So," I said and turned to look at him. I wasn't sure why I felt shy after what we'd shared, but I did. He'd called me dirty names, and I'd melted on his cock with each one. "I need a bath," I said, feeling the stickiness between my thighs.

"I have a better idea," he growled and rolled on

top of me.

"I'm very sore, and you smell of sex," I mumbled with a smile that was giving away too much.

"You're a horrible liar," he growled as he lifted himself up into a semi sitting position between my legs.

"It's probably because I can't," I quipped, but urgent knocking on the wide double doors interrupted any plans he had of early morning sex.

I *was* sore, and we both reeked of sex. I sat up, even as he glamoured clothes on both of us. He stalked to the doors and threw them open. "Someone had better be dying."

"Not dying, no. But your bride is here with Cornelius," Zahruk whispered, but I still heard him.

It was like a bucket of ice had been thrown over my head.

I felt sick, and angry tears welled in my eyes. It hadn't mattered what I did for him, and it wasn't going to change anything no matter how much I loved him. He was the Horde King, and I was his concubine. It was a simple fact.

The sound of the door closing jarred me from my thoughts, and when I looked up it was to catch Ryder watching me carefully.

"Pet," he whispered as he dropped his hands to his side.

"Don't," I cried, shaking my head. "Leave me alone," I said as I stepped back to get away from him as he advanced to where I stood.

"She means nothing to me," he growled.

"Then don't marry her! Marry me!" I was shocked at the words that left my mouth.

"It's not that easy," he said, still stalking me as I walked backwards until I was flush against the wall. His arms pinned me easily, as his mouth lowered.

"You are mine, you screamed it last night. You will scream it for me every night from here on out, Synthia. She means nothing to me. She's a contract I made before I knew you, and that's it," he replied angrily.

"And I'm just your fucking whore!" I screamed, and pushed against his arms as I tried to escape him.

"You're not a fucking whore, Synthia," he said as he pinned me against the wall to keep me from escaping him. "I agreed to marry her before I killed my father. To get out of this contract would hurt this kingdom, and I can't do that. My first move as the fucking Horde King can't be to break a fucking contract. It would be going against everything I stand for."

"So what, you marry her and then what? She just goes to the harem, and we go on like nothing happened?" I asked through tears that burned in my throat.

"It's not that simple," he admitted.

"You sire a child with her? Just like you have done with me, just like your fucking father," I snarled.

His arms dropped and his eyes burned with fire that had nothing to do with hunger. "It is my duty. I don't have to like it, but I will take her to bed, and then she will join the others in the pavilion, and you will come back to my bed. I demand it," he said coldly.

"You can demand all you want, Fairy, but the only thing you will get is a cold bedmate with no fire left for you in her soul. If you marry her, you should stay with her," I said and lowered my eyes.

"You don't get to tell me no anymore, Pet. You are mine!" he growled and punched the wall beside my head. I cringed inwardly, but didn't back down.

"Or what? You'll beat me into submission? Go ahead! Try it, fucking Fairy! Just fucking try it!" I was screaming as tears spilled from my eyes.

He flinched and dropped his hands once more to his sides. "I would never hurt you, Synthia Raine, and I will never let you go."

"You should have left me alone from the start," I said as I turned away from him so he couldn't see the tears that flowed unabashed now. He was ripping out my heart, and I'd given in to his needs last night. I'd felt like I was his entire world. Only to have it stripped from me in the dawn hours.

"I couldn't leave you alone. You became an obsession, and you still are. Go to your room; I'll come to you tonight," he said softly, frustration clear in his voice.

"No, you won't," I said and stiffened my spine as I left the room.

Inside the connecting bedroom, I dropped to my knees the moment the door closed and sobbed. I'd been so stupid to think he would love me. He wasn't even capable of love. It had been beaten out of him as a child, and the only thing that mattered to him was his beloved Faery, and becoming the King to the Horde.

I cried until my eyes were rimmed in red and raw. I crawled up from the floor and headed to the empty tub that was off to the side of the room. I looked at it for several moments before walking to the door and trying to open it.

It was locked. Ryder had locked me in like a freaking prisoner. Again. I pounded on the door until Aodhan opened it. "Synthia," he said, but wouldn't meet my eyes.

"Darynda?" I asked.

"I can help you with what you need," he said, still staring at the floor.

"I need a bath and someone to help me," I replied boldly, watching a blush flood his cheeks.

"I'll see if I can get Darynda for you."

He closed the door, and I listened as the bolt was locked again. I'd been wrong about everything, and I couldn't change it now. I thought I could fight for him, and that he would love me enough to break the contract. Now, the only thing I could do was keep my head up and figure out a way to get away from Ryder.

Screw Faery, and screw saving it. I wanted to go home, even if I didn't have a home to go to. Anything would be better than sitting in this place, knowing Ryder would mate with someone else. The tap at the door a moment before it swung open brought me from my musing, back to reality.

"Flower," Ristan said.

"You knew he had to marry her, and you knew what that entailed, and yet no one thought to tell me he was still going through with it?" I demanded angrily.

He exhaled and shook his head. "I knew, yes, but if you had been raised here, it wouldn't be such a big thing. This was arranged a long time before you were born, and he really doesn't want to make one of his first acts as King to break an oath. Alazander broke oaths all the time, and this is not the kind of king he wishes to be."

"I asked for Darynda, and you showed up. Ryder is going to let you scrub my back, Demon?" I spat, fed up with everything that I was helpless to change.

"Not quite. I don't think Ryder, much less Danu, would let us play around like that; no matter how much fun it might be." He smiled thinly. "Ryder sent me while he goes to handle his bride. He wanted you to speak to someone who knows what is going on, rather than working yourself up venting to someone who doesn't really know the details. Something about the building not surviving your wrath should you get yourself too worked up," he smirked.

"Not helping, Demon."

"Sorry, but I have spent a lot more time in the world that you grew up in than anyone else around you right now, so I will probably understand your anger better. You said we were friends, so this is me being a friend. Let's get you cleaned up and in bed, and then we will talk. You have had a long few weeks and earlier in the maze was pretty bad. You need rest; if not for you, for the babes." I stepped back as he pushed his big body into the room and closed the door. He turned and waved his hand over me, cleaning me up, and leaving me in a tiny pink nightie. At my raised eyebrow, he just chuckled.

"I am who I am, Flower. Come, let's get you in bed. He led me over to the enormous bed and waited as I climbed under the covers. He tucked me in, and then climbed in the bed himself and wrapped himself around me.

"What are you doing?" I squeaked with surprise as his long frame cuddled against me.

"Adam and Larissa are gone, and this is what Ryder would want to be doing rather than what he is dealing with, so shush." He finished situating us, and I had to admit that snuggling up with a Demon was comforting.

"I won't stand by and watch him get married to someone else. I will find a way to leave; I don't care what he says," I vowed angrily.

"I wouldn't expect anything less of you, Princess. You did not grow up here, and I'm sure you realize that had you grown up here, you would be a very different person. Go back to everything you have learned about this place and what you have discovered about the Horde. Fae don't marry unless it is to gain somehow. They don't really understand what love is, and children are raised in sort of an emotionless vacuum in comparison to what you were raised in. Alazander made the deal with her family to seal a very powerful alliance. Her family is very large and influential in the Horde Kingdom, and this deal made sense at the time, and in our world, time is rarely of the essence. Fae marriages can be agreed upon and take years to come to pass. Ascending to the throne wasn't the only thing Ryder has been pushing back." Ristan sighed and continued. "Personally, I can't stand the family, and I do not trust them. I have yet to meet Abiageal. However, Claire is in this for the prestige and standing it would give her. She and Abiageal share a mother, which was why Cornelius was eager to gift her—at her request. This isn't something Danu showed me. It is where being a soul sucker comes in handy, though. It is easier for me to see through that shit, so I passed on what Claire was offering. Although, the rest have been sampling since she came to us. She is very good at disguising her true motives and desires."

"I'd wondered why she was so willing to become nothing more than food. She seems to have the rest of the guys thinking she is the shit."

"Well, she does have her uses." He gave a little snort. "She showed up shortly after the deal with her family was made, as a gift from Cornelius. Claire said it was so that she would be able to stay with her sister, and Alazander didn't see any reason to say no." Ristan made a face. "I think that is a load of crap, even though it is not a lie. Being a concubine to a monarch is a very powerful place to be, even though you may not think so now. Oftentimes a concubine can have more power, affection, and attention than a wife can, and I am pretty sure Claire was trying to get to the position of a second wife or a first concubine. The one that you now occupy, even if it is unofficial," he said against my ear, as if he was trying to convince me I was important to Ryder.

"So she wants to be the head whore; that's her deal?" I snapped. "That's what Ryder wants me to be?"

"The Fae don't have the same social morals that Humans do, so they do not view a concubine as a whore," he said patiently. "It is typically a place of honor, especially if the monarch does not attend to any other females as often as he does his favorite concubine."

"It's medieval and stupid," I growled

"It is our way," he said simply.

"I just don't understand why he would think it is

ok to do this. I am a Princess. Doesn't that count for anything? You guys knew that I would eventually be the Heir because of the prophecy. Doesn't *that* count for anything?"

"Danu's visions set events in motion. He couldn't offer for you in marriage because he was already promised, so he had to offer for you as a concubine to fulfill what the vision entailed. You have met her; you know she does not make these things easy, which leads me to the next part—Ryder does not love his bride, nor does he hold any affection for her, Flower. I wouldn't put too much stock in what he thinks of her. If she is anything like Claire, she will go into the pavilion with the others, and she will be granted rights to dally where she wishes. He is obsessed with you; he might even be in love with you. Of course, he is Fae so he doesn't recognize it as such, but it is all over him. We can all see it. He wants you and he will not let you go. He can't break this contract; we have been trying to find a way. But I know something you don't seem to have caught yet."

"What; did your psycho Goddess give you another vision?"

He gave me a huge knowing grin. "She dropped a few clues in the maze. She called you the right choice for the Queen of Faery and told you to find something worth fighting for and your powers would come forth. Is he worth fighting for?" My heart stopped as I shifted back and stared at his patterned eyes. "You have to stop thinking like a Human, and start thinking like the Fae, Flower. They always stack the cards in their favor."

"And what if I want to play a different game? Normally when the cards are stacked against you, it's best to play a different game," I whispered.

"Could you walk away from him? You carry his children, and I don't foresee him allowing you to walk away."

"I can't just allow him to marry someone else, and keep me as his toy. I'd be nothing more than his whore, and I'm not stupid, Ristan. I know that a wife would be who he shared his life with, and I would be his bedmate. I deserve better than that, and even if it means walking away from him, I'd do it. I can't be the other woman, and I know what I want. I want him, and I want to share his life; not just his bed."

"Then fight for him," he said.

"I can fight for love, Demon. I just won't compete for it. I shouldn't have to."

Chapter
THIRTY~ONE

I was in that weird state between being awake and asleep when Ryder sifted back to the room. He was silent as he sat on the bed across from me. He remained perfectly quiet until I finally turned over and leveled him with a glare.

"We need to talk," he stated the obvious.

"There's nothing to talk about, Ryder. Unless you went down there and figured out some miracle that ended with you not being married, well then, we'd have a shit ton to talk about," I snapped angrily.

"Syn," he warned.

"It fucking hurts! I can't breathe, Ryder, because of you! Before you I was fine. I was living. I could breath and without you I can't! When Adrian died it hurt like hell, but I could breathe, damn it!"

He pulled me across the bed before I could speak, and the tears that welled in my eyes ran freely down my face. "Put me down!"

"No," he whispered.

"Stop touching me! I can't think with you close.

I wasn't raised like this and you can't expect me to just jump in line and figure it out. I can't. I can't erase what I was raised to believe in overnight."

"I am not trying to force it, Syn. I'm trying to figure a way out of this contract. It just takes time. Just give it to me and I will figure it out."

"Like the harem?" I barked, fed up with the lines. I didn't trust that he would find a way out and it hurt. It really hurt.

"That's not up for discussion," he replied on a sigh.

"Why? Why isn't it up for discussion? It's off limits, that's all you say. Explain it, and then maybe, just maybe I can understand why it's off limits."

"Because...Fuck! They are not just Alazander's concubines! Synthia, think about it; what the fuck could make me keep women my father had?" he snapped.

"I don't understand," I whispered, taking in his defensive posture.

"My mother is in there, along with many others my father hurt. I can't just release them; it's not that simple. Some of those women have been crushed and are just starting to come out of the shells my father beat them into. My mother is lost. She is trapped in her own body and becomes hysterical when she is around groups of people. He finally broke her the day I killed him. Yes, some are mine, Synthia, but I don't fuck them. I only want one woman in my bed. You."

"Why didn't you just say that to begin with, Ryder? I'm Human, or I was raised as one anyway; I have helped save women from Fae like your father as a Witch. That? What you just told me? I understand

and can accept it. I don't know why it's so hard for you to trust me, but if you could just give me the benefit of the doubt and trust me, I might just surprise you," I replied. Ristan tried to tell me about the pavilion. Hearing it from Ryder's lips helped me to understand that the Demon wouldn't lie for him just to make me feel better.

He ran his hands through his thick midnight hair and smiled. "You amaze me every day, Pet. I gave you to another man, and you should hate me for that, but you don't. You haven't even screamed at me for it yet. I went fucking crazy, Syn. I held it together by a thin thread to maintain the peace, but on the inside I was as crazy as the beast. So I get it. The thought of you fucking Adam drove me insane. That he would touch you like I had, or that he would kiss those sweet lips that I'd become obsessed with. The only fucking thing that kept that thread from breaking was knowledge that I was sacrificing my desires for Faery. I thought I deserved it, for everything I had done. And even though I was prepared to give you to him, I was plotting how to take you back."

"This is different, though, Ryder. There isn't a chance that it's a mistaken identity. Your father made this contract, and if it was written by him, I don't see a chance of you getting out of it."

"That's where you need to trust me. My father always had a way out of everything. I just have to find it. I'm only asking you to give me enough time to find it."

"We both need time. You've put me through hell, and no, you're right. I haven't freaked out, but then again, I'm not that type of girl. I was taught to be a good man in a storm. I don't explode without thinking shit through. You need time to get out of this mess, and I need time to think. You knew this was coming, and yet you never told me anything. It's a betrayal; maybe not to you, but to me it is. You got me pregnant. It may have been the beast that got the job accomplished, but it's your children growing inside of me. Now I get this dropped in my lap because you decided not to trust me, and that I see as a betrayal. I haven't asked for much from you. So give me time. I realize I need to feed, but you also promised to show me other ways to feed as well, and have yet to deliver on your words. Teach me so that I can have the time to think without you mucking it all up."

"Mucking it all up?" he asked pointedly.

"Yes, Ryder. When you're this close, I can't think. You come in all tall, dark, and deadly and my lady parts go all cuckoo for cocoa puffs and shit."

"Is that so?" he asked silkily.

"Not even, Fairy." I stood my ground, watching him.

"Fine, but that time is going to be here. You will be in danger if you leave this place without me. Here, I can guard you and the babes. I have enemies everywhere, and you would be their best tool to use against me while you are pregnant. I can't show too much emotional attachment in front of anyone in this castle outside of my elite guard. It's dangerous, as I have enemies here as well."

"Then why fight so hard for it?" I asked.

"Because I need to fix what I helped my father perpetuate. I need to save this world, and if it means sacrificing my own needs, I wouldn't hesitate, you already know that. Destiny didn't fight this hard to bring us together just to tear us apart, Pet. She has a plan."

"I've met Destiny. She's a mind freak who loves a game twister, seriously," I mumbled.

"Ristan said she was interested in you. She didn't bring you here just to torment you. Danu has a plan, and even though she can't intervene directly, she will throw us some sort of a lifeline. We just need to figure out what it is."

He scooted off the bed and held out his hand for mine. "I want to take you somewhere. Think you have enough energy to go, or shall I feed you first?" he smirked wickedly.

I took his hand and stood up as he glamoured a soft blue baby doll dress over my skin. It went to just above my knees, and stopped with a soft length of lace. He pulled me to him and I flinched as his hands came up, but then I realized he was reaching for my hair.

"What are you doing?" I asked quietly.

"I'm putting your hair up." He pulled it up gently and placed a rubber band at the base of my neck efficiently.

"I can do my own hair," I said as he looked at the ponytail that was situated too high on my head, like a late 80's hair-do. All it was missing was a scrunchie.

He pulled me toward the door, and when he opened it, I narrowed my eyes at the entire Elite Guard that stood ready for war behind the door. "You did my hair to *off me*?" I asked jokingly.

"No, it's just a precautionary measure for your safety. I figured it might be good for you to get out of the castle for a short trip, but that doesn't mean I'm going to do it without measures for you and the babes' safety."

As I moved closer into the full Elite Guard's path, I caught sight of Adam. "Where are we going?" I asked, wondering where in the world we were heading that he needed to take such measures as to enlist the entire guard of thirteen men, plus Adam.

"It's a secret," he whispered as he turned me into his arms and smiled.

I hated surprises, but the thought of getting out of this place was tempting. I melted against his body as he wrapped his arms around me protectively. It felt nice to be secure in his arms, cherished even. He sifted us out of Faery and to a busy industrial area in California; if the palm trees and license plates were anything to go off of.

It wasn't home, but it was close. I looked around the area and noticed a few things. One: it was a factory in the industrial park and the smell coming from it was horrible. Two: there was a woman waiting for our group at the front of the business.

Great, he'd brought me back to my world just to remind me how much it could stink here? I watched as the woman approached us and noticed she had pointy ears. Her eyes were large on her oval face and sparkled like fresh dew in the morning after a storm. Fae? I hadn't seen any with ears like that yet.

"Elven," Ryder said with a small smile that twisted his lips up. "Arista, this is Synthia. She's here for what I ordered," Ryder spoke to the woman softly.

Jealousy reared her ugly head, but it was more to do with the way the woman laid her hand on Ryder's chest and leaned in to kiss his lips. "Good to see you, my King," she said sweetly.

I lifted an irritated brow at Ryder. Great surprise!

He'd brought me here to watch another woman swoon at his feet. This was just what I needed.

"If you will follow me, Princess," she said and smiled softly.

At the front doors of the cement building she inserted her key card and pushed a few buttons into a code panel. She fluffed her short blonde curls and opened the door, which the men quickly took for her and held it open.

I shook my head because of the look she gave them in thanks. It was more of a *see yourself to my bedroom* look. Inside, the smell grew worse, but the sign that hung over the front desk made all the stink in the world fade away. It read simply OPI Headquarters.

I felt hot tears push behind my eyes.

Holy fairy farting buckets!

"This way please," Arista said, and I followed her silently.

Inside the hallway, we were guarded on both sides by the men. The entire building was silent as we made our way through it. I was trying to swallow past the thickness that was clogging my throat. It wasn't until she stopped at a door and clicked numbers into another panel that the tears welled up and dropped.

Inside the room was shelf after shelf of my favorite nail polish. It wasn't just nail polish, though, it was OPI nail lacquer. My Fairy had remembered that I was obsessed with it, and that my entire collection had been destroyed with my house.

"You can pick from any shade. If you leave the bottles you want, I will have them sent to Faery for you," Arista said politely.

"All of them; I want them all," I whispered brokenly, even as I turned and threw myself in Ryder's arms. "Thank you!" I cried, unsure if it was hormones or that he was extending an olive branch and trying to give some of the comforts I'd thought to never have again. There was a lot I could live without, but my nail polish and coffee were both something I needed to just feel like I was myself again.

"We will take one hundred of every color," Ryder said over my head to Arista.

"Seriously? That's a lot of polish," she replied.

"Synthia wants it," he whispered into my hair, "and I want her to be happy."

Arista sighed at his romantic comment. Shit, *I* was sighing! He'd brought me to the freaking OPI factory. Shit! I was at the OPI factory, and was too busy hugging on the Fairy to be grabbing bottles. I ripped myself from his arms and darted my gaze, looking for my favorite shades.

"Can I take a few bottles back with us?" I asked as my fingers itched and my palms sweated to touch them all.

"He is paying for them." She laughed and shook her head. "So feel free, Princess, to take any of them that you want."

A few bottles? I left with thirty shades of polish, hand lotions, polish remover, and countless other things that I'd never been able to afford before. When we sifted back to Faery and the men had piled all the goods into a cabinet that he glamoured for me, Ryder turned and smiled.

"Good surprise?" he asked.

"Best surprise."

"I knew you loved the lacquer, and I'm trying, Pet. It's not safe for you to go home while your brother is hunting you, but this was something I could do. Ristan has history with Arista, so he reached out and made sure she could help. So, how do you plan on thanking me?" he asked with a boyish grin.

"Nice try, Fairy. I still need time to think," I replied. "Maybe I'll thank you later, in a way we can both enjoy."

"I like that idea," he purred.

"I didn't say drop your pants and get naked. I said later; as in not right now," I replied as he took a calculated step toward me, only to stop at my words.

"Pet," he growled.

"Fairy," I smiled.

"I don't like to be kept waiting," he replied.

"Neither do I, so I guess you better get to figuring out how to void that contract."

Chapter
THIRTY-TWO

I spent a few days learning more about the Demon. Not by choice, but because he said he had been getting erratic visions about the Mages and my brother, Faolán, that he couldn't pinpoint. So he, which really meant Ryder, wanted to make sure I was safe at all times, so I got stuck with over six and half feet of Demon as a babysitter. Well, *they* called it extending his duties as a bodyguard.

At least he made it interesting, and instead of cooping me up and making me crazy, it looked like he and Ryder must have discussed entertainments for me other than 'spin the Fairy,' and my days weren't as boring as a result.

In the mornings, he would escort me to Zahruk, who would spend an hour sparring with me. Nothing too strenuous because of the babies. But I got some payback of my own for that little stabbing incident a while back. For some reason, Darynda and the rest of my handmaiden posse begged to go to these workout sessions personally, I thought it was to see Zahruk and any of the other guards that might have been working out in the armory without their shirts on.

Darynda would not take her eyes off Zahruk, and

Meriel didn't just track Ryder like he was dinner; all the males were a buffet to her. I found out the first day of our sessions that she was half-Nymph and she was always hungry, or so it seemed.

After sparring, he would escort me to one of the many libraries where we would meet up with Dristan, who would bring out all sorts of dusty books and scrolls to help me understand Fae history and politics. It seemed that he had more talents than just being a flirt, and he was hoping that Ryder would utilize him as more of an ambassador. He was also very protective of the books in the libraries, and treated them like treasures. I learned a lot from these two as sessions usually devolved in them arguing about one topic in history or another. Although they both dodged questions about how old they were, it seemed that for some of this history, one or both of these two were present as they were both part of Alazander's guard before they were part of Ryder's. I wasn't sure why my handmaiden posse would always scatter, and seemed to have other things to do when history or politics were involved.

Adam had returned to the Dark Kingdom with the promise to return soon, and I did not see Adrian now that the trial was over. The trial had taken both Adrian and Vlad out of Tèrra for over two weeks, and they had to get back to their duties of monitoring the Mages. It seemed that the Mage activity had not slowed down there, even with the increase of more Mage trouble here in Faery. It was an indication that there might be a lot more of them than Ryder had initially suspected.

This afternoon Ristan had been entertaining me with classic movies—since we had *Fae-per-View*, which was way better than *Pay-per-View*. He could think of a movie, and it would play on the wall like a projector.

He bet me that I couldn't beat him at chess, so I had. The first time, at least. He'd won the second, and I'd won the third. Each had a price…and we got to choose what it was. I planned on tormenting him with chick flicks, and indulging in some perfect girl time, since he insisted on babysitting me.

We watched Beaches first, which backfired. I bawled my eyes out and he patted my back awkwardly. He made me watch Goonies next, which had me rolling with laughter as he recited each of the characters' dialogue in a replicated voice. He was a sport and painted my nails, which in the end looked like I had allowed a one year old to go wild on my digits.

"You are the worst nail painter, ever," I said, holding my hand up to inspect it.

"Who's the idiot that wanted me to paint their nails? And shit, this stuff stinks like Pixie farts," Ristan complained.

"Wait until you catch a whiff of the remover," I said, smiling evilly.

"Nice try." He barked with laughter as he glamoured the polish off with a twist of his fingers. "Hungry yet?" he asked, yet again. He had been dropping these not so subtle hints every couple of hours since he had gotten here. I was starting to think Ryder was paying him to ask that question. Either that or he couldn't wait for Ryder to take over.

"I fed from him yesterday," I replied flippantly. I'd done more than feed; I'd jumped him as soon as he'd come to my room, ripping his clothes off before he could even grasp what I was doing and gorging on him. Not that he'd complained when he'd figured it out.

He'd slammed me against the wall, even though he'd made sure to not hurt my midsection, and after I called him dirty names for being gentle, he'd made me scream his name until I'd lost my voice. He'd also broken the bed, which, hey, you wouldn't hear me complaining about it.

"Why are you always so nice to me?" I asked Ristan as he leaned back and put his hands behind his head on the bed leisurely. "Out of everyone here, you seem to be the most willing to help me."

"You make Ryder happy, Flower. I like him better when he is happy. He hasn't had an easy life, and I like seeing him happy with you. I am also here to protect you from anyone seeking to harm you. Besides, it gets me out of the tedious bullshit that the others have to sit through, like holding court and listening to everyone bitch and moan over what they think they are entitled to."

"Oh," I replied and exhaled slowly, considering what he'd said.

"Still—" he was cut off; his eyes flashed red and began swirling.

"Ristan?" I asked. When he didn't answer, I moved to touch him.

"I wouldn't do that," Danu's voice said from behind me. "You touch him, and you will follow him into the vision, child."

I spun around and leveled my gaze on her. She was dressed in an elegant, light blue outfit of lace, and silk. Her black hair hung loose, falling in gentle waves around her slim hips. "You," I said, barely above a whisper.

"Me," she agreed with a beautiful smile on her full

mouth. "It's time to choose, Sorcha. Life or death?"

"That's pretty vague, Danu; even for you," I replied, placing myself firmly between her and the Demon who seemed lost inside the vision.

Her eyes went from Ristan's slumped form on the bed, to me, and back again. "Interesting."

"Still waiting," I continued. I didn't trust her, and I sure as hell didn't trust her with the Demon after the shit he'd told me.

"It's time to choose whether or not you will allow Faery and your children to die because you insist on hanging onto that last thread of humanity you have inside of you. That last little bit of disbelief. It's your choice. I cannot make it for you. I had thought, given who I had paired you up with, that you would be an easy sell. Adam caught on and embraced it, even as he was in Transition," she replied softly as she took in the wide variety of nail polish.

"I can just choose to accept you?" I asked guardedly. I wasn't born yesterday.

"Of course, Sorcha," she said, holding up bottle after bottle and examining each one at her leisure. As if she had all the time in the world. "There really isn't a catch, so please stop assuming I am a monster. You are being rather rude, considering I am here to help you."

"No one in this world does anything for free."

"We do, my child, if our existence depends on this world surviving," she replied inside my head.

"Stay out of my head," I warned.

"I've been inside of your head since the day you

were created. I set the events in motion that created who you are and who you were meant to be. Ryder was only following what I'd given him for his path. He had to see the evil, which he'd been born of to stop. You had to endure hell to become a warrior and protector. Sometimes living through something so horrible will shape our minds and make us stronger in the end. Like you." She turned and continued her perusal of the polish. "Of course I didn't want them to die; they were a perfect match for you. The Guild was the perfect place to hide you while you came into womanhood. Transition came much faster than I expected, but of course Ryder figured out the clues and found you sooner than I had intended him to."

"So, you are saying you planned it all?" I raised a brow and took a step closer.

"Much of it. You exceeded most of my expectations. I couldn't stop the Mages, or Joseph. Faolán put a little kink in my neck; however, his greed fulfilled what he was supposed to do. I can see the future and how each choice shapes things. I can set events into motion. However, I cannot directly interfere with free will and I can't stop bad things from happening. Sometimes those bad things are necessary, like what you saw in the maze. From death comes rebirth, from fire comes reshaping and reseeding. Fire shapes and molds in the forge. What are trials in life but fire? They shape and mold. There are some things that even I cannot foresee. Like your participation in the Wild Hunt, although that swan dive was a nice touch." She smiled, and dipped her head to me at her words.

"Why me?" I asked.

"You have a fire in you that most of the High Fae lack these days. They grow careless in age, bitter even. Many have lost their compassion along with their emotions. They lose touch with what I created them for. They are the keepers of this world I have created. I used part of my soul when I created it. If Faery dies, that part of me will die as well. All creatures of Faery have a small piece of me within them. While many Gods have perfected their own worlds, mine was built to be…interesting. Perfect is so boring, don't you agree?" she asked, turning to look out the window beside her.

"Yes," I answered hesitantly, wondering where she was going with this.

"Good. I'm glad we agree on this," she replied. "Sorcha, I can hear you loud and clear. I can hear your thoughts louder than anyone else in this world. You are special to me; I gave you a part of me no one else has. In fact, I gave you enough that you could be considered my own daughter."

Wow…put the brakes on Becky! She did not just say that!

"Oh, but I did." She smiled and shook her head. "He's right; you are quirky and fun."

"Who is right?" I asked slowly.

"The Demon; he has a soft spot for you."

"What did you give me?"

"That's a story for another time. Right now, we need to worry about what is coming, and less about the details of how we got here. There are, shall we say, several concerns conspiring right now and you need to let me in. If you don't, you and the babes won't live through it. One of these concerns is Faolán. He's a power hungry Fae, and trust me, there is nothing worse. He has discovered what you are carrying and even now he is trying to figure out how to get into the coronation," she stated.

"Do you ever bring good news?" I scoffed.

"I'm a Goddess. I never bother myself unless it's important. I could tell you how the whole world of Faery is depending on those infants, but you've already been told that. Adam was open; he allowed me in and embraced the power I had to give him. He is ready for his trials. It's your turn, Sorcha. Let me in so I can protect you. Accept me so those infants have a fighting chance."

"Fine; tell me how," I growled.

"I can only tell you that you have to want to accept me, to accept Faery. I wanted you in the Human world partially so that you could learn the things that the Fae lack. One drawback to living as a Human, is accepting that a Goddess can help you. Humans can be either sheep or cynics, and with what you have been through to create your strength, it has made you self-reliant and compassionate. It also made you skeptical and a bit cynical, child. You need to have a lot of faith, and to trust me."

"When is Faolán coming, and how will I know he is here?" I was getting frustrated, as her idea of help was causing more questions in my mind than answers.

"Sorry, I can't interfere directly. I can only push you in the right direction. When the time is right, you will know," she whispered with an impish smile on her lips. "You will survive this, Sorcha. You are a survivor; you were born with the right tools to get the job done. Let me in."

She sifted out, and I watched as Ristan jolted upright in the bed and shook his head.

"What the fuck, Flower!? What happened while I was under?" he asked as his eyes scanned me from head to toe, ensuring I was unharmed. "Are you alright?"

"I'm okay. You just kinda got all swirly eyed, and went all *lights are on yet no one's home* on me." It wasn't a lie, because he'd done just that, right before Danu had sifted in.

Chapter

THIRTY-THREE

I was dressed and standing in front of the mirror. Darynda had Faelyn glamour a dress in crimson red, which was a work of art. I looked like a work of art. My hair was in an updo, which still gave me a soft look. It had been decorated with strands of gold weaved throughout it. The red dress was silk, which hugged each curve. I had gold and platinum bands over my forearms and upper arms.

She'd allowed me my way about applying very little makeup beyond the Big Apple Red OPI polish and lipstick. They'd gone on and on about how I had the pregnancy glow, but I hadn't told them it was more of a *Ryder stopped by for dinner* glow.

Those curves were showing a lot more this week. According to Eliran, I was firmly in my second trimester, which had me looking for each change every minute of the day. Right now, the dress hugged the tiny little baby bump that kept reminding me I was no longer fighting my own battle.

I was fighting theirs as well, which was okay since they were mine. Ryder's, too, but for now, they were all mine. I waited until the room was empty before I allowed myself a side view of my blossoming body.

My boobs were out of control and sore enough that I noticed them a lot more. I hadn't gained much weight, which seemed to upset Eliran, but I was okay with it. My hand smoothed over the gentle swell that was proof that I was pregnant.

"Wow," Adam said from where he'd snuck in behind me.

"Hey," I whispered as his eyes flowed over my body, taking in the changes.

"You look amazing," he replied with a boyish grin.

"You look pretty good yourself, Dark Fairy." I smiled, taking in his formal clothing. He was dressed in his midnight colored cloak and matching black pants. His hair was slicked back, and his brands were visible from the sleeveless shirt he wore beneath the cloak. Fae didn't have formal wear. They wore their cloaks and Caste color. Kind of like the Scots, with their family Clan's plaid.

"I'm your escort…along with half the Elite Guard. He keeps you hidden from the world."

"The Mages keep him on his toes," I replied.

"Are you happy?"

"I will be," I grinned wickedly, "soon."

"Oh-oh," Adam said with a sparkle in his green eyes.

"I'm going to fight for him. He's my ever after, Adam. I'm willing to fight to keep him," I said with enough force that he knew I wasn't playing around.

"He's also the man who knocked you up and is engaged to another woman."

"He is, but it isn't something he himself set into motion. He's going to get out of it, and he's going to do it soon."

"If he hurts you…" he let the threat hang in the air unsaid.

"If he hurts me, you won't have to kick his ass, Adam, because I will."

"That's my girl," he said proudly.

I smiled and hooked my arm through his. I allowed him to escort me to the door where several others of the Elite Guard stood waiting for us. Ristan took in the dress with a low whistle. Zahruk and Sevrin smiled politely, even though their eyes widened at my approach.

I took in their wicked looking armor. The armor seemed to be multi-functional as they wore it to my presentation, all formal court events, as well as the trial. Dristan had shared that Ryder was more liberal about the guard not wearing the helmet and mask headgear than his father had been. Ryder felt that the headgear should only be worn when heading for, or into battle. They also wore weapons as usual; though these were jeweled with black and red stones, the only indicator that they were 'dressing up' for tonight's events.

"Flower, you look good enough to eat," Ristan whispered as we started down the hallway.

"If you bite me, I will bite you back, Demon."

"What makes you think I won't consider that foreplay?" he asked, raising a brow high on his forehead.

"Is that all you think about?" I asked as his lips

turned up, and a devilish smile splayed across his mouth.

"I think about tying my females up, making them scream, and beg for more. I also like hot wax and long walks in the sand. Does that count?" he asked with heat burning in his eyes as he said it.

"Kinky fuckery, Demon. Keep that shit to yourself." I laughed and shook my head at him.

"I like it. What can I say? It does it for me."

The men around us laughed as I joined in with them. Ristan settled down as he slipped into bodyguard mode.

"Okay, so first things first: it has been decided that the coronation will be more of a casual event than what has happened in the past. Ryder has decided to attend in Fae form rather than his Horde King form. He wants to send a message that this will be a very different rule than what Faery has experienced with the Horde King's in the past. There will be a small feast that is really just for the Horde, no outsiders at this time. They will go on and on about who is who and then it is nothing more than a sit down formality. Ryder is going to have to be seated beside his intended future bride. No going all Witchy on her. It's only for show, and he needs to act like the Horde King more than ever tonight, even though he will not be in that form. Then he will hear the challenges, not that they could take him. This is a formality as the Heirs are chosen by Danu. This is just a chance to air out past grievances so that the new monarch will better understand what was not liked about the old monarchy," he snorted, "and there was a lot not to like, so this could take a while. Keep in mind that it will become an open house, so to say, so it won't just be the Horde airing their grievances; it will be those from the other Castes, too. After the challenges will be the coronation where Danu's high priest will come in and bless his reign, yadda, yadda, ceremony over, and then we can party. You are still to stay within his sight at all times, even with the precautions being taken tonight. We don't know if your parents will be here, but Liam is already inside the castle. Just keep in mind that when this gets heated, they can't sway the outcome, but it's going to give us a good idea of who is going to give Ryder the most trouble."

"He isn't going to fight Ryder, period. I'll handle that part. Liam was abused here, but he seemed pretty damn stable when I was last with him." I hoped.

"He has every right to challenge him. We're getting off subject, though. You are being introduced tonight as well," he said.

"I had a feeling about that," I said as we entered the great hall through the wide doors.

"Good, because it's show time," he said as he took in the mass of people lining the walls. "This is a cluster fuck," he said to Savlian, who nodded his head in agreement. "Formation. Z, you can let Ryder know she has been appraised of the niceties and she will be a good girl now."

Zahruk rolled his eyes at Ristan's flippancy. "Keep her close. Adrian and Vlad will be in right after you and will add another layer of security. Silas is sniffing out everyone in attendance tonight. Synthia, behave, please," Zahruk said as his blue eyes searched mine, and then went to my bump. "And for the love of the Goddess, don't do anything stupid."

"Afraid you might have to stab me again?" I questioned with an impish smile spreading over my lips.

"Not quite; just don't want to have to worry about you tonight. Plates full, Babe." He smiled back as he turned and made his way to Ryder.

"Cue music," I replied to Ristan, who scoffed but smiled all the same.

"Cue the Prozac; we should have brought some back with us for the Light King. He looks like he is about to explode with anticipation. He is assuming Ryder will accept the existing contract with him. Highly doubting it myself," Ristan said with a devious smile now plastered to his face.

"Good. The guy is an asshole. He needs to go boom," Adam said as his finger absently rubbed over my wrist.

"Oh shush, Adam; he was almost your father in-law," I joked.

"That would have made him your father," he countered and hit his mark.

"Yes, that would have sucked," I replied as I turned to look at him.

Something touched my shoulder, and I turned to find Adrian and Vlad decked out in their Fae finery. Both wore crisp white linen shirts over their wide chests, and they also wore elegant crimson cloaks loosely clasped at their throats. It seemed like jeweled weaponry was the order of the evening as both Vlad and Adrian had elaborately jeweled swords in scabbards at their waists.

"Fancy Face, you look well," Adrian said as his eyes slid down slowly to land on my abdomen. I briefly wondered if he was bothered by the small bump that announced my pregnancy. "Wow, pregnancy looks good on you."

"Thanks," I replied easily as I turned and hugged him quickly. "You look good."

He smelled great, and his hair was a tinge darker than it had been last time I'd seen him. I had to admit, being a Vampire made him look older and more handsome than he had when he'd been Human.

"I'm part of your protection for tonight, which means that I can actually talk to you."

"Funny boy," I said as I turned back at Ristan's urging.

It was time.

I felt the butterflies moving in my stomach and held my head high as we took our places to enter the enormous throne room.

"Synthia, Princess to the Blood Kingdom. Also carrying the Heir to the Horde Kingdom," a short red cap announced in a booming voice. He continued as we started in, announcing everyone who was with us. The entire crowd erupted at my name, and with what followed.

"Adam, Heir and reigning Prince of the Dark Kingdom."

"Vlad the Third, Prince of Wallachia, cousin to the Horde King."

I almost stopped, but Ristan's hand on mine kept me moving.

"Ristan, third son of Alazander, Prince of the Horde Kingdom."

My head snapped to attention and twisted until I was staring with my mouth open, looking at Ristan.

"Aodhan, eighth son of Alazander, Prince of the Horde Kingdom."

He continued, ticking off each of Ryder's men. Z was Alazander's second son, and I was getting whiplash from my head turning to each name that was ticked off. Ryder's Elite Guard was made up entirely with his brothers. Why hadn't I put that together before? Vlad was his cousin?

"Seriously!" I asked, staring at Ristan.

"Yes, Flower, seriously. Our father liked to fuck, a lot. He fucked anyone he thought would bring him strong sons and daughters."

"Ciara, Daughter of Alazander, and Princess of the Horde."

"You have sisters?" I gaped at him.

"Only one, a half-sister, but she's enough." He grimaced, but managed to smile.

Ciara was beautiful. She had raven hair that fell to her hips, and eyes of violet and turquoise. She wore a white dress styled much like the one I wore, and hers was trimmed with gold. I looked around the room as all of the Elite Guard took note of her entrance.

I'd hate to be the guy she dated. Ryder said Dristan was his brother, and that he was the youngest. She had Horde brands, so obviously she'd made it through Transition—I was curious to see if those who had helped bring her through had lived, considering who her brothers were, and how many of them were here. Dristan was announced as being Alazander's one hundred and twenty eighth of his sons. Which meant either there were always a ton of brothers, or male relations, that protected her.

"You guys could have told me," I hissed.

"And missed seeing your reaction? Not a chance in hell, Flower."

Drums sounded from all around us, as if an entire marching band was descending on the assembly. Those who had been talking stopped, as people pushed and fought to see above the crowd.

"Abiageal, daughter of the high noble Cornelius, and fiancée to the Horde King."

"And the Horde King, Ryder, first born son of Alazander. He is Danu's chosen Heir, born of Alazander of the Horde, and Kiara, the Dark Princess, sister to Kier, the reigning Dark King."

The entire assembly went insane. Howls erupted, as screams of pride and happiness from the Horde extended and drowned out any other noise from those unhappy with Ryder being King.

I exhaled slowly as the beautiful female beside him bowed low at the waist and demurely placed her hand out for Ryder. She had platinum hair much like Claire's, but that was where the resemblance stopped. Instead of the two shades of brown that Claire had, Abiageal had a line of brown and another of lilac in her eyes. She was thin and delicate, and everything a Fae woman should have looked like. I swallowed past the pain that hammered against me, even as my heart beat violently in my chest.

"It is okay, Synthia. Breathe," Ristan encouraged me as he patted my hand resting on his wrist.

I closed my eyes as Ryder accepted her hand and focused on just getting air into my lungs. I wasn't upset. Quite the opposite; I wanted to jump on the dais, smash her head in, and claim my King. It just seemed like the wrong time to do so.

I opened my eyes to find Ryder standing in front of me. "Come, Princess, you sit with me for the feast," he said with a crooked smile on his beautiful face.

He walked us to the second hall, which was right off from the great hall and held many tables. It was a huge room, decorated in a pale shade of grey with black trim. Huge chandeliers were lit above the tables, which were hand-crafted from oak and polished to a high shine. It was a beautiful room, and the chair Ryder pulled out for me was comfortable.

Abiageal and her father, who looked no more than thirty, sat on his right, as I was seated to Ryder's left with Ristan on my other side. Adam was beside him, and the others sat around us protectively. Adam's father and mother sat a little way down the table from us, and Kier acknowledged my arrival with a small smile and a nod of his head.

An entire boar rested on a platter on the table in front of us with an apple shoved in his mouth. I felt my stomach flutter and pitch at the sight of it. Ryder noticed. "Synthia?"

"It's the pig," I said from beneath my hand, which I'd placed over my mouth and nose. "It smell's horrible."

Ryder snapped his fingers and servants came running to remove it and place it further down the long table. "Better?"

"Thank you," I said, removing my hand.

"My King, I was under the impression in the contract your father agreed to, that Abiageal would be the one to birth the heir. She will be the first wife, as was your mother," Cornelius said with a glare that could have melted the iceberg that sank the *Titanic*. It was leveled at me.

"The contract stated that I should take your daughter as my first wife. Danu designates the Heirs, so this is an assumption on your part," Ryder said, leveling the dark haired man with an equal deadly glare. "I've been reading over the contract between you and my father. You wanted to ensure that it was unbreakable."

Cornelius narrowed his green and yellow eyes crudely. "Are you trying to find a way out of it? I assure you, there isn't one."

"I didn't say that now, did I?" Ryder growled from deep in his chest.

"My daughter was to be the queen, and with the title comes the opportunity of the Heir. The previous three generations of Heirs were born from the first wife."

"That was an assumption on your part rather than being in the contract, as Alazander did not think he would ever die. Synthia wasn't planned. She is, however, my choice. Have care how you proceed, Cornelius."

"Are you threatening me?" he sputtered.

"No, I'm warning you. If I was threatening you, you'd know it. I don't plan on ruling as my father has, and that means there will be a lot of changes. I took Synthia, Princess of a Royal Caste. She may not be from the Horde, but she is my choice as the mother to my children, Cornelius. That was not addressed in the contract, nor was it my father's right to give. It is my choice alone, and she is my choice."

Okay, so dinner was awkward!

"She is lovely," Abiageal said sweetly, her big brown and lilac eyes still plastered to the table.

"Thank you, Abiageal. She is exquisite," Ryder said as his hand slid down my leg beneath the table.

I almost jumped as his fingers fluttered over the silk dress and his heat sank into my skin, setting it ablaze. This wasn't the place to set me on fire, considering how unbalanced my sex drive was. I couldn't get enough of him as it was.

"Still, the first pregnancy should go to my daughter! I was promised it!" Cornelius slammed his hands on the table, forcing more eyes from around the room to look at us.

"There was no promise of it," Ryder said in that voice that brooked no argument.

"It's irrelevant, as I'm in the second trimester of my pregnancy," I pointed out.

"There are herbs to take care of unwanted bairns!" Cornelius said in a high pitched nasal voice.

Ryder moved so fast that no one saw him until Cornelius screeched in terror from across the room. Ryder had him pinned to the wall with his hands around the guy's neck. "That child will not be harmed. If anyone so much as attempts it, I will kill them in a way that makes my father look weak!" Ryder roared in his multi-layered voice.

"Ristan, I think dinner is done," I said, looking at poor Abiageal, who looked about as tan as a ghost. "He won't hurt him," I assured her. I hoped he didn't, since every Royal of the Horde was watching him.

"My father had no right to say that to you. It was meant as a barb, and shouldn't have been even whispered out loud. There are too few children in Faery now, and to even say that in jest was cruel," Abiageal murmured softly.

Well shit. She was sweet. So much for hating her. She was the opposite of Claire.

Chapter
THIRTY-FOUR

We entered the grand hall and came face to face with the last people on earth or Faery that I ever wanted to see again. Dresden and Tatiana both glared at me as they blocked my way.

"Well, aren't you just full of surprises," Dresden spewed harshly as his eyes roamed from my breasts to my abdomen.

"Such a joy pregnancy is," Tatiana said as her husband's eyes got stuck on my breasts.

"I guess I am," I replied, feeling a little bold, considering who was behind me guarding my back. "And this pregnancy has been a joy," I said, making sure I had replied to them both. The pregnancy had been a surprise that had both shocked and joyed me.

"Had I known you were so fertile, I would have kept you around," Dresden pressed.

"That wasn't one of your options," I indulged him, but only because I wanted to see his face when Ryder joined us.

I didn't have long to wait as Ryder rounded the

corner and stood beside me. His eyes went from my stiff posture, to Dresden who had yet to look up. Sensing Ryder's presence, he finally did, thankfully.

"You!" he growled as recognition dawned on him that the new Horde King named Ryder was the very same Ryder he had thought was one of Kier's sons. It also didn't help that Ryder was no longer disguising how much power he had when he was in his Fae form.

"Dresden," he bowed slightly, "Tatiana. What an unwanted surprise," Ryder purred.

"You lied to us!" Dresden sputtered in outrage.

"I'd be very careful of your words, Light King, as we have a very precarious treaty right now. This event is under truce and has been declared as a Sanctuary. If you overstep your welcome, I will have you removed from this gathering. I'd also be very careful of how you treat Synthia."

"I had a treaty with your father! He gave it to me when he killed Anise. It is still binding, and I hold you to it."

"You are wrong. Most of the treaties my father made died with him. You've had peace because I chose to use my time to gain allies and secure other things needed before claiming my birthright. I suggest you start thinking of terms for a new treaty that we can both agree on, and remember, Dresden, I am not my father. I think he made a rash decision in killing Anise, which set your spoiled, self-indulged ass on the throne. It can be easily rectified should you prove to be a thorn in my side."

He dismissed Dresden and Tatiana, both of whom looked like they were about to be sick. They sifted out together before I could manage an in-your-face to them both. The look on his face had been priceless when he'd seen Ryder.

"Synthia, go with Ristan; you do not need to be present or suffer through this. It will be a lot of posturing and other bullshit. You can visit with Adam and Adrian as well." To Ristan he said, "Stay within my sight."

"Can do," Ristan said, slipping his arm through mine as Abiageal and her father trailed behind Ryder. I wasn't privy to what Cornelius was telling the man to his left, but his eyes were on me as he did it.

We sat between the others with the Elite Guard as Ryder stood on the dais and listened to those who had grievances about the way Alazander had ruled. No one could actually challenge Ryder's claim since he'd been chosen by Danu to be the Heir.

There were too many of them; all expressing their displeasure, although no one challenged him outright. But Ristan had been right; this would give Ryder a better idea of who opposed his rule. I watched as Liam glared at Ryder, and if looks could kill, Ryder would be dead. He looked as if he wanted to protest as well, but he kept whatever was on the tip of his tongue in its place.

Some opposed Ryder for what his father had done, and it made me proud with how he deflected them as to why he would be a better monarch than Alazander was. He wouldn't follow in his father's footsteps; he'd make his own path. One that would benefit all of the Castes as he intended to repair what had been ruined and replace the bridges his father had burned.

I felt it in my bones that he was the right choice for this. He'd been born to rule this deceptively dangerous land, and it was why he was such a brute. He'd been raised here, and his father had been brutal, but he'd also seen what ruling as his father had left behind.

He would be a better ruler than any before him had, because he cared for this world, and he would make sacrifices to fix to it. He could make the hard choices that would need to be made. The mere fact that he was presiding over this assembly in his Fae form rather than the form of the Horde King spoke volumes as to the kind of monarch he wanted to be known as.

I watched as a Fae male with long black hair and wearing flowing robes that looked like the Milky Way got lost in them, approached Ryder at the dais. He was escorted by four Fae males, armed with ceremonial weaponry. As if a signal had been given, they knelt as one in front of Ryder.

Ryder placed his hand on the robed Fae's shoulder and he stood proudly, as his voice rang out.

"Ryder, first born son of Alazander, do you accept the responsibility of ruling the Horde, as well as the smaller Castes who depend upon the Horde for protection?"

"I accept the responsibility of this, and more. I will protect the Horde from those who seek to harm my own. I will protect those of the weaker Castes, and those who depend on us for their livelihoods. I vow to repair what my father left behind in his wake, and the destruction he brought upon our kind with his greed and merciless pandemonium."

Zahruk stepped up, his blue eyes smiling as he presented the gold crown to the mass of the crowd, and then turned to face his brother. "Kneel before your people, my brother, and be crowned as King of the Horde before all," Z's voice rose to be heard above the crowd as the High Priest stepped up and accepted the crown that Zahruk held in his hands.

"Who is your second in command?" The Priest asked, as his robes were held out of the way, by those who stood beside him.

"Zahruk, second son of Alazander, will serve as my second. He will walk beside me, but never behind me."

Ryder held his hand up for Zahruk to take and knelt before the High Priest. Z towered above Ryder now, which almost made it comical, except no one else thought it was funny. Zahruk bent low and kissed his brother's hand, with a wicked smile planted on his face as he did so.

"Zahruk, second son of Alazander, do you pledge your life to protect your King? Would you follow him willingly into battle to protect the Horde?" The Priest asked.

"Without thinking twice," he replied with a wicked little smirk on his face for the entire crowd to see.

"Ryder, you kneel before me and accept this crown and the responsibilities that come with it. Danu has chosen you as her Heir, the King of the Horde. Follow my lead and give us your pledge, and accept this crown as a symbol of the bond you will share with your people."

"I will," Ryder said, still on his knees.

"Do you take this crown, and vow to protect this land and its people from harm?"

"I take this crown, and vow to protect this land and its people."

"In times of war, do you vow to defend your people until your last dying breath?"

"I vow to protect them even in my death," Ryder growled. The crowd gave wild hoots of encouragement at his words.

"Do you vow to give back to this land, for which you take?"

"If I take from this land, I will plant new seeds, I will replenish what we need, and in doing so, always protect the interest of this land. No harm shall befall Faery, or the Horde Kingdom from my hand, or any other under my rule."

"Then with Danu's blessing, I crown you Ryder, first born son and Danu's chosen warrior heir, King of the Unseelie, and the Horde alike. Rise as the King, and face your people."

The entire room erupted into boisterous cheers as Ryder faced them as their newly crowned King. The crown changed as it formed to Ryder's head. Gemstones of amber formed in the front as black onyx and ruby appeared behind them. It was beautiful and mysterious, everything that Ryder was.

I turned my head a little and found Cornelius watching me and it was unnerving. The crowd started to disperse as people drifted to the open doors of the hall. Some went outside for fresh air, as others went to the hall where refreshments were served. People moved around freely as music started up from across the room. People started mingling, and soon couples started moving toward the dance floor that had been glamoured with decorations.

"He gives me the creeps," I said quietly after a quick glance showed he was still staring at me.

"Cornelius has considerable strength, but he needs Ryder as bad as we need his alliance. He has some pretty powerful connections as well," Ristan mused.

"So do I," I mused and caught Ristan regarding me with a curious look. "Hey, I have half of Spokane that owes me for saving their asses."

"I bet you do," he said as we headed into the room where dancing had started up. It was a celebration set to last for the entire night. We were on the outside of the people dancing so it was easier for the men to guard me. Adam came strolling up with a smile from ear to ear.

"Wanna shake shit up?" he asked, wiggling his eyebrows.

"I'd say they need a new DJ, and a couple of dance lessons," Adrian stated as he and Vlad came in from the same direction we had.

"We can't dance to this," I said as the weird sounding song continued to cut through the room. It had no beat, and the Fae looked more like they needed a room as they slow danced.

Ristan smiled and snapped his fingers, and the song changed to OneRepublic's *Counting Stars*. Many of the Fae immediately departed the dance floor, and I smiled. Idiots wouldn't know a good song if it slapped them all upside the head.

"Might need to liven it up with a music war," Ristan mused from beside me.

I knew they'd done music wars at *Sidhe Darklands*, where Fae would 'fight' by changing the songs just like Ristan had and the winner was determined by cheers, but this was Faery, and music from the Human world wasn't something that everyone here liked.

Many still held on to the old ways as was apparent from the music that sounded like bagpipes and other ancient instruments.

I moved to stay within sight of Ryder, as Adrian and Adam started dancing on either side of me, both smiling, or more to the point, goofing off as we used to. It was how we used to relieve stress after a mission. It wasn't long before Adrian had pulled Meriel out onto the dance floor, and I saw Adam was dancing with Darynda. I saw Keeley and Faelyn off to the side dancing with each other as they cast glances to the males around us, hoping that one of them would cut in and dance with them.

I smiled until my face hurt as we danced to the songs Ristan picked. Soon, we had a lot more of the Fae out dancing as we were. Which, let's just say we all looked like idiots bobbing our heads and shaking it to the beat.

I caught sight of Ryder smiling at me as I danced between Adrian and Adam. He shook his head, but something beyond his shoulder caught my eye and it left me breathless, in a bad way. Danu was behind him, her eyes on me as she nodded her head and looked around the room.

Sinjinn and Silas were making their way toward Ryder with urgency marked in their stride. I looked around and back at the direction they had come from. Nothing. Danu walked in my direction as I came to a standstill.

"Time to choose," she whispered with a crooked smile on her full red lips, before she moved to stand behind Adrian.

No one else seemed to notice her presence. Ryder shouted out orders in that language that I still couldn't

understand, and as I turned to look in his direction—
everything happened at once.

Adrian and Adam were both thrown across the
room as if someone had just picked them up and
tossed them away. Screams erupted as Ristan grabbed
hold of me, and began moving swiftly toward Ryder
as he shouted out urgent orders to those around us in
the same language Ryder had just used.

I knew it was useless.

They couldn't stop what was coming.

Ristan was still shouting directions as he moved
when he slammed into an invisible barrier that
knocked us both back.

"Fuck, they blocked us," Ristan growled as his
eyes searched and found Ryder's. They were doing
their little mind to mind thing when Ristan's eyes
flashed and swirled red. Before I could process what
was happening, he crushed me against himself as he
wrapped his body around mine.

Something sounded like it exploded, or had inside
the invisible bubble we were in. Ristan's body shook,
and he gasped out a curse of pain as his body absorbed
the impact. I felt something pull against my skin, like
something was trying to bite it. Ristan lifted my chin;
his hand tugged at Ryder's necklace and pulled it free.
"Flower," he whispered.

"It's going to be okay, Ristan," I whispered back
through hot tears.

It wasn't okay.

Everything was moving fast, but I felt as if it was
in slow motion. I could see Zahruk battling Fae that
wore the colors of the Blood Kingdom with a long

sword in one hand and a dagger in the other. Dristan, Sinjinn, and the rest of the guard were also engaging Fae in similar colors. Across the hall, I could see Vlad and Adrian fighting with swords and their fangs were out, mouths bloody as they fought.

Ryder had gone into full Horde King form and was battling to get to me. I saw him pick up one of the Blood Fae with his magic and literally rip the male apart. There was something else there other than the Blood Fae combatants that the men were seeking.

Even now, I could see the men shifting, turning to beast. Zahruk had become a hound, the same one who had nipped at my heels at the hunt. Others turned easily, including Silas who had become a growling wolf with blood red eyes.

There had to be Mages outside of the bubble that held Ristan and me that must have been wearing some sort of camouflage or invisibility glamour, and the men were fighting against them to get to us. I could hear no sound. The only noise was my heart pounding in my ears, and Ristan's against mine as he used his body to save me from something I couldn't see.

I felt tears in my eyes as something wet and sticky spread across my stomach. No! Not the babies. *Danu, now!* Nothing happened. Ristan made a sound of pain, and pushed me toward the invisible barrier with a force that shocked me.

His black armor was dripping with blood from thousands of cuts to it. I thought nothing could get through that armor. My lips quivered with an idea of what had happened. I looked down, and none of it was my blood. "No!" I screamed. Something was here, inside the bubble with us, and we couldn't see it.

Ristan looked like he was being stabbed. His body

was jerked one way, and then another. I moved closer, but he held up his hand and shouted. "Stay back, Syn, spell," he growled as he was being slashed, stabbed, and torn with whatever spell the Mages were using.

As quickly as the attack began, it stopped. Ristan coughed, and blood exploded from his mouth as he went to the ground—hard. I went down to the floor with him. I was on my hands and knees, slipping in blood from the wounds he'd endured. His body was mutilated with cuts, and he was choking on his own blood from the wound that had gone straight through his back to his chest. I tried to pull my magic around me and like my last attempts since coming here, nothing happened. "Ristan, get up! Get up, Demon. Now! Don't do this to me. Don't you fucking do this to me, please?" I begged on a broken sob.

"Get up!" No, this wasn't happening, not again! "Danu!"

The bubble darkened and I looked up at Ryder, wings spread wide as he pushed on the shield, trying to find a weak point or how to remove it safely. Some would explode into a glass like material when broken by anyone other than the person who cast it; others could be crushed by these types of shields.

Ristan shuddered and suddenly became still as more blood poured from his mouth. His eyes stared blankly. The patterns in his eyes didn't move, swirl, or shift for the first time since I'd met him. I pressed my head to his chest—nothing.

I lifted my hands that were covered in blood, and met Danu's eyes which were welling with tears that slid down her face. "Now, Synthia. Now will you accept me? Please."

It was the first time she'd called me by my chosen

name.

"I accept," I growled, finding the fight I had left in me, even as tears fell freely from my eyes. They'd sent Joseph to my home, they killed innocents indiscriminately, and now they had killed Ristan to get to me.

They needed to die, and in a really bad way.

I opened myself to her.

"I want it now."

"You have it, child; you always have."

Chapter
THIRTY~FIVE

I shook my head at Danu. I couldn't feel shit, and I had a sinking feeling she'd wanted me to feel helpless and scared. "Help me!" I growled at her, but mid-growl I felt it. I felt it inside my bones, down to my very being. A warm rush of pleasure, that tingled and mixed with pain.

Danu sifted to me, even as the shield vibrated with the force of Ryder's assault. His men were behind him, fighting against the Blood Fae and Mages that had emerged from the crowd. They had appeared from nowhere, and Ryder's men were now fighting behind him in a protective semi-circle as he continued his assault on the barrier. "You can do this, Synthia! You need to accept me, *really* accept what I am trying to give you!" she screamed as something sailed toward us, and Ryder knocked it out of the way easily.

"They are coming after you. Dammit, child, accept me. I can't hold them back or it is considered interfering. Even I have rules I must follow," she warned crossly.

I wasn't listening anymore. I had closed my eyes and extended my arms—shedding the last of my fears, misgivings and accept that I had to stop trying to escape my destiny, and embrace it with open arms. I had to do this to save what I treasured; my new friends and my growing wee little beasties.

I could feel the pull to Darkness. The taste of light on my face, as the Light came in and settled. The Blood Fae in me, it wanted blood. The Horde wanted everything dead who threatened me, or my soon to be family.

"That's it, daughter," she encouraged.

"I need a moment," I said through the power as it radiated through me and around me.

"You don't have a moment," she said, shaking her head. "You need to focus and figure out how to fight them. Ristan didn't deserve what they did to him, any more than the rest who have been slain from getting in their way. They need to die. You need to do this so that they can't hurt anyone else." She smiled sadly.

"They are going to die screaming. I promise you that," I said, but I was no longer worried about what I had to do. I knew it deep in my bones how to use my powers, and how to make them pay. I took a second to peek at Ryder, who was now issuing orders to those around him as he pointed at the weak points of the barrier. Smart, he'd found them fast in the utter chaos around him.

I smiled sadly and turned to face those who had thought to harm my unborn children. All at once the power I'd been denying surged forth and the air crackled with the power and electrical charge. Thin lines of silver, black, and gold shot along my crimson brands and spread over my flesh as my vision became blurry and then crystal clear. I blinked and I could see all of the different types of aural signatures from everyone in the room. I could see the Horde Fae shining gold, Adam radiated green, and the Blood Fae radiated a deep crimson color. The Mages radiated black, as if their souls were corrupted and it had stained their auras.

There were four Mages that were still using a type of invisibility glamour, one moving closer to me as I watched. Ryder broke through, shattering the shield's spell. The wicked taint of it drifted to my nose. It was the same scent that had radiated through the barrier when they'd taken Ristan down. As I watched, the four mages shed their glamour and became fully visible before me.

I wasted no time before moving into action. I sifted behind the closest Mage, and pulled him against me until his back was against my chest. I lifted my hands to his neck, and twisted. I didn't flinch at the cracking or snapping of his bones. Instead, I closed my eyes and smiled.

I opened my eyes and met Ryder's shocked face, smiling. His eyes were taking me in, and I watched as his eyes grew large with surprise as I reached out and held him immobile with my power. Well, at least for a moment before he shook free with a blinding grin.

"Less flirting, more fighting," Danu snapped as another Mage stepped forward, walking right through her. I noticed Ryder reaching out for me and flicking his fingers at the Mage, who disintegrated into ashes, clothes and all. I was beginning to see why no one fucked with the Horde King. He'd simply flicked his wrist and ended the Mage's life. It shouldn't be that simple to end anyone, but I wasn't going to bring that up anytime soon, not to him.

I sifted to stand in front of the next Mage, and smiled coldly. "You have no idea what you messed with, and now you die," I said, and extended the fangs inside of my mouth. I watched as he stood helpless to move from my magic as it froze him in place. I brought my tongue out to lick one of the extended incisors.

I wanted him to become mute—and he was. I imagined all of the blood inside of him; isolating every one of his blood cells, and redirecting it away from where it kept his heart beating in one fast push—and it did. It exploded from his body through his mouth, eyes, ears, and nose. I stepped back as it began to pool around his feet and headed for the next Mage as he collapsed.

"You guys like shields? Let's see if you like one of mine." I cast a bubble around him. He turned, trying to get away from me, and ran into the barrier on the other side. I brought my hand out and pulled with the power surging through me. Unwillingly, he came sliding across the floor back toward me.

As he got closer, he spun around and sliced out with his sword. I dodged it as if he had attacked in slow motion. I sifted in close and my hand had shot out before I could have thought better of it, and gripped something hot and wet. A sickening noise filled my ears as I pulled my arm out of his chest—with his heart in my hand. He fell to the floor lifelessly.

I looked up to see Faolán watching me. His eyes were wide with fear as he started chanting a spell in Latin that sounded an awful lot like one of the ones that the Guild used to make shields like the one Ristan and I had been trapped in. I threw the heart at him as hard as I could and watched as he caught it and tossed it to the ground.

I wasn't stupid; he had more magic than I could deal with right now. Maybe in this form I could kill him, but I was draining from using too much, too soon. Ryder was on me before I could decide what to do, and Faolán sifted out as the remaining Blood Fae sifted out after him. I glanced around and couldn't see any more Mage aural signatures in the hall.

"What the hell, Synthia!?" Ryder asked as he took me in slowly, with a carefully guarded look in his eyes.

"Ryder," I whispered as the power vibrated inside of me, wanting to come out. It was the same feeling I'd felt by touching Ryder, only this was my own, and it was coming from me.

"Impossible," Ryder argued with a note that was more disbelief than anything else. He looked me over and touched his fingers along the multitude of colors from the brands.

"Ristan," I said and pushed my way through the crowd to where the Demon was lying on his back, covered in blood.

"*Bring him back,*" I begged of Danu, and watched as she narrowed her eyes on him, as if she was considering what to do. I sank to the floor and pulled the huge Demon onto my lap. "*Please!*" I screamed it in my mind, knowing she would hear it loud and clear.

"Synthia, he's a Demon, and one I really like, but I still can't interfere. It's against the rules," she said sadly. I saw Eliran push through the crowd to kneel beside Ristan, as well as the little Demoness, Alannah.

Eliran glamoured off the jerkin from Ristan's body armor and bent to examine the multitude of ugly stab wounds all over his chest, arms, and throat as Alannah gently stroked Ristan's hair. His lifeless eyes stared blankly, and my heart broke for her. I couldn't bear it and reached down and closed his eyes.

"I hate these types of spells," Eliran muttered. "Nasty things—once it acquires its victim, it keeps slashing until they bleed out. He can't regenerate as long as it is in place." Eliran chanted for a few minutes as I held my breath. His eyes met with Alannah's and nodded gently. Both of them shot power into the Demon, and his wounds began to close at a rapid rate. His chest rose as he took a deep breath, and I almost cried out with relief from it. He coughed and choked for a few moments before his eyes opened and his lips parted to release a vivid curse.

"Fuck!" Ristan shouted as he tried to sit up but fell back down. His eyes landed on me, and he closed them with noted relief.

"Demon," I cried as tears ran down my face. My heart gave a happy lurch and I smiled at him and tilted my head in a way which wasn't Human at all. I'd seen Ryder do it a million times before.

"I was given a vision of you dying…" Ristan growled, covering his face with his hands. "Fuck," he said again as he scrubbed his face and looked back at me. He looked at my new brands and smiled sardonically as he shook his head slightly. "That bitch," he said softly. "I told you, she gets her way, fucks with my head, and still she abides by the rules." He turned his head and looked at Eliran, and then Alannah.

"Mother?" he questioned, and I blinked, startled. Alannah tousled his hair like a little boy and laughed at him.

"Remember our talks about seeing the future?" Danu said to me gently. "So many choices that could lead to many different outcomes. One future was of you dying by the same spell and all we have done would have easily been lost. Another possibility would have been me sending him a vision that stopped the Mages before they ever attacked. That one would have saved him from the spell, and the pain of it, but then you would not have embraced your destiny until it was too late to save your children, Ryder, or yourself. You are loyal to your friends and those you love. You go a little crazy and use anything you can when they are being hurt. I just gave him the first vision of a possible future, and he reacted exactly how I wanted him to." She shrugged like it was no big thing.

I needed to remind myself that the Fae were not so easily killed. Seeing Ristan harmed had made me lose it. She was correct in that, but she was wrong. I wasn't crazy; I'd held it together until the enemies had been dispatched.

I felt sick and totally understood why Ristan had issues with this lady. She was sadistic and relentless in her ways.

Ryder pulled me against him as the men helped Ristan to his feet. Danu moved to stand beside me. I glanced at her briefly and wondered what the reaction of those present would think if they knew their Goddess was in their midst.

The moment Ristan was up, I threw myself into his arms and shook with visible relief.

"Wow, Flower," he said with a small laugh as he wrapped his arms around me.

"I watched you die, which means I get to hug you, Demon," I muttered against his chest. He squeezed me tight, and then released me but held me at arm's length.

"The spell they used would have killed you," he smiled softly. "It was a choice, and an easy one at that.

Now that you have come into your own, you will be a lot tougher to kill." He winked as he reached out to touch my new brands.

"Ryder," Cornelius said, coming up to stand close to us with his eyes angry and narrowed on me. "We have a traitor in our midst," he accused with those yellow and green eyes still firmly on me. "Those were Blood Fae attacking our people!"

"Cornelius, I'd be very careful with what you say next. Synthia is and has been under my protection since the moment I laid eyes on her. I know exactly who was leading those warriors and I will be having words with the Blood King about this soon enough. Moreover, I think we need to talk about the contract you and my father made. I'd like for you to meet with me tomorrow."

"Why do we need to wait until tomorrow? I am here right now," he argued.

"Because I said that is when we will talk. You will meet with me tomorrow in my office, and until then you can stay in one of the guest chambers."

"I'd rather we do it tonight," Cornelius pressed.

"I suggest you heed my words, and leave it until tomorrow! Do you want to argue the matter and challenge me?" he demanded.

"No," Cornelius answered quickly.

"Good. Synthia, come with me," he growled and didn't wait for me. Instead, he sifted to me and smiled as his hands touched my skin. We sifted out of the chaos, leaving it for the men to take care of. He took us to his chambers, and pulled me close against his body, still in the Horde King form, his wings comforting me with their heated touch. "You scared the fuck out of me," he growled softly, "I am going to eradicate the Mages and Faolán from this world and any other one that they are occupying."

"Good," I whispered against the warmth of his body.

Ryder stared at me for a few moments before he sat me on the bed and moved away. He had been quiet, as if he was mulling over a puzzle.

"What the hell are you, Synthia?" he growled softly, as he ran his hands through his hair and his wings rustled behind him as they rose a bit higher.

"I'm still Fae. I'm still me, Fairy," I whispered through the lump now forming in my throat at the thought of his rejection.

"No, Synthia, there has to be more to this. You came into your Heir brands tonight and instead of an emblem like the rest of the Heirs, you have the markings for all four Castes on you. The red glow in your eyes tonight, when you came into your powers, I half expected. That would have been normal for the Blood Heir. Your father does the same in anger. But the rest, no. No one has ever in the history of the Fae possessed more than one brand. This," he ran a finger down my brands on my arm. "Horde brands are normally black, gold is the Caste color for the Horde, this is something very different. Did Danu speak to you and let you know what was going on?" His tone was taking on more of a frustrated growl, like I was holding out on him or something. Like I was the one keeping secrets. I shook my head solemnly.

"She didn't say why she did this. She was here tonight, though. She told me that if I didn't accept her, our children would die. She said you could die as well, if I didn't accept her and embrace what I was. She warned me tonight, and egged me on, encouraging me to accept her and then Ristan—shit I thought he was dead and she played me, Ryder. She said she's been the one setting events into motion from the start of this. My parents—everything. She said I couldn't become what she needed me to be here in Faery," I replied sadly. His features softened a little as he absorbed and considered what I had told him.

"Sometimes I think you were created to be my perfect drug," he growled from deep in his chest as his arms reached out and pulled me close until I was pressed hard against his burning skin. "I can't stay away from you, and I'm drawn to you like a fucking addict." His mouth lowered even as his hands came up to hold my face up, locked in their sheer dominance.

I moaned against his mouth as he ground his erection against me. He pulled his mouth away from mine, and turned me around, pressing me against the wall with my face pressed against it. He removed the dress, leaving me only in a thin pair of soft pink lace panties.

"I often wonder why I couldn't walk away from you when I first set eyes on you," he whispered as his magic pulsed over me, removing the updo. My hair cascaded down my naked back freely. His hand came up to rest on my neck, as the other one played with my hair. He lifted it up, and kissed the back of my neck tenderly. His free hand came around and held my face with his fingers on one side, and his thumb easily pressed against the other side.

"I plan on fucking you, Pet; slow, hard, and for hours on end. Think you can handle it?" he purred against my ear as his mouth sent heated breath fanning against my neck.

"Yes," I replied as I ground my ass into him, seeking his cock.

"Good, get on your knees," he urged as I turned toward him as his hands allowed it.

"Ryder—"

"Chain of command, Synthia. I say it. You do it. End of chain, am I clear?" he growled as his wings expanded behind him.

"Yes," I said as I lowered myself to my knees without breaking eye contact.

"Good girl," he replied even as he glamoured his clothes off and waited for me to do as I had been told.

My hand went up to grab his cock, and I stroked it softly as I licked my lips with anticipation. I realized as my lips slid over his silky smooth skin that I'd been starving until I'd met him. For his taste, for the one thing only he could give me. He's my drug of choice, and I don't think there's a rehab for it. There's only the addiction; one so strong that without it, I'd die.

"Fuck," he growled as I started moving my mouth against him, pulling him further into my throat as his hips moved forward and back. I moaned against him, using my tongue to stroke the thick vein on the underside of his massive cock. "I love the feel of your lips upon my skin." He gripped my hair and held it in place as he continued to move his cock deeper. And then he pushed me again.

"Get on the bed, now," he ordered as his hand

came down and stroked his throbbing cock.

I got up from the floor and moved to the bed, crawling on top of the enormous mattress and then turning back around to face him as I lay against the pillows. He moved onto the bed slowly as he began to change back to his more familiar Fae form. His wings were the last to vanish as his eyes burned into me.

"Turn over and get on your knees with your ass in the air, Synthia, now. I want you to slowly remove your panties, and show me everything that's mine."

"Yours?" I asked, raising a delicate brow at him.

He moved fast, stretching himself on top of me as he pushed my hands over my head with one hand and his other firmly planted between my legs on what he was claiming as his own. "It may be between *your* legs, Pet, but make no mistake, this belongs to *me*. Understand?"

"Yes," I whispered, meeting his gold eyes which had begun to glow with hunger.

"Good girl; now do as I told you. Show me what is mine, and make me want to fuck it," he growled before his head lowered and his teeth slid over my flesh at the side of my neck, making my skin tingle in their wake.

I turned over easily, and lifted my ass seductively in the air. I spread my legs until I heard him growl with approval. I placed my head on the bed, turning it to the side and then used my hands to undo the two small bows on either side of the panties, and enjoyed the hiss of air he gave as I exposed myself to his growing hunger.

"Tell me what you want," he ordered.

"You; I want you to fuck me," I replied in a voice thick from lust.

I loved when he played with me, when he took control and became the master of the bedroom. He was a natural Dom, without needing to say it or demand obedience. He had it without trying. "I've been craving you all day. I wanted it to end, just so I could fuck that sweet haven," he purred.

"Why are you still talking?" I demanded, as I swayed my ass invitingly to him.

I was ready for him to enter me. I was soaked already. I wasn't, however, ready for the slap that landed on my cheek from behind, or the one he issued to the other side. "That's for scaring the shit out of me."

"Ouch," I said playfully. "Oomph!" I cried as his magic entered me, filling my core until I could take no more.

"Fuck, you're tight," he ground out as his magic penetrated me, and started to move.

"Mmm," I moaned as he flipped me over and held my legs apart. I looked to where his eyes were locked. I could feel his need burning in his golden eyes, even as he licked his lips.

"Good girls get special kisses. Do you want to be kissed?" he murmured softly.

"Yes," I whimpered as the orgasm built hot and fierce inside of me with the movement of his magic alone.

He lowered his mouth and claimed my clit with his lips, and then licked from one end to the other. His magic swept over me, until my entire body tingled from it. His breath was hot as it fanned my sensitive skin. He pulled up and looked at me. "You want to come, don't you?"

"I need to," I begged.

"Then come for me," he encouraged as his magic increased its speed inside of me, and his mouth continued to kiss my exposed flesh. My entire body trembled and shook as the orgasm exploded. I screamed from the sheer turbulence of it, as he lapped at it, sucking and kissing until I thought I would shatter. He pulled his mouth up and licked his lips. "Little girl, who taught you to come like that?" he grinned wickedly.

"You did," I whispered through the hoarseness in my throat.

"Good answer," he replied as he held my legs apart and slid inside. "I love the way you take me into your body. I love the way your sweet pussy sucks my cock off while I fuck you. The way your nipples harden when I invade and conquer you. You are my perfect drug, Synthia. Your body is mine, as well as your soul," he whispered as he rocked his hips and increased the pace. I came again, violently, as he rode my body.

"I didn't say you could come again," he growled and flipped me over until I was on my stomach, and my legs were lifted from behind me in his hands. He spread them until he fit between my legs. He rammed himself home and buried his throbbing need to the hilt. I cried out with the intense pleasure from it. "Take it," he growled as he increased speed and held my legs up further, giving him further depth as he fucked me. "So fucking good. So mine," he growled.

He exploded, and I felt my body feeding from

him, right up until we both collapsed on the bed. "You have five minutes before I turn you over and fuck you again. I suggest you use it wisely."

"Is that so?" I asked as I fought to catch my breath.

"It's so," he said, smiling as he lowered himself down beside me. "You are mine now, and nothing will change that. I won't let anything stand in my way."

"Mmm," I said with a smile on my lips and waited expectantly.

"Three minutes," he whispered as his eyes locked with mine.

I felt my heart stutter, and my stomach flutter.

He didn't say anything more as he ticked off the minutes until he entered me again. We slept in the same bed, but my heart was heavy. I'd expected more. I wasn't sure why, since he'd said he wanted to renegotiate the contract with Cornelius. I had just thought that if he wouldn't let anything stand in his way, he'd ask to marry me.

Chapter
THIRTY-SEVEN

~ *Ryder* *~*

I walk in the direction of my office, considering what I have to do. I want Synthia. It's as simple as that. She's mine, and soon she will become the mother of my children. I can't make her just another concubine. She won't allow it, and even if she would, I couldn't do that to her.

My mind brings back the events of last night. How Syn's eyes changed from blood red to blue and purple after the heat of battle had passed. Her brands remained as representation of all four Castes in one beautiful package. It's best to leave the knowledge of what she said between us. No one else needs to know how important she might be to this world—not yet anyway.

Cornelius will concede to what I am going to offer; he has to. I am the fucking King. I could easily become the tyrant my father had been. Easily. Abiageal deserves better. Why these assholes throw their daughters at us—fuck it, it's disturbing. I respect the Blood King. He was the only one who refused to cave until we gave him no choice.

His daughter is a lot like him, strong of mind and pure of will. She's everything I want, and need. Marrying Abiageal could undo what we have, and I refuse to lose Syn. Not when I have the power to take care of this easily. I push through the door of the wide office and head for the old oak desk that my father used.

It's the third time I have used his office since I took his head. The beast stirs as I approach the polished desk and pull back the wide chair that is big enough for wings when I take that form. He likes this room; he likes what happens here. He likes the power that is exerted here. Even now, he is pushing and prodding me to take the form of the Horde King. He wants me to frighten Cornelius, cow him into submission. I scan the shelves of scrolls. My father had many contracts. It's filled with them. Scrolls created on the skins of traitors. Syn would hate seeing this place. She would hate what has happened in here.

A knock sounds at the door and I growl. "Come in."

I sit behind the desk, settling into the chair as Cornelius walks in like a fucking peacock ruffling his feathers. I don't respect him. He's loose with his words and thinks he's entitled. He sent Claire to us like a fucking gift basket.

He smiles when he sees me behind the desk and closes the door. "Your father would be proud of you, at what you have become," he says, attempting to remind me that he was close with my father. If he thinks that, he wasn't as close as he believes he was.

"Would he? Would he be proud that I took his head as well?" I remind him that I killed my father. His eyes narrow.

"Your father was a complicated being," he replies easily. I hold my tongue as he seats himself in the chair that is strategically placed on my left. It makes those who sit in it feel safe. They forget that when I am in the form of the Horde King, that my wing span could easily kill them from where I sit. "Now, let's talk about your marriage to my daughter. I want the Blood Heir removed from this kingdom. She is a threat to my daughter."

"Synthia is not a threat to anyone who doesn't fuck with her first," I reply with a calculated look. He has a plan. I'm curious what he thinks he has that I want. I want Syn, period. He can't give her to me, so anything he thinks he has is worthless.

"By marrying my daughter you will gain my alliance," he points out.

"Do I not have your alliance now?" I ask. He knows this question is loaded. He's smart, but not smart enough to fuck with me.

"Of course, but Abiageal's dowry comes with forty thousand troops."

"I want you to consider other options for your daughter and the contract you and my father negotiated," I say, and watch as his face turns red with rage.

"No, I will not! You will marry my daughter and she will become the Queen of the Horde! I've worked too fucking hard for you to fuck this up. You will do as I say!" he shouts.

"Do I need to remind you of who I am, and what I can do? I am the Horde King, and I can easily rule as my father did. There are many ways for us to settle this. You and my father agreed to these terms, not me.

I signed because it was my father's wish for me to do so. Do you not wish better for your daughter than a life spent in the pavilion?"

"She's a daughter! The only thing they are good for is building alliances. That contract is unbreakable! You will marry her, or you will step aside and let one of your brother's rule!" His face was turning mottled with his outrage.

I smile at him. "Cornelius, you forget yourself and how Danu works. None of my brothers is an Heir. I was being polite. You will consider one of my brothers for your daughter's hand. You will seriously consider it. I've already abolished arranged marriages. I wrote it into our laws last week. These are your options: Allow your daughter to select her own husband from one of my many brothers, or go to war. Do you really wish to make an enemy of the Horde? I'm trying to be reasonable. The first option that I offer, it allows you to keep your head. You need to remember who my father was, and how he ruled because I can easily become that. I would rather bring the entire Horde together, and unite the Realm. You are either on my side, or in my way. I suggest you choose the right path for your people, Cornelius."

"This is outrageous!"

I smile as I allow the beast form to take over. The fear in his eyes excites the beast, and I smile inwardly. "I suggest you sleep on it. I have many brothers suitable for your daughter's hand in marriage. I recommend that you consider your daughter's future in your choice. If you want to keep in my good graces, then choose wisely for only one of the choices presented today ends with your head on your shoulders."

"So I either bow to you and your concubine or I lose my head?" He puffs his chest out and glares.

"Synthia is not my concubine, Cornelius. She's so much more than you can see right now. She's also higher ranking than you and your family, and I intend to offer the Blood Kingdom an olive branch through her. We are at war with the Mages, and soon they will attack in force. If the Four Castes of the Realm of Faery do not work together, we may not have anything left when they are finished."

"They are Changelings! Easily killed," he says.

"Easily killed? Did you not notice that they breached our fucking defenses last night? They have been brewing in hate for centuries. If you do not see them as a potential threat, then open your eyes. They can conceal who they are from us, as they did with Arianna. They breached my defenses, which you yourself know is an impossible feat. They have centuries of preparations on us. This isn't some half-assed plot they just worked up. There has been centuries of planning on their part. There aren't a handful of them bent on revenge, there are *thousands* of them. If we plan to save this world, and I do, we need to stick together."

"Zahruk," Cornelius sputters. "I choose the second born prince for my daughter's hand."

"You weren't listening. I will not force your daughter on any of my brothers. I will not sign their fate over to you. I will allow your daughter to court them, and if they make a match, I will honor it. I will allow her free choice, as will you."

"That's ludicrous!"

"That's how it will be. I am the Horde King, and this is my will. Agree to the terms, Cornelius. Do not make me become my father to see them fulfilled. That would become messy and I'd rather not slip into that role anytime soon. I will, however, if pushed."

"I will take it under consideration. However, I need to pass it by my advisors."

"Do so, and remind them that they can be found, and replaced, *easily*."

I woke up early to find Ryder already gone from his chambers. I sat up and felt another presence in the room. Danu turned around and pushed the hair from her face before she spoke.

"I am sure you have more questions," she said quietly.

"Um, yes, how about we start with the whole, you could even be considered my daughter business. You're my mother?"

"In a way, yes, Synthia. You were created from an egg that I took from my womb and planted into your mother's. Easy feat for a Goddess, but I needed to be sure you would be strong enough to fight for this world. You are tied to it more than anyone else, and yet you seem to fight it harder than anyone. You hold onto humanity, when you were born without a shred of it in your being. You are my daughter, you are the child of a Goddess, and yet you are pure. Your heart is untouched by the influence of me, or anyone else in Faery. You fight for what you love, and I needed you to have something that I knew you would be willing to fight for. So I set Ryder on your path. I made you for him so you have everything that he needs and wants. He just doesn't understand it. His beast doesn't have to understand it, he just accepts it. He is everything you want, and I need you for the stability of this world if it is to survive. Strong of mind and pure of heart is the only way to hold the relics. You need them to fight the Mages. You need them to protect your unborn children."

"Back up; *you* are my *mother*!?" I stammered, even though she'd said it. It was sinking in fully now.

"I said you are the perfect Queen for Faery. As a whole. Ryder could be the King of Faery and I want that for him, but I can't allow him to have it unless he is balanced. Like his father before him, he has the drive to take it by force, and he's not pure of heart. He would be easily corrupted if he doesn't have something to keep him leveled. That's you. You are his equal in every way. Stronger, well he does have you there. He does have every creature of the Horde pouring through his veins. You; well, you have me. You have the blood of a Goddess running through your veins and countless others who are part of me. It's why you can heal, and also why you feel so much and fall so hard. It's a bitch to balance, but you do well, considering."

"Ryder's beast mentioned that he was all of the creatures of the Horde, and that's what makes the difference between Fae and the Horde King."

"It is also what makes him the strongest creature in Faery. Unfortunately, the beast can be unstable because of it. This is not how I intended for it to be. I love the Horde. All of the creatures of the Horde are… different and diverse. Some are truly hideous and dangerous, others are beautiful, and you underestimate the danger inherent with these creatures. I intended for the Horde King to be their champion and also to keep them within the boundaries of the Horde Kingdom. I also created many others of the Fae, and they were always special to me, but nothing like the Horde. Bilé fouled it all up."

"Bilé?"

"He has many names that he is known by. Right now, most of the ones I use for him are bad. He was my husband," she said with a small pout on her lips. "Consort, whatever…let's just say things didn't go so well and during one of our spats, he decided to curse the spirit of the beast of the Horde King. He did this because he knew he was my favored creation in this world. Considering I choose who receives the beast, it was one of the many ways he had tried to screw with me."

"So you're talking about God wars here?" I asked as a small shiver ran down my spine. Gods, when they got pissy, destroyed shit. They corrupted minds, and could easily destroy worlds.

"You have the idea. The curse was that the Horde King would need a match to balance him or he would become insane. Considering the strength of the spirit, there wasn't any one who could be considered a match for him, and that is why Alazander became the tyrant that he did. Alazander was the strongest of the Horde Fae at the time; the only one worthy of being chosen. His beast could not find balance and Alazander wasn't strong enough, or steady of mind to control him. Bilé knows I can't undo the curse. He also knows I cannot directly interfere with my creations."

"So what does that have to do with me?"

"Bilé might have unbalanced my Horde King, but I can influence, and I can create something new, so I made a match for Ryder by making you, Synthia," she said conspiratorially.

"You said one of many ways he's tried to screw with you," I replied, rubbing my temples from the implications of everything she was saying.

"He and I have been at odds for a long time. Everything that has been happening in Faery points to him. He is the Hades to my Demeter, death to life. As I told you before, there are something's I can't foresee, but I can see what will balance and repair what he has done. Your children will be born with the Four Royal Caste's blood pulsing in their veins. They will help stabilize this world until the others are put into play. By then, you should have the relics needed to close this world off from the Human world, Synthia. Which you will do. You will still be able to travel between this world and theirs, but those not of pure blood won't be able to find a portal into this world. They won't be able to continue to poison it."

"Wow," I said from a lack of what to say to all of that.

"I tell you that you are a Goddess and my daughter, and all you can say is wow?" she asked with wide blue eyes.

"It's a lot to take in! I went from being Human, to being Fae, and now you tell me I am a Demi-Goddess, so you gotta give me a second here to absorb it all."

"Being a Goddess isn't everything it's made out to be. I can't interfere with freewill. I also can't do things like make the Mages disappear. I could, but there are all sorts of nasty repercussions for interfering that way. I could make things much worse than they currently are, and I have faith in my creations and know that in the end, they will prevail."

"You can't directly interfere, got it," I said, sitting up and throwing my legs over the side of the bed as I glamoured on cotton bottoms, and a matching baby blue top. "It's best that he doesn't know," I breathed.

"He would give you everything you wanted if he

knew," she said as she sifted to sit beside me. She lowered her eyes to where my bump was obvious through the tight cotton. "He would marry you without question."

"Why should I tell him, and why should it matter to him if I am a Demi-goddess? No thank you. If he marries me, I want it to be because he wants it. Not because of what I am," I said quietly.

A lot had happened, but I'd felt the power of what was inside of me. It was both exhilarating, and scary. But with power, came a lot of problems. It was best no one knew just how powerful I was right now.

"You are smart," she said simply. "Smart and beautiful, my daughter. I was afraid you might not wish to have anything to do with me. I could respect it if you did not want me around."

"Hey, I've had three different mothers and a mother in-law in less than two months. I thought Syrina was my mother, and then Tatiana. Thankfully that one only lasted a minute and half. Then I was given to Adam as the Light Heir, so I inherited a mother in-law who had been planning to hate me. Then I met Madisyn, and knew I had a connection with her. I'm glad to know you are my mother, Danu, but I don't plan on you being all maternal on me. I also think it would crush the woman who thinks I am her daughter. She has mourned for me for a very long time. With time, maybe the secret can come out, but now isn't the time."

"You have an old soul for someone so young, daughter. Most would be singing their Goddess parentage from the rafters."

"Most are power hungry saps who would abuse it. I just want to save this world and make it someplace I want to raise my babies in."

"That will be a long journey, child; one that won't be only yours to take. It will take all of the Heirs to solve the problems with Faery. The damage is deep, and many will die before the cure is established. Ryder is fighting an enormous battle. It's one that needs time to heal, as well as all of the Castes to come together and work for it. This world will not be healed when the babes come. I will be here if I can, but I am needed elsewhere as well."

"Can you tell me...?" I couldn't finish it; the thought of even one of them not living sent emotions storming through me.

"No; I wish I could. I can't see those connected to me as well as I'd like to. If they are meant to live, Synthia, they will. It's one of the downsides of being powerful. Even I have rules that must be followed, and if I refuse to follow those rules, I pay dearly for it."

"So being a Goddess isn't all its chalked up to be?" I joked.

"Hardly, but there are some perks. Synthia, Ristan will get a vision soon. Heed it. Prepare for it, and be careful of what choices you make. Do nothing in haste, and do not go after Faolán."

"What's that supposed to mean?" I asked.

"Another time...but I mean it, child. Do nothing in anger or haste. Your beast comes." She leaned over and kissed my forehead. I felt her lips as she sifted out. *"Revenge is not worth the lives you will change. Some things must be let go to move on,"* floated through my mind as softly as a gentle caress.

"Pet," Ryder said, coming into the room with a

steaming cup of coffee in his hand. "I didn't wish to wake you, yet. I figured you'd be tired from last night."

I extended my arms and accepted the steaming cup with a smile. He was sniffing the room; I could see it in the way his nostrils flared and his eyes scanned the room. He didn't ask if anyone had been here, but his eyes were burning with curiosity.

"It smells like ambrosia in here," he said as he sat beside me.

"Mmm, did you bring some in after I fell asleep?" I asked innocently. I was getting way better at playing with words.

"Minx. The men want to know how you feel," he said as he reached over and set the cup of bliss I'd just sipped from onto the small oak table beside the bed.

"Just the men?" I asked with a saucy smirk. "I'm perfectly fine." I smiled as he leaned over and kissed me gently. "Now I am more than fine. Maybe breakfast is in order?" I whispered as he laughed against my lips.

"Wanton little thing in the mornings," he growled hungrily.

"I had a great Transition teacher. He assured me I would be ravenous for the first few months after it. Add pregnancy to it, and man did he hit the target spot on," I replied as my hands slid over his wide back.

"Mmm, he must have been a smart creature," he assured me.

"Why do the men want to know if I'm okay?" I asked, remembering he'd asked.

"They want to throw a party. The coronation was... disturbed. My brothers want to use it as an excuse to get wild and obnoxious."

"Brothers...all of them are your brothers?" I asked.

"Vlad is my uncle's son; he is born from Blood and Horde. My uncle took a fancy to her, but she was actually married to a Human at the time. It's a long story. The others are from different mothers. Only Dristan, I, and Ciara have the same mother. Ciara was the last to be born, Dristan right before her. My father visited the pavilion frequently, and fed from several women a day."

"That's a lot of siblings," I said.

"I'm Fae; we can have thousands. Alazander was abusive to his concubines and wives. He didn't care who birthed his bastards either. There are many more that we may not even know about out there."

"Special," I said as I felt sorrow for those who had been under Alazander's rule. "I understand the need to keep the pavilion. I only ask that you don't use it. I'm not into sharing you, Fairy. If you want me to be faithful to you, then you have to give me the same respect."

He smiled and brought my forehead to his. "Good God, woman; you drive me crazy."

"I plan to drive you crazy for a long time to come."

"Good," he said and placed his hand on my leg and noticed I was clothed. "I am sorry the torque prevented you from casting. It was necessary when you first arrived. There are many with the Horde that are easily antagonized, and until you learned our ways, I didn't want you to use magic that might get you into trouble. It is one of the reasons you have always had a guard present."

"I understand why you did it, but now if you put it on me, you better make sure you put it on me because it's pretty and it carries your mark and not because you want to control me, or I'll remove it. It's time for you to trust me, and my choices. I was taught to make smart choices. The only one questionable was signing your contract," I whispered.

"I made sure you had no other choice," he rumbled as he leaned over and nuzzled my neck.

"I had choices; I just couldn't think with you around. Still can't," I said wickedly.

"If you keep smiling with that damn grin on your lips, I'm going to fuck you."

"That's a bad thing, how?"

Chapter
THIRTY-EIGHT

Several hours later, we bathed in the tub together. He hadn't promised marriage, but I had a plan to wear him down and make him so in love with me that he couldn't live without me. Danu's words played in my head as we headed to one of the smaller meeting halls which the men had set up recently.

Being in the Human world for as long as they were, they had begun to appreciate the gathering and meeting places that had been set up for them there, like *Sidhe Darklands* and *Nightshade*.

The room was decked out with nightclub lights, and the men were gathered around a small bar where, of course, Vlad stood behind it laughing at something Adam had said. I smiled and took in those in the bar. They'd all become important to me. I wasn't sure when it had happened, but these men were my family.

"Flower," Ristan said as he sifted in beside us.

"Demon," I replied with a subtle nod of acknowledgment.

"How are my nephews?" Savlian asked with twinkling eyes and a wicked grin.

"Your nieces are growing," I countered, "and planning on how to drive you all insane for messing with their mother. You have been warned," I replied with a brilliant grin of my own. I was going to curse them all, and give them girls that would drive them insane while trying to keep up with them. My kids would be awesome, and sassy.

"Twin girls," Savlian said with a look that teetered on panic.

"Yes, so that Uncle Savlian…and the rest of you can chase them. Just think about it, when they start dating…" I stopped abruptly. If I did have girls, they'd have all these men guarding them, and dating was going to be crazy for them. Poor darlings.

"Yes, you just think about that thought," Savlian said, victorious.

"Well, shit," I said after a moment of picturing it inside my head. *Poor girls!*

"Vlad," I nodded at him as we sat at the bar and he poured me a glass of sparkling water.

"Hey you, long time no see," he joked.

"Yeah, you gotta get out more," I chimed back. "They all make you serve drinks, makes a boy boring."

"Boring is good," he replied. "Besides, they start manifesting their own drinks and it just gets weird. Not to mention, I enjoy it. Good spot to see what's going on around you."

I looked around the bar and noticed he was right. He could see everyone, and watch everything going on without anyone noticing that he was doing so. "Adrian?" I asked.

"Chasing Alden," Vlad replied and hurriedly supplied the answer to the question burning on my tongue. "Got word he had info for us, and Adrian offered to go and get him. It's too dangerous for him to stay inside the Guild now. Ristan got in with one of the librarians there. She seems to become tongue tied with him around, and gives it up easily."

"I hope you are talking info, and not something else," I said, placing my hand absently against my abdomen.

"I am," he smiled and flicked a fang as he leaned against the smooth bar top and folded his hands together. "I would discuss sex in the presence of a beautiful woman, but I do have manners," he replied. "Adrian's doing well, Syn. He's improving on the hunger and moving on. You don't have to worry about him anymore. I will watch him and protect him now."

"That's good," I said before taking a big drink from the glass.

"It is," he said as he turned away to fill Sevrin's drink.

"Synthia," Sevrin said with a nod of his head and a smile playing along his lips.

I nodded at him and turned to watch Ryder, who had left the bar to talk with Ristan at one of the small tables. The entire group was happy and congratulating Ryder. Silas had been invited, and nodded as I walked past where he stood on my way to the guys.

"Oh I don't think so," Adam's voice sounded from behind me as he twirled me around and smiled down at me. "No hello for me?" He sounded wounded, but I knew better.

I smiled and fell into his waiting arms. "How did it

go with your dad?" I asked. He'd sifted back to fill his father in on what had happened soon after the fight.

"He's kicking himself in the ass for leaving before the fight started; he's been dying to see a little action. He would have loved to have seen you come into your own last night," he shook his head and laughed.

I watched from beside Adam as one after another, Ryder's brothers began approaching him and pledging their loyalty and devotion to him. It wasn't something I understood, but in the end I wouldn't have missed it.

It was unsettling. I'd lived my life looking for revenge, and now it seemed like a waste of time.

I wanted Faolán dead for what he had done to my adoptive parents, but it no longer mattered who dished out his death. He wasn't the type to just slink into the shadows and die. He'd have to be hunted down and killed, and it needed to happen before my children were born since he still thought he could take my powers, and since he would know that one of my children would be the next Heir because of the prophecy, he'd go after them as well. No, he needed to die and it was time to allow the others to help me with him.

"You seem happy," Adam said.

"I am. I just wish Larissa was here with us to see how this has turned out. She would have made an amazing aunt."

"She would have, but she's not gone," he said as he pulled me closer. "She's in our hearts, and she will always be there."

"True," I said as I watched Savlian nod at one of the women who had just arrived in the hall a few moments ago. She smiled and followed him out of the room. Sevrin followed close behind them.

"So this is how the Fae party?" I asked curiously.

"Mostly," he smiled. "Unless it is a feeding party, which I hear is wild, but they still keep it classy," he said smoothly.

"Wild and classy don't normally mix," I replied.

"Vlad normally keeps the peace. He serves, and the men talk to females, choosing one or more for the night, and then they leave. They got some major swagger. I'm trying to pick and choose a few techniques from each of them. Vlad only has to nod his head, and the women will go to the man who wants them for the night. I'm trying to talk him out of his secrets."

I laughed, but Ristan caught my eye as his eyes changed and his face went blank. "Shit," I said and headed in his direction. Ryder tried grabbing his hand to see the vision, but the shake of his head told me he hadn't been successful.

We all circled around him, waiting for him to come back from wherever Danu had sent him for the vision. Everyone was silent as we waited, and Adam's hand slid into mine even as Ryder protected Ristan, even though he was in a room full of his brethren.

When Ristan finally started to come back, his eyes searched for me and leveled me with a concerned look that sent warning bells off in my head. Had Danu showed him what I was? I seriously hope she didn't after the talk we had earlier.

"What did you see?" Ryder asked even as his eyes went from Ristan's demeanor to me.

"We go to war," Ristan whispered.

"With?" Ryder asked.

"The Mages," he answered.

"We are already at war."

"Not like this one, Brother. Not like this."

"How many are coming this way?" Silas asked.

"Thousands led by Faolán. They obtained a few relics and think they have the ones needed to kill all of us. We need to prepare for a war like we have never seen before. It's time to prepare."

I shivered as his words slithered down my spine.

"What else did you see?" Ryder asked.

"We have a secret weapon; one that will turn the tables and change this world forever."

I held his eyes and smiled. He hadn't seen me, he'd seen my mother. He had also seen what she'd wanted him to. This was a fight unlike any we had ever encountered before, but we would meet it head on and come what may, we'd survive it.

I took a deep breath and jumped in uneasily. "Adam, go inform your father that we have need of him. We'll need the Shadow Warriors for this fight. I'll also send a letter to my father in the Blood Kingdom, and request an audience with him since he is unwilling to come here. We need to send someone to Dresden, and warn him of what is coming. He won't think this is his fight, but if he fails to come, tell him *I'll* be showing up to replace him as Alazander did with Anise," I said, taking control as I watched Ryder for a sign that I was over stepping. I didn't see it. Instead, I saw pride shining back in his eyes. He stood and addressed the group.

"Call for the Horde to mobilize, and have them start making preparations for war. Tell them to start collecting the supplies from the Damned Mines. We will need everything we have. The smaller Castes will need to head in this direction so that we can easily protect them from coming to harm. Call the Unseelie and the Sluagh in; tell them it's time to play with the Mages." Ryder gave a battle cry as he finished and the entire assembly picked up the call and sounded it with him.

I placed my hand over my abdomen and wondered what kind of a world would be left when we were done. They had taken away any chance of peace, and now I was glad I was beside Ryder. This entire time I'd been running and trying to escape my destiny. It was time to embrace it, and do what I had been created for. It was time to prepare for war, and make my beast love me.

~~*~*~*~THE END~*~*~*~*~*

~FOR NOW~

AUTHOR

Amelia Hutchins lives in the beautiful Pacific Northeast with her beautiful family. She's an avid reader and writer of anything Paranormal. She started writing at the age of nine with the help of the huge imagination her Grandmother taught her to use. When not writing a new twisting plot, she can be found on her author page, or running Erotica Book Club where she helps new Indie Authors connect with a growing fan base.

Come by and say hello!

www.facebook.com/authorameliahutchins

www.facebook.com/EroticaBookClub

www.goodreads.com/author/show/7092218.
Amelia_Hutchins

Made in the USA
Coppell, TX
22 September 2023